JOHN BANVILLE

The Book of Evidence
TWENTY-FIFTH ANNIVERSARY EDITION

With an Introduction by
COLM TÓIBÍN

Supplementary Material compiled and edited by
RAYMOND BELL

PICADOR CLASSIC

First published 1989 by Martin Secker & Warburg Limited

First published in paperback 1998 by Picador

This Picador Classic edition first published 2014 by Picador
an imprint of Pan Macmillan, a division of Macmillan Publishers Limited
Pan Macmillan, 20 New Wharf Road, London N1 9RR
Basingstoke and Oxford
Associated companies throughout the world
www.panmacmillan.com

ISBN 978-1-4472-7536-7

Visit **www.picador.com/classic** to read more about all our books
and to buy them. You will also find features, author interviews and
news of any author events, and you can sign up for e-newsletters
so that you're always the first to hear about our new releases.

Contents

Introduction
COLM TÓIBÍN

In his book *Doubles*, Karl Miller wrote about a time in fiction when 'a hunger for pseudonyms, masks, new identities, new conceptions of human nature, declared itself.' Thus Robert Louis Stevenson's Dr Jekyll could announce: 'This, too, was myself' as he became 'a stranger in his own house'. Jekyll wrote that he 'learned to recognise the thorough and primitive duality of man; I saw that, of the two natures that contended in the field of my consciousness, even if I could rightly be said to be either, it was only because I was radically both.'

London in the years around the publication of Stevenson's novel and Wilde's *The Picture of Dorian Gray* was the site where many other artists, including W. B. Yeats, George Bernard Shaw, Joseph Conrad and Henry James, allowed their doubled selves, and their work full of masked selves, secret agents, secret sharers, and sexual secrets, to flourish and further duplicate. Everywhere they went, they left behind in some attic of the mind an opposite self, recently discarded.

Every man, W. B. Yeats pointed out, had 'some one scene, some one adventure, some one picture that is the image of his secret life.' In 1909, Joseph Conrad wrote his story 'The Secret Sharer', in which the captain of a ship is confronted with his precise double. 'It was, in the night, as though I had been faced by my own reflection in the depths of a sombre and immense mirror.' Conrad's narrator's double refers to the interloper as 'my second self'. No self in these years was stable. Robert Louis Stevenson wrote: 'I am a fictitious article and have long known it. I am read by journalists, by my fellow novelists and by boys.'

In August 1891, as he stayed at the Marine Hotel in Kingstown in Ireland, Henry James, described by his biographer as someone 'in search of, in flight from, something or other', had the idea for his story 'The Private Life' in which the sociable writer in the drawing room could at the exact same moment be found alone with his other self in his study. In 1908, James would also publish 'The Jolly Corner', in which a man who had been away thirty-three years returns to New York to find his maimed double moving in the very rooms of the house where he was born. Thus began the idea that a character in fiction was either two people, or was nobody.

John Banville's novel *The Book of Evidence* contains, and indeed predicts, the many selves and doublenesses of Banville's own fiction, and offers strange premonitions of the division of Banville himself into the high novelist John Banville, concerned with style, order, irony, chaos, authenticity and beauty, and the less high novelist Benjamin Black, who is interested in murder and crime.

Freddie Montgomery, the narrator of *The Book of Evidence*, is a figure of masks and second selves. Having committed a brutal and senseless murder, as he prepares to prowl the streets of Dublin, he puts on new clothes which he calls 'my new mask!' and then he steps 'forth gingerly, a quavering Dr Jekyll, inside whom that other, terrible creature chafed and struggled, lusting for experience.' In his new doubleness, Freddie feels a strange power. 'It sprang not from what I had done, but from the fact that I had done it and *no one knew*. It was the secret, the secret itself, *that* was what set me above the dull-eyed ones among whom I moved as the long day died, and the streetlights came on, and the traffic slid away homeward, leaving a blue haze hanging like the smoke of gunfire in the darkening air. And then there was the constant, hot excitement, like a fever in the blood, that was half the fear of being unmasked and half the longing for it.'

This sense of doubleness belongs not merely to the criminal in Freddie but to the artist in him, as he follows the example of Borges in his short text 'Borges and I': 'The other one, the one called Borges, is the one things happen to. I walk through the streets of Buenos Aires and stop for a moment, perhaps mechanically now, to look at the arch of an entrance hall and the grillwork on the gate; I know of Borges from the mail and see his name on a list of professors or in a biographical dictionary. I like hourglasses, maps, eighteenth-century typography, the taste of coffee and the prose of Stevenson; he shares these preferences, but in a vain way that turns them into the attributes of an actor.'

Freddie Montgomery, as both murderer and narrator, criminal and dandy, is animated by the conflict between the absurd notion of the authentic self and the lovely emptiness of the invented self. The self, for him as narrator, is fluid, shifting and deliciously inauthentic. When he becomes a sort of servant to his host Charlie French, Freddie writes: 'I fell into a certain manner that was not my own and that yet seemed, even to me, no less authentic, or plausible, at least, than my real self. (My real self!)'. In that same sequence, he observes: 'What an actor the world has lost in me!'

In an earlier passage, he also muses on acting not merely as craft or profession but as an almost proper way of being in the world. 'Yes, that's what I should do, I should live henceforth among actors, practice among them, study their craft, the grand gesture and the fine nuance. Perhaps in time I would learn to play my part sufficiently well, with enough conviction, to take my place among the others, the naturals, those people on the bus, and all the rest of them.'

Montgomery's strange guiltless guilt, his moving from one role into another, the lure for him of being found out, would make its way into the body of John Banville's later work, including *The Untouchable* (1997) which deals with the masking and unmasking of Victor Maskell, based on one of the Cambridge spies, and *Shroud* (2002), which also treats secrecy, disguise and the drama of being found out.

Both Maskell in *The Untouchable* and Vander in *Shroud* function as actors in their own lives until their roles become them. All disguise and invention, they are filled with the ambiguous energy which has gone into their own making. There is a sort of hushed awe in their way of noticing the world, as though nothing can ever be taken for granted. Like Freddie Montgomery, for them the act of self-inventing is all the more delicious because nothing much lies underneath except the bare canvas on which they, with such relish, have painted themselves. There is no stability, no truth. Writing too is a form of acting, all surface gesture, tricks, illusion; making phrases and sentences are forms of strutting and fretting.

Freddie Montgomery commits a murder, but, from his own point of view, this hardly makes him anything as simple as a murderer. The killing of the woman, in this version, was a form of acting too. It has made his tone more urgent and haughty, his perception sharper, his narrative more disturbing. He is inspired and almost amused, awed and transfixed by his own ability to act the part, which may be real, of a man without a motive.

He is fascinated too, and indeed impelled, by the painted image as much as he is by the real world. He notices the absence of the paintings in the house where he was born more than he does his father's actual absence; the sight of a painting in a friend's house offers him a sort of motive, or a whetting of the appetite, as nothing else does.

Freddie's shadow life as an actor and his interest in painting takes on greater substance in Banville's later novels. *Eclipse* (2000) and *Ancient Light* (2012) will deal with the actor Alexander Cleave;

Ghosts (1993) and *Athena* (1995), dramatize the power of painting, the illusions created by illusion. These latter two novels can be read as part of a cycle of novels which begins with *The Book of Evidence*; they meditate on crime and art, on the lure of what is fake, whether it be a personality or a painting.

Just as *The Book of Evidence* prefigures what will concern Banville – and indeed Benjamin Black – the novel also nods slyly to Banville's previous work. The faintly menacing, oddly raffish Mediterranean world in which we first see Freddie Montgomery has echoes in Banville's early novel *Nightspawn* (1971); the ruined Irish ancestral house to which Freddie returns is vaguely reminiscent of the eponymous house in *Birchwood* (1973); and Freddie's efforts as a scientist make a wink at the trilogy of novels about science and scientists which Banville published between 1976 and 1982.

The matters which have concerned Banville in his novels and which emerge with such unsettling clarity and feline force in *The Book of Evidence* have been of interest to many other writers, and indeed to philosophers. But what distinguishes Banville from them, and also from Benjamin Black, his baleful other, is his style. There is a comic edge in his tone, a knowing grace in his cadences mixed with fierce and pointed observation, especially of light and air, but also of what people and things look like, and also, dare we say it? – since something as banal as psychology does not interest him much – of motives and feelings.

The first person voice he uses has time on its hands and adjectives at its disposal; it belongs to someone educated and leisured, a connoisseur of the world's strangeness. But it also belongs to someone under pressure to notice, remember and speak. It has elements of the voice of Oscar Wilde in his prose masterpiece, the most exquisite and pained of the unreliable narrations, *De Profundis*. It is almost as amused by the world, as in love with words and as filled with sensuous longing and a disregard for others as the voice of Humbert Humbert in *Lolita*. It is trying to piece together some facts, many of them puzzling, which throw light on treachery and secrecy, with elements close to the voice of Dowell in Ford Madox Ford's *The Good Soldier*. It is also as impatient with piety and solemnity, fed up with the foolish tricks of fiction, and with metaphysics and ethics, as the figures who speak or remain silent or who generally mutter about the body in Beckett's trilogy. It has some of the lyrical, melancholy, bewildered tone of Neil Jordan's *The Dream of a Beast*, and, in the way in which characters in *The Book of Evidence* have claws rather than hands and are filled with odd, feral appetites, some of the same interest in the connection between animal and man in a slowly fading universe.

But the cadences, and the observations, in all their fearless interest in both wryness and beauty, belong to Banville alone. While he is interested in bowing to the world's beauty while insisting on its unknowability and our own mysterious place in it, his work is distinguished by the command of rhythm, by rhythmic energy and variation. As Freddie returns to Ireland, for example, he witnesses a sunset. He describes this with luscious care and thought and lovely cadences before including a stark, forlorn, startling sentence made up of eleven words, eight of them with only one sad, sharp syllable: 'This sunset, for instance, how lavishly it was laid on, the clouds, the light on the sea, that heartbreaking, blue-green distance, laid on, all of it, as if to console some lost, suffering wayfarer. I have never really got used to being on this earth.'

And then there is the way of noticing, the sheer accuracy in ways of rendering experience. Freddie, for example, is lying in bed in a strange room. Much of what he feels and sees is familiar both to him and to the reader, such as 'the usual barking of dogs and bellowing of cattle' or the observation that 'Now and then a car or a lorry passed by'. But this tired way of remembering is merely there so it can be all the more fruitfully ambushed by the next image, which tells what the lights of a quickly passing lorry do to a darkened room at night: 'a box of lighted geometry slid rapidly over the ceiling and down the walls and poured away into a corner.' This is what holds us, this reading of the known world, this finding something true to say about where we have been. This rich system of registering what is seen attaches Freddie's uncommon experience to our own.

But it is fleeting. Freddie's ways of finding enough in the world to wonder at and puzzle about give him his solitary and troubled voice. His own confusion over the gap between what is random and what makes sense allows his voice its bewildered eloquence and its high tone. He is an exalted witness to his own tormented self. He senses that the damage he has done, the violence in him, has its roots in some primary damage, in the crime committed at the very start of things, events about which Freddie can merely find faint traces of in his own inconclusive and affecting book of evidence.

A Note on the Text

The present text follows, with the exceptions noted below, that of the first edition published by Martin Secker & Warburg Limited in March 1989, and from which the majority of all later impressions were offset, not only in the UK and Ireland, but also in the US. The text has been reset twice since first publication, and with varying degrees of negligence: a few regrettable errors were introduced into the *Frames* trilogy (comprising *The Book of Evidence*, *Ghosts* and *Athena*) published by Picador in 2001, whilst those of a more conspicuous sort blighted an otherwise well-intentioned promotional edition made available in 2005.

The copy-text for this anniversary edition of *The Book of Evidence* is that of the first edition, and which the author has revisited to make some two hundred emendations, a partial record of which may be found in the Appendix (pp. 273–8). In addition to a small number of word changes, these emendations relate chiefly to the capitalisation of certain nouns (Guard, Sergeant, Inspector) and polite forms of judiciary address (my Lord, your Honour); punctuation; the removal of unnecessary hyphens (dust-mote, car-horn, fore-token, etc.); the correction of misspellings (Pomerol for Pommerol, hangars for hangers, Stoneybatter for Stoney Batter, etc.); and, in one instance, a complete rechristening (Eddie for Billy), although this same character reappears, in spirit if not now in name, in the author's *Ghosts*. As to the house-styling favoured for the first edition, this has been silently modified in only one respect: the en dashes of the original have been replaced by em dashes.

The Book of Evidence

My Lord, when you ask me to tell the court in my own words, this is what I shall say. I am kept locked up here like some exotic animal, last survivor of a species they had thought extinct. They should let in people to view me, the girl-eater, svelte and dangerous, padding to and fro in my cage, my terrible green glance flickering past the bars, give them something to dream about, tucked up cosy in their beds of a night. After my capture they clawed at each other to get a look at me. They would have paid money for the privilege, I believe. They shouted abuse, and shook their fists at me, showing their teeth. It was unreal, somehow, frightening yet comic, the sight of them there, milling on the pavement like film extras, young men in cheap raincoats, and women with shopping bags, and one or two silent, grizzled characters who just stood, fixed on me hungrily, haggard with envy. Then a Guard threw a blanket over my head and bundled me into a squad car. I laughed. There was something irresistibly funny in the way reality, banal as ever, was fulfilling my worst fantasies.

By the way, that blanket. Did they bring it specially, or do they always keep one handy in the boot? Such questions trouble me now, I brood on them. What an interesting figure I must have cut, glimpsed there, sitting up in the back like a sort of mummy, as the car sped through the wet, sunlit streets, bleating importantly.

Then this place. It was the noise that impressed me first of all. A terrible racket, yells and whistles, hoots of laughter, arguments, sobs. But there are moments of stillness, too, as if a great fear, or a great sadness, has fallen suddenly, striking us all speechless. The air stands motionless in the corridors, like stagnant water. It is laced with a faint stink of carbolic, which bespeaks the charnel house. In the beginning I fancied it was me, I mean I thought this smell was mine, my contribution. Perhaps it is? The daylight too is strange, even outside, in the yard, as if something has happened to it, as if something has been done to it, before it is allowed to reach us. It has an acid, lemony cast, and comes in two intensities: either it is not enough to see by or it sears the sight. Of the various kinds of darkness I shall not speak.

My cell. My cell is. Why go on with this.

Remand prisoners are assigned the best cells. This is as it should be. After all, I might be found innocent. Oh, I mustn't laugh, it hurts too much, I get a terrible twinge, as if something were pressing on my heart—the burden of my guilt, I suppose. I have a table and what they call an easy chair. There is even a television set, though I rarely watch it, now that my case is *sub judice* and there is nothing about me on the news. The sanitation facilities leave something to be desired. Slopping out: how apt, these terms. I must see if I can get a catamite, or do I mean a neophyte? Some young fellow, nimble and willing, and not too fastidious. That shouldn't be difficult. I must see if I can get a dictionary, too.

Above all I object to the smell of semen everywhere. The place reeks of it.

I confess I had hopelessly romantic expectations of how things would be in here. Somehow I pictured myself a sort of celebrity, kept apart from the other prisoners in a special wing, where I would receive parties of grave, important people and hold forth to them about the great issues of the day, impressing the men and charming the ladies. What insight! they would cry. What breadth! We were told you were a beast, cold-blooded, cruel, but now that we have seen you, have heard you, why—! And there am I, striking an elegant pose, my ascetic profile lifted to the light in the barred window, fingering a scented handkerchief and faintly smirking, Jean-Jacques the cultured killer.

Not like that, not like that at all. But not like other clichés either. Where are the mess-hall riots, the mass break-outs, that kind of thing, so familiar from the silver screen? What of the scene in the exercise yard in which the stoolie is done to death with a shiv while a pair of blue-jawed heavyweights stage a diversionary fight? When are the gang-bangs going to start? The fact is, in here is like out there, only more so. We are obsessed with physical comfort. The place is always overheated, we might be in an incubator, yet there are endless complaints of draughts and sudden chills and frozen feet at night. Food is important too, we pick over our plates of mush, sniffing and sighing, as if we were a convention of gourmets. After a parcel delivery word goes round like wildfire. *Psst! She's sent him a Battenberg! Homemade!* It's just like school, really, the mixture of misery and cosiness, the numbed longing, the noise, and everywhere, always, that particular smelly grey warm male fug.

It was different, I'm told, when the politicals were here. They used to goose-step up and down the corridors, barking at each other in bad Irish, causing much merriment among the ordinary criminals. But then they all went on hunger strike or something, and were moved away to a place of their own, and life returned to normal.

Why are we so compliant? Is it the stuff they are said to put in our tea to dull the libido? Or is it the drugs. Your Honour, I know that no one, not even the prosecution, likes a squealer, but I think it is my duty to apprise the court of the brisk trade in proscribed substances which is carried on in this institution. There are screws, I mean warders, involved in it, I can supply their numbers if I am guaranteed protection. Anything can be had, uppers and downers, tranqs, horse, crack, you name it—not that you, of course, your Worship, are likely to be familiar with these terms from the lower depths, I have only learned them myself since coming here. As you would imagine, it is mainly the young men who indulge. One recognises them, stumbling along the gangways like somnambulists, with that little, wistful, stunned smile of the truly zonked. There are some, however, who do not smile, who seem indeed as if they will never smile again. They are the lost ones, the goners. They stand gazing off, with a blank, preoccupied expression, the way that injured animals look away from us, mutely, as if we are mere phantoms to them, whose pain is taking place in a different world from ours.

But no, it's not just the drugs. Something essential has gone, the stuffing has been knocked out of us. We are not exactly men any more. Old lags, fellows who have committed some really impressive crimes, sashay about the place like dowagers, pale, soft, pigeon-chested, big in the beam. They squabble over library books, some of them even knit. The young too have their hobbies, they approach me in the recreation room, their calf eyes fairly brimming, and shyly display their handiwork. If I have to admire one more ship in a bottle I shall scream. Still, they are so sad, so vulnerable, these muggers, these rapists, these baby-batterers. When I think of them I always picture, I'm not sure why, that strip of stubbly grass and one tree that I can glimpse from my window if I press my cheek against the bars and peer down diagonally past the wire and the wall.

Stand up, please, place your hand here, state your name clearly. Frederick Charles St John Vanderveld Montgomery. Do you swear to tell the truth, the whole truth and nothing but the truth? Don't make me laugh. I want straight away to call my first witness. My wife. Daphne. Yes, that was, is, her name. For some reason people have always found it faintly comic. I think it matches very well her damp, dark, myopic beauty. I see her, my lady of the laurels, reclining in a sun-dazed glade, a little vexed, looking away with a small frown, while some minor god in the shape of a faun, with a reed pipe, prances and capers, vainly playing his heart out for her. It was that abstracted, mildly dissatisfied air which first drew my attention to her. She was not nice, she was not good. She suited me. Perhaps I was already thinking of a time to come when I would need to be pardoned—by someone, anyone—and who better to do that than one of my own kind.

When I say she was not good I do not mean she was wicked, or corrupt. The flaws in her were nothing compared with the jagged cracks that run athwart my soul. The most one could accuse her of was a sort of moral laziness. There were things she could not be bothered to do, no matter what imperatives propelled them to her jaded attention. She neglected our son, not because she was not fond of him, in her way, but simply because his needs did not really interest her. I would catch her, sitting on a chair, looking at him with a remote expression in her eyes, as if she were trying to remember who or what precisely he was, and how he had come to be there, rolling on the floor at her feet in one of his own many messes. Daphne! I would murmur, for Christ's sake! and as often as not she would look at me then in the same way, with the same blank, curiously absent gaze.

I notice that I seem unable to stop speaking of her in the past tense. It feels right, somehow. Yet she often visits me. The first time she came she asked what it was like in here. Oh, my dear! I said, the noise!—and the people! She just nodded a little and smiled wanly, and looked about her idly at the other visitors. We understand each other, you see.

In southern climes her indolence was transformed into a kind of voluptuous languor. There is a particular room I remember, with green shutters and a narrow bed and a Van Gogh chair, and a Mediterranean noon pulsing outside in the white streets. Ibiza? Ischia? Mykonos perhaps? Always an island, please note that, clerk, it may mean something. Daphne could get out of her clothes with magical swiftness, with just a sort of shrug, as if skirt, blouse, pants, everything, were all of a piece. She is a big woman, not fat, not heavy, even, but yet weighty, and beautifully balanced: always when I saw her naked I wanted to caress her, as I would want to caress a piece of sculpture, hefting the curves in the hollow of my hand, running a thumb down the long smooth lines, feeling the coolness, the velvet texture of the stone. Clerk, strike that last sentence, it will seem to mean too much.

Those burning noons, in that room and countless others like it—my God, I tremble to think of them now. I could not resist her careless nudity, the weight and density of that glimmering flesh. She would lie beside me, an abstracted *maya*, gazing past me at the shadowy ceiling, or at that chink of hot white light between the shutters, until at last I managed, I never understood exactly how, to press a secret nerve in her, and then she would turn to me heavily, quickly, with a groan, and cling to me as if she were falling, her mouth at my throat, her blind-man's fingertips on my back. She always kept her eyes open, their dim soft grey gaze straying helplessly, flinching under the tender damage I was inflicting on her. I cannot express how much it excited me, that pained, defenceless look, so unlike her at any other time. I used to try to have her wear her spectacles when we were in bed like this, so she would seem even more lost, more defenceless, but I never succeeded, no matter what sly means I might employ. And of course I could not ask. Afterwards it would be as though nothing at all had happened, she would get up and stroll to the bathroom, a hand in her hair, leaving me prostrate on the soaked sheet, convulsed, gasping, as if I had suffered a heart attack, which I suppose I had, in a way.

She never knew, I believe, how deeply she affected me. I was careful that she should not know it. Oh, don't mistake me, it was not that I was afraid I would give myself into her power, or anything like that. It was just that such knowledge would have been, well, inappropriate between us. There was a reticence, a tactfulness, which from the first we had silently agreed to preserve. We understood each other, yes, but that did not mean we knew each other, or wanted to. How would we have maintained that unselfconscious grace that was so important to us both, if we had not also maintained the essential secretness of our inner selves?

How good it was to get up then in the cool of afternoon and amble down to the harbour through the stark geometry of sun and shadow in the narrow streets. I liked to watch Daphne walking ahead of me, her strong shoulders and her hips moving in a muffled, complex rhythm under the light stuff of her dress. I liked to watch the island men, too, hunched over their pastis and their thimbles of turbid coffee, swivelling their lizard eyes as she went past. That's right, you bastards, yearn, yearn.

On the harbour there was always a bar, always the same one whatever the island, with a few tables and plastic chairs outside, and crooked sun-umbrellas advertising Stella or Pernod, and a swarthy, fat proprietor leaning in the doorway picking his teeth. It was always the same people, too: a few lean, tough types in bleached denim, hard-eyed women gone leathery from the sun, a fat old guy with a yachting cap and grizzled sideburns, and of course a queer or two, with bracelets and fancy sandals. They were our crowd, our set, our friends. We rarely knew their names, or they ours, we called each other pal, chum, captain, darling. We drank our brandies or our ouzos, whatever was the cheapest local poison, and talked loudly of other friends, characters every one, in other bars, on other islands, all the while eyeing each other narrowly, even as we smiled, watching for we knew not what, an opening, perhaps, a soft flank left momentarily unguarded into which we might sink our fangs. Ladies and gentlemen of the jury, you have seen us, we were part of the local colour on your package holiday, you passed us by with wistful glances, and we ignored you.

We presided among this rabble, Daphne and I, with a kind of grand detachment, like an exiled king and queen waiting daily for word of the counter-rebellion and the summons from the palace to return. People in general, I noticed it, were a little afraid of us, now and again I detected it in their eyes, a worried, placatory, doggie sort of look, or else a resentful glare, furtive and sullen. I have pondered this phenomenon, it strikes me as significant. What was it in us—or rather, what was it *about* us—that impressed them? Oh, we are large, well-made, I am handsome, Daphne is beautiful, but that cannot have been the whole of it. No, after much thought the conclusion I have come to is this, that they imagined they recognised in us a coherence and wholeness, an essential authenticity, which they lacked, and of which they felt they were not entirely worthy. We were—well, yes, we were heroes.

I thought all this ridiculous, of course. No, wait, I am under oath here, I must tell the truth. I enjoyed it. I enjoyed sitting at ease in the sun, with my resplendent, disreputable consort at my side, quietly receiving the tribute of our motley court. There was a special, faint little smile I had, calm, tolerant, with just the tiniest touch of contempt, I bestowed it in particular on the sillier ones, the poor fools who prattled, cavorting before us in cap and bells, doing their pathetic tricks and madly laughing. I looked in their eyes and saw myself ennobled there, and so could forget for a moment what I was, a paltry, shivering thing, just like them, full of longing and loathing, solitary, afraid, racked by doubts, and dying.

That was how I got into the hands of crooks: I allowed myself to be lulled into believing I was inviolable. I do not seek, my Lord, to excuse my actions, only to explain them. That life, drifting from island to island, encouraged illusions. The sun, the salt air, leached the significance out of things, so that they lost their true weight. My instincts, the instincts of our tribe, those coiled springs tempered in the dark forests of the north, went slack down there, your Honour, really, they did. How could anything be dangerous, be wicked, in such tender, blue, watercolour weather? And then, bad things are always things that take place elsewhere, and bad people are never the people that one knows. The American, for instance, seemed no worse than any of the others among that year's crowd. In fact, he seemed to me no worse than I was myself—I mean, than I imagined myself to be, for this, of course, was before I discovered what things I was capable of.

I refer to him as the American because I did not know, or cannot remember, his name, but I am not sure that he was American at all. He spoke with a twang that might have been learned from the pictures, and he had a way of looking about him with narrowed eyes while he talked which reminded me of some film star or other. I could not take him seriously. I did a splendid impression of him—I have always been a good mimic—which made people laugh out loud in surprise and recognition. At first I thought he was quite a young man, but Daphne smiled and asked had I looked at his hands. (She noticed such things.) He was lean and muscular, with a hatchet face and boyish, close-cropped hair. He went in for tight jeans and high-heeled boots and leather belts with huge buckles. There was a definite touch of the cowpoke about him. I shall call him, let me see, I shall call him—Randolph. It was Daphne he was after. I watched him sidle up, hands stuck in his tight pockets, and start to sniff around her, at once cocksure and edgy, like so many others before him, his longing, like theirs, evident in a certain strained whiteness between the eyes. Me he treated with watchful affability, addressing me as friend, and even—do I imagine it?—as *pardner*. I remember the first time he sat himself down at our table, twining his spidery legs around the chair and leaning forward on an elbow. I expected him to fetch out a tobacco pouch and roll himself a smoke with one hand. The waiter, Paco, or Pablo, a young man with hot eyes and aristocratic pretensions, made a mistake and brought us the wrong drinks, and Randolph seized the opportunity to savage him. The poor boy stood there, his shoulders bowed under the lashes of invective, and was what he had always been, a peasant's son. When he had stumbled away, Randolph looked at Daphne and grinned, showing a side row of long, fulvous teeth, and I thought of a hound sitting back proud as Punch after delivering a dead rat at its mistress's feet. Goddamned spics, he said carelessly, and made a spitting noise out of the side of his mouth. I jumped up and seized the edge of the table and overturned it, pitching the drinks into his lap, and shouted at him to get up and reach for it, you sonofabitch! No, no, of course I didn't. Much as I might have liked to dump a table full of broken glass into his ludicrously overstuffed crotch, that was not the way I did things, not in those days. Besides, I had enjoyed as much as anyone seeing Pablo or Paco get his comeuppance, the twerp, with his soulful glances and his delicate hands and that horrible, pubic moustache.

Randolph liked to give the impression that he was a very dangerous character. He spoke of dark deeds perpetrated in a far-off country which he called Stateside. I encouraged these tales of derring-do, secretly delighting in the aw-shucks, 'tweren't-nuthin' way he told them. There was something wonderfully ridiculous about it all, the braggart's sly glance and slyly modest inflexion, his air of euphoric self-regard, the way he opened like a flower under the warmth of my silently nodding, awed response. I have always derived satisfaction from the little wickednesses of human beings.

To treat a fool and a liar as if I esteemed him the soul of probity, to string him along in his poses and his fibs, that is a peculiar pleasure. He claimed he was a painter, until I put a few innocent questions to him on the subject, then he suddenly became a writer instead. In fact, as he confided to me one night in his cups, he made his money by dealing in dope among the island's transient rich. I was shocked, of course, but I recognised a valuable piece of information, and later, when—

But I am tired of this, let me get it out of the way. I asked him to lend me some money. He refused. I reminded him of that drunken night, and said I was sure the *Guardia* would be interested to hear what he had told me. He was shocked. He thought about it. He didn't have the kind of dough I was asking for, he said, he would have to get it for me somewhere, maybe from some people that he knew. And he chewed his lip. I said that would be all right, I didn't mind where it came from. I was amused, and rather pleased with myself, playing at being a blackmailer. I had not really expected him to take me seriously, but it seemed I had underestimated his cravenness. He produced the cash, and for a few weeks Daphne and I had a high old time, and everything was grand except for Randolph dogging my steps wherever I went. He was distressingly literal-minded in his interpretation of words such as *lend* and *repay*. Hadn't I kept his grubby little secret, I said, was that not a fair return? These people, he said, with an awful, twitching attempt at a grin, these people didn't fool around. I said I was glad to hear it, one wouldn't want to think one had been dealing, even at second-hand, with the merely frivolous. Then he threatened to give them my name. I laughed in his face and walked away. I still could not take any of it seriously. A few days later a small package wrapped in brown paper arrived, addressed to me in a semi-literate hand. Daphne made the mistake of opening it. Inside was a tobacco tin—Balkan Sobranie, lending an oddly cosmopolitan touch—lined with cotton wool, in which nestled a curiously whorled, pale, gristly piece of meat crusted with dried blood. It took me a moment to identify it as a human ear. Whoever had cut it off had done a messy job, with something like a bread-knife, to judge by the ragged serration. Painful. I suppose that was the intention. I remember thinking: How appropriate, an ear, in this land of the toreador! Quite droll, really.

I went in search of Randolph. He wore a large lint pad pressed to the left side of his head, held in place by a rakishly angled and none-too-clean bandage. He no longer made me think of the Wild West. Now, as if fate had decided to support his claim of being an artist, he bore a striking resemblance to poor, mad Vincent in that self-portrait made after he had disfigured himself for love. When he saw me I thought he was going to weep, he looked so sorry for himself, and so indignant. You deal with them yourself now, he said, you owe them, not me, I've paid, and he touched a hand grimly to his bandaged head. Then he called me a vile name and skulked off down an alleyway. Despite the noonday sun a shiver passed across my back, like a grey wind swarming over water. I tarried there for a moment, on that white corner, musing. An old man on a burro saluted me. Nearby a tinny churchbell was clang-ing rapidly. Why, I asked myself, why am I living like this?

That is a question which no doubt the court also would like answered. With my background, my education, my—yes—my culture, how could I live such a life, associate with such people, get myself into such scrapes? The answer is—I don't know the answer. Or I do, and it is too large, too tangled, for me to attempt here. I used to believe, like everyone else, that I was determining the course of my own life, according to my own decisions, but grad-ually, as I accumulated more and more past to look back on, I realised that I had done the things I did because I could do no other. Please, do not imagine, my Lord, I hasten to say it, do not imagine that you detect here the insinuation of an apologia, or even of a defence. I wish to claim full responsibility for my actions—after all, they are the only things I can call my own—and I declare in advance that I shall accept without demur the verdict of the court. I am merely asking, with all respect, whether it is feasible to hold on to the principle of moral culpability once the notion of free will has been abandoned. It is, I grant you, a tricky one, the sort of thing we love to discuss in here of an evening, over our cocoa and our fags, when time hangs heavy.

As I've said, I did not always think of my life as a prison in which all actions are determined according to a random pattern thrown down by an unknown and insensate authority. Indeed, when I was young I saw myself as a master builder who would one day assemble a marvellous edifice around myself, a kind of grand pavilion, airy and light, which would contain me utterly and yet wherein I would be free. Look, they would say, distinguishing this eminence from afar, look how sound it is, how solid: it's him all right, yes, no doubt about it, the man himself. Meantime, however, unhoused, I felt at once exposed and invisible. How shall I describe it, this sense of myself as something without weight, without moorings, a floating phantom? Other people seemed to have a density, a thereness, which I lacked. Among them, these big, carefree creatures, I was like a child among adults. I watched them, wide-eyed, wondering at their calm assurance in the face of a baffling and preposterous world. Don't mistake me, I was no wilting lily, I laughed and whooped and boasted with the best of them—only inside, in that grim, shadowed gallery I call my heart, I stood uneasily, with a hand to my mouth, silent, envious, uncertain. They understood matters, or accepted them, at least. They knew what they thought about things, they had opinions. They took the broad view, as if they did not realise that everything is infinitely divisible. They talked of cause and effect, as if they believed it possible to isolate an event and hold it up to scrutiny in a pure, timeless space, outside the mad swirl of things. They would speak of whole peoples as if they were speaking of a single individual, while to speak even of an individual with any show of certainty seemed to me foolhardy. Oh, they knew no bounds.

And as if people in the outside world were not enough, I had inside me too an exemplar of my own, a kind of invigilator, from whom I must hide my lack of conviction. For instance, if I was reading something, an argument in some book or other, and agreeing with it enthusiastically, and then I discovered at the end that I had misunderstood entirely what the writer was saying, had in fact got the whole thing arse-ways, I would be compelled at once to execute a somersault, quick as a flash, and tell myself, I mean my other self, that stern interior sergeant, that what was being said was true, that I had never really thought otherwise, and, even if I had, that it showed an open mind that I should be able to switch back and forth between opinions without even noticing it. Then I would mop my brow, clear my throat, straighten my shoulders and pass on delicately, in stifled dismay. But why the past tense? Has anything changed? Only that the watcher from inside has stepped forth and taken over, while the puzzled outsider cowers within.

Does the court realise, I wonder, what this confession is costing me?

I took up the study of science in order to find certainty. No, that's not it. Better say, I took up science in order to make the lack of certainty more manageable. Here was a way, I thought, of erecting a solid structure on the very sands that were everywhere, always, shifting under me. And I was good at it, I had a flair. It helped, to be without convictions as to the nature of reality, truth, ethics, all those big things—indeed, I discovered in science a vision of an unpredictable, seething world that was eerily familiar to me, to whom matter had always seemed a swirl of chance collisions. Statistics, probability theory, that was my field. Esoteric stuff, I won't go into it here. I had a certain cold gift that was not negligible, even by the awesome standards of the discipline. My student papers were models of clarity and conciseness. My professors loved me, dowdy old boys reeking of cigarette smoke and bad teeth, who recognised in me that rare, merciless streak the lack of which had condemned them to a life of drudgery at the lectern. And then the Americans spotted me.

How I loved America, the life there on that pastel, sun-drenched western coast, it spoiled me forever. I see it still in dreams, all there, inviolate, the ochre hills, the bay, the great delicate red bridge wreathed in fog. I felt as if I had ascended to some high, fabled plateau, a kind of Arcady. Such wealth, such ease, such innocence. From all the memories I have of the place I select one at random. A spring day, the university cafeteria. It is lunchtime. Outside, on the plaza, by the fountain, the marvellous girls disport themselves in the sun. We have listened that morning to a lecture by a visiting wizard, one of the grandmasters of the arcanum, who sits with us now at our table, drinking coffee from a paper cup and cracking pistachio nuts between his teeth. He is a lean, gangling person with a wild mop of frizzed hair going grey. His glance is humorous, with a spark of malice, it darts restlessly here and there as if searching for something that will make him laugh. The fact is, friends, he is saying, the whole damn thing is chance, pure chance. And he flashes suddenly a shark's grin, and winks at me, a fellow outsider. The faculty staff sitting around the table nod and say nothing, big, tanned, serious men in short-sleeved shirts and shoes with broad-rimmed soles. One scratches his jaw, another consults idly a chunky wristwatch. A boy wearing shorts and no shirt passes by outside, playing a flute. The girls rise slowly, two by two, and slowly walk away, over the grass, arms folded, their books pressed to their chests like breastplates. My God, can I have been there, really? It seems to me now, in this place, more dream than memory, the music, the mild maenads, and us at our table, faint, still figures, the wise ones, presiding behind leaf-reflecting glass.

They were captivated by me over there, my accent, my bow-ties, my slightly sinister, old-world charm. I was twenty-four, among them I felt middle-aged. They threw themselves at me with solemn fervour, as if engaging in a form of self-improvement. One of their little foreign wars was in full swing just then, everyone was a protester, it seemed, except me—I would have no truck with their marches, their sit-downs, the ear-splitting echolalia that passed with them for argument—but even my politics, or lack of them, were no deterrent, and flower children of all shapes and colours fell into my bed, their petals trembling. I remember few of them with any precision, and when I think of them I see a sort of hybrid, with this one's hands and that one's eyes and yet another's sobs. From those days, those nights, only a faint, bitter-sweet savour remains, and a trace, the barest afterglow, of that state of floating ease, of, how shall I say, of balanic, ataraxic bliss—yes, yes, I have got hold of a dictionary—in which they left me, my muscles aching from their strenuous ministrations, my flesh bathed in the balm of their sweat.

It was in America that I met Daphne. At a party in some professor's house one afternoon I was standing on the porch with a treble gin in my hand when I heard below me on the lawn the voice of home: soft yet clear, like the sound of water falling on glass, and with that touch of lethargy which is the unmistakable note of our set. I looked, and there she was, in a flowered dress and unfashionable shoes, her hair done up in the golliwog style of the day, frowning past the shoulder of a man in a loud jacket who was replying with airy gestures to something she had asked, while she nodded seriously, not listening to a word he said. I had just that baleful screen of which I saw myself reflected, immensely tall and thin, and curved like a bow. There was a smell of fried food. Señor Aguirre, with a little moue of distaste, examined the seat of one of the chairs and sat down. He poured out wine for us, and tipped his glass in a friendly toast. He was a businessman, he said, a simple businessman, not a great professor—and smiled at me and gently bowed—but all the same he knew there were certain rules, certain moral imperatives. One of these in particular he was thinking of: perhaps I could guess which one? Mutely I shook my head. I felt like a mouse being toyed with by a sleek, bored old cat. His sadness deepened. Loans, he said softly, loans must be repaid. That was the law on which commerce was founded. He hoped I would understand his position. There was a silence. A kind of horrified amazement had taken hold of me: this was the real world, the world of fear and pain and retribution, a serious place, not that sunny playground in which I had frittered away fistfuls of someone else's money. I would have to go home, I said at last, in a voice that did not seem to be mine, there were people who would help me, friends, family, I could borrow from them. He considered. Would I go alone? he wondered. For a second I did not see what he was getting at. Then I looked away from him and said slowly yes, yes, my wife and son would probably stay here. And as I said it I seemed to hear a horrible cackling, a jungle hoot of derision, just behind my shoulder. He smiled, and poured out carefully another inch of wine. The infant, which had been playing with my shoelaces, began to howl. I was agitated, I had not meant to kick the creature. Señor Aguirre frowned, and shouted something over his shoulder. A door behind him opened and an enormously fat, angry-looking young woman put in her head and grunted at him. She wore a black, sleeveless dress with a crooked hem, and a glossy black wig as high as a beehive, with false eyelashes to match. She waddled forward, and with an effort bent and picked up the infant and smacked it hard across the face. It started in surprise, and, swallowing a mighty sob, fixed its round eyes solemnly on me. The woman glared at me too, and took the wooden spoon and threw it on the table in front of me with a clatter. Then, planting the child firmly on one tremendous hip, she stumped out of the room and slammed the door behind her. Señor Aguirre gave a slight, apologetic shrug. He smiled again, twinkling. What was my opinion of the island women? I hesitated. Come come, he said gaily, surely I had an opinion on such an important matter. I said they were lovely, quite lovely, quite the loveliest of their species I had ever encountered. He nodded happily, it was what he had expected me to say. No, he said, no, too dark, too dark all over, even in those places never exposed to the sun. And he leaned forward with his crinkled, silvery smile and tapped a finger lightly on my wrist. Northern women, now, ah, those pale northern women. Such white skin! So delicate! So fragile! Your wife, for instance, he said. There was another, breathless silence. I could hear faintly the brazen strains of music from a radio in the bar downstairs. Bullfight music. My chair made a crackling noise under me, like a muttered warning. Señor Aguirre joined his El Greco hands and looked at me over the spire of his fingertips. Your whife, he said, breathing on the word, your beautiful whife, you will come back quickly to her? It was not really a question. What could I say to him, what could I do? These are not really questions either.

I told Daphne as little as possible. She seemed to understand. She made no difficulties. That has always been the great thing about Daphne: she makes no difficulties.

It was a long trip home. The steamer landed in Valencia harbour at dusk. I hate Spain, a brutish, boring country. The city smelled of sex and chlorine. I took the night train, jammed in a third-class compartment with half a dozen reeking peasants in cheap suits. I could not sleep. I was hot, my head ached. I could feel the engine labouring up the long slope to the plateau, the wheels drumming their one phrase over and over. A washed-blue dawn was breaking in Madrid. I stopped outside the station and watched a flock of birds wheeling and tumbling at an immense height, and, the strangest thing, a gust of euphoria, or something like euphoria, swept through me, making me tremble, and bringing tears to my eyes. It was from lack of sleep, I suppose, and the effect of the high, thin air. Why, I wonder, do I remember so clearly standing there, the colour of the sky, those birds, that shiver of fevered optimism? I was at a turning point, you will tell me, just there the future forked for me, and I took the wrong path without noticing—that's what you'll tell me, isn't it, you, who must have meaning in everything, who lust after meaning, your palms sticky and your faces on fire! But calm, Frederick, calm. Forgive me this outburst, your Honour. It is just that I do not believe such moments mean anything—or any other moments, for that matter. They have significance, apparently. They may even have value of some sort. But they do not mean anything.

There now, I have declared my faith.

Where was I? In Madrid. On my way out of Madrid. I took another train, travelling north. We stopped at every station on the way, I thought I would never get out of that terrible country. Once we halted for an hour in the middle of nowhere. I sat in the ticking silence and stared dully through the window. Beyond the littered tracks of the upline there was an enormous, high, yellow field, and in the distance a range of blue mountains that at first I took for clouds. The sun shone. A tired crow flapped past. Someone coughed. I thought how odd it was to be there, I mean just there and not somewhere else. Not that being somewhere else would have seemed any less odd. I mean—oh, I don't know what I mean. The air in the compartment was thick. The seats gave off their dusty, sat-upon smell. A small, swarthy, low-browed man opposite me caught my eye and did not look away. At that instant it came to me that I was on my way to do something very bad, something really appalling, something for which there would be no forgiveness. It was not a premonition, that is too tentative a word. I knew. I cannot explain how, but I knew. I was shocked at myself, my breathing quickened, my face pounded as if from embarrassment, but as well as shock there was a sort of antic glee, it surged in my throat and made me choke. The *campesino* was still watching me. He sat canted forward a little, hands resting calmly on his knees, his brow lowered, at once intent and remote. They stare like that, these people, they have so little sense of themselves they seem to imagine their actions will not register on others. They might be looking in from a different world.

I knew very well, of course, that I was running away.

I had expected to arrive in rain, and at Holyhead, indeed, a fine, warm drizzle was falling, but when we got out on the channel the sun broke through again. It was evening. The sea was calm, an oiled, taut meniscus, mauve-tinted and curiously high and curved. From the forward lounge where I sat the prow seemed to rise and rise, as if the whole ship were straining to take to the air. The sky before us was a smear of crimson on the palest of pale blue and silvery green. I held my face up to the calm sea-light, entranced, expectant, grinning like a loon. I confess I was not entirely sober, I had already broken into my allowance of duty-free booze, and the skin at my temples and around my eyes was tightening alarmingly. It was not just the drink, though, that was making me happy, but the tenderness of things, the simple goodness of the world. This sunset, for instance, how lavishly it was laid on, the clouds, the light on the sea, that heartbreaking, blue-green distance, laid on, all of it, as if to console some lost, suffering wayfarer. I have never really got used to being on this earth. Sometimes I think our presence here is due to a cosmic blunder, that we were meant for another planet altogether, with other arrangements, and other laws, and other, grimmer skies. I try to imagine it, our true place, off on the far side of the galaxy, whirling and whirling. And the ones who were meant for here, are they out there, baffled and homesick, like us? No, they would have become extinct long ago. How could they survive, these gentle earthlings, in a world that was made to contain *us*?

★

The voices, that was what startled me first of all. I thought they must be putting on this accent, it sounded so like a caricature. Two raw-faced dockers with fags in their mouths, a customs man in a cap: my fellow countrymen. I walked through a vast, corrugated-iron shed and out into the tired gold of the summer evening. A bus went past, and a workman on a bike. The clocktower, its addled clock still showing the wrong time. It was all so affecting, I was surprised. I liked it here when I was a child, the pier, the promenade, that green bandstand. There was always a sweet sense of melancholy, of mild regret, as if some quaint, gay music, the last of the season, had just faded on the air. My father never referred to the place as anything but Kingstown: he had no time for the native jabber. He used to bring me here on Sunday afternoons, sometimes on weekdays too in the school holidays. It was a long drive from Coolgrange. He would park on the road above the pier and give me a shilling and slope off, leaving me to what he called my own devices. I see myself, the frog prince, enthroned on the high back seat of the Morris Oxford, consuming a cornet of ice cream, licking the diminishing knob of goo round and round with scientific application, and staring back at the passing promenaders, who blanched at the sight of my baleful eye and flickering, creamy tongue. The breeze from the sea was a soft, salt wall of air in the open window of the car, with a hint of smoke in it from the mailboat berthed below me. The flags on the roof of the yacht club shuddered and snapped, and a thicket of masts in the harbour swayed and tinkled like an oriental orchestra.

My mother never accompanied us on these jaunts. They were, I know now, just an excuse for my father to visit a poppet he kept there. I do not recall him behaving furtively, or not any more so than usual. He was a slight, neatly-made man, with pale eyebrows and pale eyes, and a small, fair moustache that was faintly indecent, like a bit of body fur, soft and downy, that had found its way inadvertently on to his face from some other, secret part of his person. It made his mouth startlingly vivid, a hungry, violent, red-coloured thing, grinding and snarling. He was always more or less angry, seething with resentment and indignation. Behind the bluster, though, he was a coward, I think. He felt sorry for himself. He was convinced the world had used him badly. In recompense he pampered himself, gave himself treats. He wore expensive shoes and Charvet ties, drank good claret, smoked cigarettes specially imported in airtight tins from a shop in the Burlington Arcade. I still have, or had, his malacca walking-cane. He was enormously proud of it. He liked to demonstrate to me how it was made, from four or was it eight pieces of rattan prepared and fitted together by a master craftsman. I could hardly keep a straight face, he was so laughably earnest. He made the mistake of imagining that his possessions were a measure of his own worth, and strutted and crowed, parading his things like a schoolboy with a champion catapult. Indeed, there was something of the eternal boy about him, something tentative and pubertal. When I think of us together I see him as impossibly young and me already grown-up, weary, embittered. I suspect he was a little afraid of me. By the age of twelve or thirteen I was as big as he, or as heavy, anyway, for although I have his fawn colouring, in shape I took after my mother, and already at that age was inclined towards flab. (Yes, m'lud, you see before you a middling man inside whom there is a fattie trying not to come out. For he was let slip once, was Bunter, just once, and look what happened.)

I hope I do not give the impression that I disliked my father. We did not converse much, but we were perfectly companionable, in the way of fathers and sons. If he did fear me a little, I too was wise enough to be wary of *him*, a relation easily mistaken, even by us at times, for mutual esteem. We had a great distaste for the world generally, there was that much in common between us. I notice I have inherited his laugh, that soft, nasal snicker which was his only comment on the large events of his time. Schisms, wars, catastrophes, what did he care for such matters?—the world, the only worthwhile world, had ended with the last viceroy's departure from these shores, after that it was all just a wrangle among peasants. He really did try to believe in this fantasy of a great good place that had been taken away from us and our kind—our kind being Castle Catholics, as he liked to say, yes, sir, Castle Catholics, and proud of it! But I think there was less pride than chagrin. I think he was secretly ashamed not to be a Protestant: he would have had so much less explaining, so much less justifying, to do. He portrayed himself as a tragic figure, a gentleman of the old school displaced in time. I picture him on those Sunday afternoons with his mistress, an ample young lady, I surmise, with hair unwisely curled and a generous décolletage, before whom he kneels, poised trembling on one knee, gazing rapt into her face, his moustache twitching, his moist red mouth open in supplication. Oh but I must not mock him like this. Really, really, I did not think unkindly of him—apart, that is, from wanting deep down to kill him, so that I might marry my mother, a novel and compelling notion which my counsel urges on me frequently, with a meaning look in his eye.

But I digress.

The charm I had felt in Kingstown, I mean Dun Laoghaire, did not endure into the city. My seat at the front on the top deck of the bus—my old seat, my favourite!—showed me scenes I hardly recognised. In the ten years since I had last been here something had happened, something had befallen the place. Whole streets were gone, the houses torn out and replaced by frightening blocks of steel and black glass. An old square where Daphne and I lived for a while had been razed and made into a vast, cindered car park. I saw a church for sale—a church, for sale! Oh, something dreadful had happened. The very air itself seemed damaged. Despite the late hour a faint glow of daylight lingered, dense, dust-laden, like the haze after an explosion, or a great conflagration. People in the streets had the shocked look of survivors, they seemed not to walk but reel. I got down from the bus and picked my way among them with lowered gaze, afraid I might see horrors. Barefoot urchins ran along beside me, whining for pennies. There were drunks everywhere, staggering and swearing, lost in joyless befuddlement. An amazing couple reared up out of a pulsating cellar, a minatory, pockmarked young man with a crest of orange hair, and a stark-faced girl in gladiator boots and ragged, soot-black clothes. They were draped about with ropes and chains and what looked like cartridge belts, and sported gold studs in their nostrils. I had never seen such creatures, I thought they must be members of some fantastic sect. I fled before them, and dived into Wally's pub. Dived is the word.

I had expected it to be changed, like everything else. I was fond of Wally's. I used to drink there when I was a student, and later on, too, when I worked for the government. There was a touch of sleaze to the place which I found congenial. I know much has been made of the fact that it was frequented by homosexuals, but I trust the court will dismiss the implications which have been tacitly drawn from this, especially in the gutter press. I am not queer. I have nothing against those who are, except that I despise them, of course, and find disgusting the thought of the things they get up to, whatever those things may be. But their presence lent a blowsy gaiety to the atmosphere in Wally's and a slight edge of threat. I liked that shiver of embarrassment and gleeful dread that ran like a bead of mercury up my spine when a bevy of them suddenly exploded in parrot shrieks of laughter, or when they got drunk and started howling abuse and breaking things. Tonight, when I hurried in to shelter from the stricken city, the first thing I saw was a half dozen of them at a table by the door with their heads together, whispering and giggling and pawing each other happily. Wally himself was behind the bar. He had grown fatter, which I would not have thought possible, but apart from that he had not changed in ten years. I greeted him warmly. I suspect he remembered me, though of course he would not acknowledge it: Wally prided himself on the sourness of his manner. I ordered a large, a gargantuan, gin and tonic, and he sighed grudgingly and heaved himself off the high stool on which he had been propped. He moved very slowly, as if through water, billowing in his fat, like a jellyfish. I was feeling better already. I told him about the church I had seen for sale. He shrugged, he was not surprised, such things were commonplace nowadays. As he was setting my drink before me the huddled circle of queers by the door flew apart suddenly in a loud splash of laughter, and he frowned at them, pursing his little mouth so that it almost disappeared in the folds of his fat chin. He affected contempt for his clientele, though it was said he kept a bevy of boys himself, over whom he ruled with great severity, jealous and terrible as a Beardsleyan queen.

I drank my drink. There is something about gin, the tang in it of the deep wildwood, perhaps, that always makes me think of twilight and mists and dead maidens. Tonight it tinkled in my mouth like secret laughter. I looked about me. No, Wally's was not changed, not changed at all. This was my place: the murmurous gloom, the mirrors, the bottles ranged behind the bar, each one with its bead of ruby light. Yes, yes, the witch's kitchen, with a horrid fat queen, and a tittering band of fairy-folk. Why, there was even an ogre—Gilles the Terrible, *c'est moi*. I was happy. I enjoy the inappropriate, the disreputable, I admit it. In low dives such as this the burden of birth and education falls from me and I feel, I feel— I don't know what I feel. I don't know. The tense is wrong anyway. I turned to Wally and held out my glass, and watched in a kind of numbed euphoria as he measured out another philtre for me in a little silver chalice. That flash of blue when he added the ice, what am I thinking of? Blue eyes. Yes, of course.

I did say dead maidens, didn't I. Dear me.

So I sat in Wally's pub and drank, and talked to Wally of this and that—his side of the conversation confined to shrugs and dull grunts and the odd malevolent snigger—and gradually the buzz that travel always sets going in my head was stilled. I felt as if, instead of journeying by ship and rail, I had been dropped somehow through the air to land up in this spot at last, feeling groggy and happy, and pleasantly, almost voluptuously, vulnerable. Those ten years I had passed in restless wandering were as nothing, a dream voyage, insubstantial. How distant all that seemed, those islands in a blue sea, those burning noons, and Randolph and Señor Aguirre, even my wife and child, how distant. Thus it was that when Charlie French came in I greeted him as if I had seen him only yesterday.

I know Charlie insists that he did not meet me in Wally's pub, that he never went near the place, but all I am prepared to admit is the possibility that it was not on that particular night that I saw him there. I remember the moment with perfect clarity, the queers whispering, and Wally polishing a glass with a practised and inimitably contemptuous wrist-action, and I sitting at the bar with a bumper of gin in my fist and my old pigskin suitcase at my feet, and Charlie pausing there in his chalkstripes and his scuffed shoes, a forgetful Eumaeus, smiling uneasily and eyeing me with vague surmise. All the same, it is possible that my memory has conflated two separate occasions. It is possible. What more can I say? I hope, Charles, this concession will soothe, even if only a little, your sense of injury.

People think me heartless, but I am not. I have much sympathy for Charlie French. I caused him great distress, no doubt of that. I were open and was looking to see if anyone had noticed. Freddie! he said. Well well! He lit a cigarette with a not altogether steady hand, and released a great whoosh of smoke towards the ceiling. I was trying to recall when it was I had first met him. He used to come down to Coolgrange when my father was alive and hang about the house looking furtive and apologetic. They had been young together, he and my parents, in their cups they would reminisce about hunt balls before the war, and dashing up to Dublin for the Show, and all the rest of it. I listened to this stuff with boundless contempt, curling an adolescent's villous lip. They sounded like actors flogging away at some tired old drawing-room comedy, projecting wildly, my mother especially, with her scarlet fingernails and metallic perm and that cracked, gin-and-smoke voice of hers. But to be fair to Charles, I do not think he really subscribed to this fantasy of the dear dead days. He could not ignore the tiny trill of hysteria that made my mother's goitrous throat vibrate, nor the way my father looked at her sometimes, poised on the edge of his chair, tense as a whippet, pop-eyed and pale, with an expression of incredulous loathing. When they got going like this, the two of them, they forgot everything else, their son, their friend, everything, locked together in a kind of macabre trance. This meant that Charlie and I were often thrown into each other's company. He treated me tentatively, as if I were something that might blow up in his face at any moment. I was very fierce in those days, brimming with impatience and scorn. We must have been a peculiar pair, yet we got on, at some deep level. Perhaps I seemed to him the son he would never have, perhaps he seemed to me the father I had never had. (This is another idea put forward by my counsel. I don't know how you think of them, Maolseachlainn.) What was I saying? Charlie. He took me to the races one day, when I was a boy. He was all kitted out for the occasion, in tweeds and brown brogues and a little trilby hat tipped at a raffish angle over one eye.

He even had a pair of binoculars, though he did not seem to be able to get them properly in focus. He looked the part, except for a certain stifled something in his manner that made it seem all the time as if he were about to break down in helpless giggles at himself and his pretensions. I was fifteen or sixteen. In the drinks marquee he turned to me blandly and asked what I would have, Irish or Scotch—and brought me home in the evening loudly and truculently drunk. My father was furious, my mother laughed. Charlie maintained an unruffled silence, pretending nothing was amiss, and slipped me a fiver as I was stumbling off to bed.

Ah Charles, I am sorry, truly I am.

Now, as if he too were remembering that other time, he insisted on buying a drink, and pursed his lips disapprovingly when I asked for gin. He was a whiskey man, himself. It was part of his disguise, like the striped suit and the worn-down, handmade shoes, and that wonderful, winged helmet of hair, now silvered all over, which, so my mother liked to say, had destined him for greatness. He had always managed to avoid his destiny, however. I asked him what he was doing these days. Oh, he said, I'm running a gallery. And he glanced about him with an abstracted, wondering smile, as if he were himself surprised at such a notion. I nodded. So that was what had bucked him up, what had given him that self-sufficient air. I saw him in some dusty room, a forgotten backwater, with a few murky pictures on the wall, and a frosty spinster for a secretary who bickered with him over tea money and gave him a tie wrapped in tissue paper every Christmas. Poor Charlie, forced to take himself seriously at last, with a business to take care of, and painters after him for their money. Here, I said, let me, and peeled a note from my rapidly dwindling wad and slapped it on the bar.

To be candid, however, I was thinking of asking him for a loan. What prevented me was—well, there will be laughter in court, I know, but the fact is I felt it would be in bad taste. It is not that I am squeamish about these matters, in my time I have touched sadder cases than Charlie for a float, but there was something in the present circumstances that held me back. We might indeed have been a father and son—not *my* father, of course, and certainly not *this* son—meeting by chance in a brothel. Constrained, sad, obscurely ashamed, we blustered and bluffed, knocking our glasses together and toasting the good old days. But it was no use, in a little while we faltered, and fell gloomily silent. Then suddenly Charlie looked at me, with what was almost a flash of pain, and in a low, impassioned voice said, Freddie, what have you done to yourself? At once abashed, he leaned away from me in a panic, desperately grinning, and puffed a covering cloud of smoke. First I was furious, and then depressed. Really, I was not in the mood for this kind of thing. I glanced at the clock behind the bar and, purposely misunderstanding him, said yes, it was true, it had been a long day, I was overdoing it, and I finished my drink and shook his hand and took up my bag and left.

There it was again, in another form, the same question: why, Freddie, why are you living like this? I brooded on it next morning on the way to Coolgrange. The day looked as I felt, grey and flat and heavy. The bus plunged laboriously down the narrow country roads, pitching and wallowing, with a dull zip and roar that seemed the sound of my own blood beating in my brain. The myriad possibilities of the past lay behind me, a strew of wreckage. Was there, in all that, one particular shard—a decision reached, a road taken, a signpost followed—that would show me just how I had come to my present state? No, of course not. My journey, like everyone else's, even yours, your Honour, had not been a thing of signposts and decisive marching, but drift only, a kind of slow subsidence, my shoulders bowing down under the gradual accumulation of all the things I had not done. Yet I can see that to someone like Charlie, watching from the ground, I must have seemed a creature of fable scaling the far peaks, rising higher and ever higher, leaping at last from the pinnacle into marvellous, fiery flight, my head wreathed in flames. But I am not Euphorion. I am not even his father.

The question is wrong, that's the trouble. It assumes that actions are determined by volition, deliberate thought, a careful weighing-up of facts, all that puppet-show twitching which passes for consciousness. I was living like that because I was living like that, there is no other answer. When I look back, no matter how hard I try I can see no clear break between one phase and another. It is a seamless flow—although flow is too strong a word. More a sort of busy stasis, a sort of running on the spot. Even that was too fast for me, however, I was always a little way behind, trotting in the rear of my own life. In Dublin I was still the boy growing up at Coolgrange, in America I was the callow young man of Dublin days, on the islands I became a kind of American. And nothing was enough. Everything was coming, was on the way, was about to be. Stuck in the past, I was always peering beyond the present towards a limitless future. Now, I suppose, the future may be said to have arrived.

None of this means anything. Anything of significance, that is. I am just amusing myself, musing, losing myself in a welter of words. For words in here are a form of luxury, of sensuousness, they are all we have been allowed to keep of the rich, wasteful world from which we are shut away.

O God, O Christ, release me from this place.

O Someone.

I must stop, I am getting one of my headaches. They come with increasing frequency. Don't worry, your Lordship, no need to summon the tipstaff or the sergeant-at-arms or whatever he's were faces hidden among the leaves, laughing. Then a whistle sounded, and the brute whined and turned guiltily towards the house. My mother was standing on the front steps. She laughed. Suddenly the sun came out, with a kind of soundless report. Good God, she said, it is you, I thought I was seeing things.

I hesitate. It is not that I am lost for words, but the opposite. There is so much to be said I do not know where to begin. I feel myself staggering backwards slowly, clutching in my outstretched arms a huge, unwieldy and yet weightless burden. She is so much, and, at the same time, nothing. I must go carefully, this is perilous ground. Of course, I know that whatever I say will be smirked at knowingly by the amateur psychologists packing the court. When it comes to the subject of mothers, simplicity is not permitted. All the same, I shall try to be honest and clear. Her name is Dorothy, though everyone has always called her Dolly, I do not know why, for there is nothing doll-like about her. She is a large, vigorous woman with the broad face and heavy hair of a tinker's wife. In describing her thus I do not mean to be disrespectful. She is impressive, in her way, at once majestic and slovenly. I recall her from my childhood as a constant but remote presence, statuesque, blank-eyed, impossibly handsome in an Ancient Roman sort of way, like a marble figure at the far side of a lawn. Later on, though, she grew to be top-heavy, with a big backside and slim legs, a contrast which, when I was an adolescent and morbidly interested in such things, led me to speculate on the complicated architecture that must be necessary to bridge the gap under her skirt between those shapely knees and that thick waist. Hello, mother, I said, and looked away from her, casting about me crossly for something neutral on which to concentrate. I was annoyed already. She has that effect on me, I have only to stand before her and instantly the irritation and resentment begin to seethe in my breast. I was surprised. I had thought that after ten years there would be at least a moment of grace between our meeting and the first attack of filial heartburn, but not a bit of it, here I was, jaw clenched, glaring venomously at a tuft of weed sprouting from a crack in the stone steps where she stood. She was not much changed. Her bosom, which cries out to be called ample, had descended to just above her midriff. Also she had grown a little moustache. She wore baggy corduroy trousers and a cardigan with sagging pockets. She came down the steps to me and laughed again. You have put on weight, Freddie, she said, you've got fat. Then she reached out and—this is true, I swear it—and took hold of a piece of my stomach and rolled it playfully between a finger and thumb. This woman, this woman—what can I say? I was thirty-eight, a man of parts, with a wife and a son and an impressive Mediterranean tan, I carried myself with gravitas and a certain faint air of menace, and she, what did she do?—she pinched my belly and laughed her phlegmy laugh. Is it any wonder I have ended up in jail? Is it? The dog, seeing that I was to be accepted, sidled up to me and tried to lick my hand, which gave me an opportunity to deliver it a good hard kick in the ribs. That made me feel better, but not much, and not for long.

Is there anything as powerfully, as piercingly evocative, as the smell of the house in which one's childhood was spent? I try to avoid generalisations, as no doubt the court has noticed, but surely this is a universal, this involuntary spasm of recognition which comes with the first whiff of that humble, drab, brownish smell, which is hardly a smell at all, more an emanation, a sort of sigh exhaled by the thousands of known but unacknowledged tiny things that collectively constitute what is called home. I stepped into the hall and for an instant it was as if I had stepped soundlessly through the membrane of time itself. I faltered, tottering inwardly. Hatstand with broken umbrella, that floor tile, still loose. Get out, Patch, damn you! my mother said behind me, and the dog yelped.

The taste of apples unaccountably flooded my mouth. I felt vaguely as if something momentous had happened, as if in the blink of an eye everything around me had been whipped away and replaced instantly with an exact replica, perfect in every detail, down to the last dust mote. I walked on, into this substitute world, tactfully keeping a blank expression, and seemed to hear a disembodied held breath being let go in relief that the difficult trick had worked yet again.

We went into the kitchen. It looked like the lair of some large, scavenging creature. Lord, mother, I said, are you *living* in here? Items of clothing, an old woman's nameless rags, were stuffed between the dishes on the dresser. The toes of three or four pairs of shoes peeped out from under a cupboard, an unnerving sight, as if the wearers might be huddled together in there, stubby arms clasped around each other's hunched shoulders, listening. Pieces of furniture had migrated here from all over the house, the narrow little bureau from my father's study, the walnut cocktail cabinet from the drawing room, the velvet-covered recliner with balding armrests in which my Great-Aunt Alice, a tiny, terrible woman, had died without a murmur one Sunday afternoon in summer. The huge old wireless that used to lord it over the lounge stood now at a drunken tilt on the draining board, crooning softly to itself, its single green eye pulsing. The place was far from clean. A ledger was open on the table, and bills and things were strewn amid the smeared plates and the unwashed teacups. She had been doing the accounts. Briefly I considered bringing up the main matter straight away—money, that is—but thought better of it. As if she had an inkling of what was in my mind she glanced from me to the papers and back again with amusement. I turned away from her, to the window. Out on the lawn a stocky girl in jodhpurs was leading a string of Connemara ponies in a circle. I recalled dimly my mother telling me, in one of her infrequent and barely literate the mattress. The view from the window—trees, a bit of sloping field, the red roof of a barn—was exact and familiar as an hallucination. Here was the cupboard I had built, and at once I had a vision of myself, a small boy with a fierce frown, blunt saw in hand, hacking at a sheet of plywood, and my grieving heart wobbled, as if it were not myself I was remembering, but something like a son, dear and vulnerable, lost to me forever in the depths of my own past. When I turned round my mother was not there. I found her on the stairs, looking a little odd around the eyes. She set off again. I must see the grounds, she cried, the stables, the oak wood. She was determined I would see everything, everything.

Out of doors my spirits rose somewhat. How soft the air of summer here. I had been too long under harsh southern skies. And the trees, the great trees! those patient, quietly suffering creatures, standing stock-still as if in embarrassment, their tragic gazes somehow turned away from us. Patch the dog—I can see I am going to be stuck with this brute—Patch the dog appeared, rolling its mad eyes and squirming. It followed silently behind us across the lawn. The stable-girl, watching sidelong as we approached, seemed on the point of taking to her heels in fright. Her name was Joan, or Jean, something like that. Big bum, big chest—obviously mother had felt an affinity. When I spoke to her the poor girl turned crimson, and wincingly extended a calloused little paw as if she were afraid I might be going to keep it. I gave her one of my special, slow smiles, and saw myself through her eyes, a tall, tanned hunk in a linen suit, leaning over her on a summer lawn and murmuring dark words. Tinker! she yelped, get off! The lead pony, a stunted beast with a truculent eye, was edging sideways in that dully determined way that they have, nudging heavily against me. I put my hand on its flank to push it away, and was startled by the solidity, the actuality of the animal, the coarse dry coat, the dense unyielding flesh beneath, the blood warmth. Shocked, I took my hand away quickly and stepped back. Suddenly I had a vivid, queasy sense of myself, not the tanned pin-up now, but something else, something pallid and slack and soft. I was aware of my toenails, my anus, my damp, constricted crotch. And I was ashamed. I can't explain it. That is, I could, but won't. Then the dog began to bark, rushing at the pony's hoofs, and the pony snorted, peeling back its muzzle and snapping its alarming teeth. My mother kicked the dog, and the girl hauled the pony's head sideways. The dog howled, the line of ponies plunged and whinnied. What a racket! Everything, always, turns to farce. I remembered my hangover. I needed a drink.

Gin first, then some sort of awful sherry, then successive jorums of my late father's fine Bordeaux, the last, alas, of the bin. I was already half-soused when I went down to the cellar to fetch the claret. I sat on a crate amid the must and gloom, breathing gin fumes out of flared nostrils. A streaming lance of sunlight, seething with dust, pierced the low, cobwebbed window above my head. Things thronged around me in the shadows—a battered rocking horse, an old high bicycle, a bundle of antique tennis racquets—their outlines blurred, greyish, fading, as if this place were a way-station where the past paused on its way down into oblivion. I laughed. Old bastard, I said aloud, and the silence rang like a rapped glass. He was always down here in those last months before he died. He had become a potterer, he who all his life had been driven by fierce, obsessive energies. My mother would send me down to look for him, in case something might have happened to him, as she delicately put it. I would find him poking about in corners, fiddling with things, or just standing, canted at an odd angle, staring at nothing. When I spoke he would give a great start and turn on me angrily, huffing, as if he had been caught at something shameful. But these spurts of animation did not last long, and after a moment he would drift off again into vagueness. It was as if he were not dying of an illness, but of a sort of general distraction: as if one day in the midst of his vehement doings something had caught his attention, had beckoned to him out of the darkness, and, struck, he had turned aside and walked towards it, with a sleepwalker's pained, puzzled concentration. I was, what, twenty-two, twenty-three. The long process of his dying wearied and exasperated me in equal measure. Of course I pitied him, too, but I think pity is always, for me, only the permissible version of an urge to give weak things a good hard shake. He began to shrink. Suddenly his shirt collars were too big for that wobbly tortoise-neck with its two slack harp-strings. Everything was too big for him, his clothes had more substance than he did, he seemed to rattle about inside them. His eyes were huge and haunted, already clouding. It was summer then, too. Light was not his medium any more, he preferred it down here, in the mossy half-dark, among the deepening shades.

I hauled myself to my feet and gathered an armful of dusty bottles and staggered with them up the damp stone steps.

Yet he died upstairs, in the big front bedroom, the airiest room in the house. It was so hot all that week. They opened wide the window, and he made them move his bed forward until the foot of it was right out on the balcony. He lay with the covers thrown back, his meagre chest bared, giving himself up to the sun, the vast sky, dying into the blue and gold glare of summer. His hands. The rapid beat of his breathing. His—

Enough. I was speaking of my mother.

I had set the bottles on the table, and was clawing the dust and cobwebs off them, when she informed me that she did not drink now. This was a surprise—in the old days she could knock it back with the best of them. I stared at her, and she shrugged and looked away. Doctor's orders, she said. I examined her with renewed attention. There was something wrong with her left eye, and her mouth drooped a little on that side. I recalled the odd way she had clutched the cigarette box and matches in her left hand when she was conducting me around the house. She shrugged again. A slight stroke, she said, last year. I thought what an odd term that is: a slight stroke. As if a benevolent but clumsy power had dealt her a fond, playful blow and accidentally damaged her. She glanced at me sidelong now with a tentative, almost girlish, melancholy little smile. She might have been confessing to something, some pecca-dillo, trivial but embarrassing. Sorry to hear it, old thing, I said, and urged her to go on, take a drop of wine, the doctors be damned. She seemed not to hear me. And then a really surprising thing happened. The girl, Joan or Jean—I'll compromise, and call her Jane—got up suddenly from her place, with a gulp of distress, and put her arm awkwardly around my mother's head, clutching her in a sort of wrestling hold, and laying a hand along her brow. I expected my mother to give her a good push and tell her to get off, but no, she sat there, suffering calmly the girl's embrace and looking at me still with that small smile. I stared back at her in startlement, holding the wine bottle suspended above my glass. It was the strangest thing. The girl's great hip was beside my mother's shoulder, and I thought irresistibly of the pony pressing against me on the lawn with that stubborn, brute weight. There was a silence. Then the girl, I mean Jane, caught my eye, and blenched, and withdrew her arm and sat down again hurriedly. Here is a question: if man is a sick animal, an insane animal, as I have reason to believe, then how account for these small, unbidden gestures of kindness and of care? Does it occur to you, my Lord, that people of our kind—if I may be permitted to scramble up and join you on the bench for a moment—that we have missed out on something, I mean something in general, a universal principle, which is so simple, so obvious, that no one has ever thought to tell us about it? They all know what it is, my learned friend, this knowledge is the badge of their fellowship. And they are everywhere, the vast, sad, initiated crowd. They look up at us from the well of the court and say nothing, only smile a little, with that mixture of compassion and sympathetic irony, as my mother was smiling at me now. She reached across and patted the girl's hand and told her not to mind me. I stared. What had I done? The child sat with eyes fixed on her plate, groping blindly for her knife and fork. Her cheeks were aflame, I could almost hear them hum. Had a look from me done all that? I sighed, poor ogre, and ate a potato. It was raw and waxen at the heart. More drink.

You're not getting into one of your moods, are you, Freddie? my mother said.

Have I mentioned my bad moods, I wonder. Very black, very black. As if the world had grown suddenly dim, as if something had dirtied the air. Even when I was a child my depressions frightened people. In them again, is he? they would say, and they would chuckle, but uneasily, and edge away from me. In school I was a terror—but no, no, I'll spare you the schooldays. I noticed my mother was no longer much impressed by my gloom. Her smile, with that slight droop at the side, was turning positively sardonic. I said I had seen Charlie French in town. Oh, Charlie, she said, and shook her head and laughed. I nodded. Poor Charlie, he is the kind of person about whom people say, Oh, like that, and laugh. Another, listless silence. Why on earth had I come back here. I picked up the bottle, and was surprised to find it empty. I opened another, clamping it between my knees and swaying and grunting as I yanked at the cork. Ah! and out it came with a jolly pop. Outside on the lawn the last of the day's sunlight thickened briefly, then faded. My mother was asking after Daphne and the child. At the thought of them something like a great sob, lugubrious, faintly comical, ballooned under my breastbone. Jane—no, I can't call her that, it doesn't fit—Joan cleared the table, and my mother produced, of all things, a decanter of port and pushed it across the table to me. You won't want us to withdraw, will you? she said, with that grin—you can think of me as a man, anyway, I'm ancient enough. I began earnestly to tell her about my financial troubles, but got into a muddle and had to stop. Besides, I suspected she was not really listening. She sat with her face half-turned to the nickel light of evening from the window, rheum-eyed and old, showing the broad brow and high cheekbones of her Dutch forebears, King Billy's henchmen. You should have a ruff, Ma, I said, and a lace cap. I laughed loudly, then frowned. My face was going numb. Jean carefully offered me a cup of coffee. No, thank you, my dear, I said gravely, in my grandee's voice, indicating my port glass, which, I noticed, was unaccountably empty. I refilled it, admiring the steadiness of the hand that held the decanter. Time passed. Birds were calling through the blue-grey dusk. I sat bemused, bolt-upright, in happy misery, listening to them. Then with a snort and a heave I roused myself and looked about me, smacking my lips and blinking. My mother and the girl were gone.

He died at evening. The room was still heavy with the long day's heat. I sat on a chair beside his bed in the open window and held his hand. His hand. The waxen feel of. How bright the air above the trees, bright and blue, like the limitless skies of childhood. I put my arm around him, laid a hand on his forehead. He said to me: don't mind her. He said to me—

Stop this, stop it. I was not there. I have not been present at anyone's death. He died alone, slipped away while no one was looking, leaving us to our own devices. By the time I arrived from the city they had trussed him up, ready for the coffin. He lay on the bed with his hands folded on his breast and his eyes shut tight, like a child being good. His hair was brushed in a neat lick across his forehead. His ears, I remember, were very white. Extraordinary:

all that anger and resentment, that furious, unfocused energy: gone.

I took what remained of the port and staggered away upstairs. My knees quaked, I felt as if I were lugging a body on my back. The light-switches seemed to have been moved, in the half-darkness I kept banging into things, swearing and laughing. Then I found my way by mistake into Joanne's room. (Joanne: that's it!) She must have been awake, listening to me barging about, I hardly got the door open before she switched on her lamp. I stood teetering on the threshold, goggling at her. She lay in a vast, sagging bed with the sheet pulled to her chin, and for some reason I was convinced that she was still wearing her jodhpurs and her baggy pullover, and even her riding boots. She said nothing, only smiled at me in fright, and for a wild moment I considered climbing in beside her, shoes and all, so that now she might cradle *my* poor whirling head in her plump young accommodating arm. I had not really noticed before her extraordinary flame-red hair, the sight of it spread out on the pillow in the lamplight almost made me cry. Then the moment was gone, and with a grave nod I withdrew silently, like an old sad grey fading ghost, and marched at a careful, dignified pace across the landing to the room where a bed had been made up for me. There I discovered that somewhere along the way I had mislaid the port.

I sat on the side of the bed, arms dangling between my knees, and was suddenly exhausted. My head fizzed, my eyes burned, but yet I could not make myself lie down to sleep. I might have been a child come home after a day of wild excursions. I had travelled far. Slowly, with underwater movements, I untied my shoelaces. One shoe dropped, and then—

I woke with a dreadful start, my ears ringing, as if there had been an explosion in my head. A dream: something about meat. It was light, but whether it was dawn or still dusk I was not sure. Grey. Nor did I know where I was. Even when I realised it was Cool-grange I did not recognise the room at first. Very high and long, with lofty windows that came down to the floor. Shabby, too, in a peculiar, offended way, as if it were conscious of once having been an important place. I got up carefully from the bed and went and looked down at the lawn. The grass was pale, and there were pigeon-coloured shadows under the trees. My brain thudded. It must be dawn: in the oak wood, under an iron sky, a solitary bird was testing out the lightening air with a single repeated flute-note. I pressed my forehead against the windowpane, and shivered at the clammy, cold touch of the glass. I had been travelling for the best part of a week, with scant food and too much alcohol, and now it was all catching up with me. I felt sick, sodden, reamed. My eyelids were scalding, my spit tasted of ash. It seemed to me the garden was watching me, in its stealthy, tight-lipped way, or that it was at least somehow aware of me, framed here in the window, wringing my hands, a stricken starer-out—how many other such there must have been, down the years!—with the room's weightless dark pressing at my back. I had slept in my clothes.

The dream. (The court will need to hear about my dreams.) It came back to me suddenly. Nothing very much happened in it. My dreams are not the riotous tumble of events that others claim to enjoy, but states of feeling, rather, moods, particular humours, gusts of emotion, accompanied often by extreme physical effects: I weep, or thrash my limbs, grind my teeth, laugh, cry out. On this occasion it had been a dry retching, the ache in my throat when I woke was what brought it back to me. I had dreamed I was gnawing the ripped-out sternum of some creature, possibly human. It seemed to have been boiled, for the meat on it was soft and white. Barely warm now, it crumbled in my mouth like suet, making me gag. Believe me, your Lordship, I do not enjoy relating these things any more than the court enjoys hearing them. And there is worse to come, as you know. Anyway, there I was, mumbling these frightful gobs of flesh, my stomach heaving even as I slept. That is all there was, really, except for an underlying sensation of enforced yet horribly pleasurable transgression. Wait a moment. I want to get this right, it is important, I'm not sure why. Some nameless authority was making me do this terrible thing, was standing over me implacably with folded arms as I sucked and slobbered, yet despite this—or perhaps, even, because of it—despite the horror, too, and the nausea—deep inside me something exulted.

By the way, leafing through my dictionary I am struck by the poverty of the language when it comes to naming or describing badness. Evil, wickedness, mischief, these words imply an agency, the conscious or at least active doing of wrong. They do not signify the bad in its inert, neutral, self-sustaining state. Then there are the adjectives: dreadful, heinous, execrable, vile, and so on. They are not so much descriptive as judgmental. They carry a weight of censure mingled with fear. Is this not a queer state of affairs? It makes me wonder. I ask myself if perhaps the thing itself—*badness*—does not exist at all, if these strangely vague and imprecise words are only a kind of ruse, a kind of elaborate cover for the fact that nothing is there. Or perhaps the words are an attempt to make it be there? Or, again, perhaps there *is* something, but the words invented it. Such considerations make me feel dizzy, as if a hole had opened briefly in the world. What was I talking about? My dreams, yes. There was the recurring one, the one in which—but no, no, leave that to another time.

I am standing by the window, in my parents' bedroom. Yes, I had realised that it was, used to be, theirs. The grey of dawn was giving way to a pale wash of sunlight. My lips were tacky from last night's port. The room, the house, the garden and the fields, all was strange to me, I did not recognise it today—strange, and yet known, too, like a place in—yes—in a dream. I stood there in my wrinkled suit, with my aching head and soiled mouth, wide-eyed but not quite awake, staring fixedly into that patch of sunlit garden with an amnesiac's numbed amazement. But then, am I not always like that, more or less? When I think about it, I seem to have lived most of my life that way, stalled between sleep and waking, unable to distinguish between dream and the daylight world. In my mind there are places, moments, events, which are so still, so isolated, that I am not sure they can be real, but which if I had recalled them that morning would have struck me with more vividness and force than the real things surrounding me. For instance, there is the hallway of a farmhouse where I went once as a child to buy apples. I see the polished stone floor, cardinal red. I can smell the polish. There is a gnarled geranium in a pot, and a big pendulum clock with the minute-hand missing. I can hear the farmer's wife speaking in the dim depths of the house, asking something of someone. I can sense the fields all around, the light above the fields, the vast, slow, late-summer day. I am there. In such remembered moments I am there as I never was at Coolgrange, as I seem never to have been, or to be, anywhere, at any time, as I, or some essential part of me, was not there even on that day I am remembering, the day I went to buy apples from the farmer's wife, at that farm in the midst of the fields. Never wholly anywhere, never with anyone, either, that was me, always. Even as a child I seemed to myself a traveller who had been delayed in the middle of an urgent journey. Life was an unconscionable wait, walking up and down the platform, watching for the train. People got in the way and blocked my view, I had to crane to see past them. Yes, that was me, all right.

I picked my way down through the silent house to the kitchen. In the morning light the room had a scrubbed, eager aspect. I moved about warily, unwilling to disturb the atmosphere of hushed expectancy, feeling like an uninitiate at some grand, rapt ceremony of light and weather. The dog lay on a dirty old rug beside the stove, its muzzle between its paws, watching me, a crescent of white showing in each eye. I made a pot of tea, and was sitting at the table, waiting for it to draw, when Joanne came in. She was wearing a mouse-grey dressing-gown belted tightly about her midriff. Her hair was tied up at the back in a thick, appropriately equine plume. It really was remarkable in colour, a vernal russet blaze. Immediately, and not for the first time, I found myself picturing how she must be flossed elsewhere, and then was ashamed, as if I had misused the poor child. Seeing me, she halted, of course, ready to bolt. I lifted the teapot in a friendly gesture, and invited her to join me. She shut the door and edged around me with a panic-stricken smile, keeping the table between us, and took down a cup and saucer from the dresser. She had red heels and very white, thick calves. I thought she must be about seventeen. Through the fog of my hangover it occurred to me that she would be bound to know something about the state of my mother's finances—whether, for instance, those ponies were making money. I gave her what was intended to be a boyish, encouraging smile, though I suspect it came out a broken leer, and told her to sit down, that we must have a chat. The tea, however, was not for her, but for my mother—for Dolly, she said. Well! I thought, Dolly, no less! She made off at once, with the saucer grasped in both hands and her agitated smile fixed on the trembling liquid in the cup.

When she was gone I poked about morosely for a while, looking for the papers that had been on the table yesterday, the bills and ledgers and chequebook stubs, but found nothing. A drawer of the little bureau from my father's study was locked. I considered forcing it open, but restrained myself: in my hungover mood I might have smashed the whole thing to bits.

I wandered off through the house, carrying my teacup with me. In the drawing room the carpet had been taken up, and a pane of glass in one of the windows was broken, and there was glass on the floor. I noticed I had no shoes on. I opened the garden door and stepped outside in my socks. There was a smell of sun-warmed grass and a faint tang of dung in the rinsed, silky air. The black shadow of the house lay across the lawn like a fallen stage-flat. I ventured a step or two on the yielding turf, the dew seeping up between my toes. I felt like an old man, going along shakily with my cup and saucer rattling and my trouser-cuffs wet and crumpled around my ankles. The rosebeds under the window had not been tended for years, and a tangle of briars rioted at the sills. The faded roses hung in clusters, heavy as cloth. Their particular wan shade of pink, and the chiaroscuro of the scene in general, put me in mind of something. I halted, frowning. The pictures—of course. I went back into the drawing room. Yes, the walls were empty, with here and there a square patch where the wallpaper was not as faded as elsewhere. Surely she hadn't—? I put my cup down carefully on the mantelpiece, taking slow, deep breaths. The bitch! I said aloud, I bet she has! My feet had left wet, webbed prints behind me on the floorboards.

I went through room after room, scanning the walls. Then I tackled the upstairs. But I knew there would be nothing. I stood on the first-floor landing, cursing under my breath. There were voices nearby. I flung open a bedroom door. My mother and Joanne were sitting up side by side in the girl's big bed. They looked at me in mild astonishment, and for a moment I faltered as something brushed past my consciousness, a wingbeat of incredulous speculation. My mother wore a knitted yellow bed-jacket with bobbles and tiny satin bows, which made her look like a monstrously overgrown Easter chick. Where, I said, with a calm that surprised me, where are the pictures, pray? There followed a bit of comic patter, with my mother saying *What? What?* and I shouting *The pictures! The pictures, damn it!* In the end we both had to shut up. The girl had been watching us, turning her eyes slowly from one to the other of us, like a spectator at a tennis match. Now she put a hand over her mouth and laughed. I stared at her, and she blushed. There was a brief silence. I will see you downstairs, mother, I said, in a voice so stiff with ice it fairly creaked.

As I was going away from the door I thought I heard them both sniggering.

My mother arrived in the kitchen barefoot. The sight of her bunions and her big yellow toenails annoyed me. She had wrapped herself in an impossible, shot-silk tea-gown. She had the florid look of one of Lautrec's ruined doxies. I tried not to show too much of the disgust I felt. She pottered about with a show of unconcern, ignoring me. Well? I said, but she only raised her eyebrows blandly and said, Well what? She was almost smirking. That did it. I shouted, I waved my fists, I stamped about stiff-legged, beside myself. Where were they, the pictures, I cried, what had she done with them? I *demanded* to know. They were mine, my inheritance, my future and my son's future. And so on. My anger, my sense of outrage, impressed me. I was moved. I might almost have shed tears, I felt so sorry for myself. She let me go on like this for a while, standing with a hand on her hip and her head thrown back, contemplating me with sardonic calm. Then, when I paused to take a breath, she started. Demand, did I?—I, who had gone off and abandoned my widowed mother, who had skipped off to America and married without even informing her, who had never once brought my child, her grandson, to see her—I, who for ten years had stravaged the world like a tinker, never doing a hand's turn of work, living off my dead father's few pounds and bleeding the estate dry—what right, she shrilled, what right had I to demand anything here? She stopped, and waited, as if really expecting an answer. I fell back a pace. I had forgotten what she is like when she gets going. Then I gathered myself and launched at her again. She rose magnificently to meet me. It was just like the old days. Hammer and tongs, oh, hammer and tongs! So stirring was it that even the dog joined in, barking and whining and dancing up and down on its front paws, until my mother gave it a clout and roared at it to lie down. I called her a bitch and she called me a bastard. I said if I was a bastard what did that make her, and quick as a flash she said, If I'm a bitch what does that make *you*, you cur! Oh, it was grand, a grand match. We were like furious children—no, not children, but big, maddened, primitive creatures—mastodons, something like that—tearing and thrashing in a jungle clearing amidst a storm of whipping lianas and uprooted vegetation. The air throbbed between us, blood-dimmed and thick. There was a sense of things ranged around us, small creatures cowering in the undergrowth, watching us in a trance of terror and awe. At last, sated, we disengaged tusks and turned aside. I nursed my pounding head in my hands. She stood at the sink, holding on to one of the taps and looking out of the window at the garden, her chest heaving. We could hear ourselves breathe. The upstairs lavatory flushed, a muted, tentative noise, as if the girl were tactfully reminding us of her presence in the house. My mother sighed. She had sold the pictures to Binkie Behrens. I breathless from the stairs, leaning down and pressing a fiver urgently into a palsied, papery hand. He accumulated a lot of trash, but there were a few pieces which I thought were not altogether bad, and probably worth something. Most of these he had wheedled out of a distraite old lady whom his own father had courted briefly when she was a girl. He was hugely proud of this piece of chicanery, imagining, I suppose, that it put him on a par with the great robber barons of the past whom he so much admired, the Guggenheims and Pierpont Morgans and, indeed, the Behrenses. Perhaps these were the very pictures that led to his meeting Helmut Behrens. Perhaps they tussled for them over the old lady's deathbed, narrowing their eyes at each other, mouths pursed in furious determination.

It was through painting also that I met Anna Behrens—or met her again, I should say. We knew each other a little when we were young. I seem to remember once at Whitewater being sent outside to play with her in the grounds. Play! That's a good one. Even in those days she had that air of detachment, of faint, remote amusement, which I have always found unnerving. Later on, in Dublin, she would appear now and then, and glide through our student roisterings, poised, silent, palely handsome. She was nicknamed the Ice Queen, of course. I lost sight of her, forgot about her, until one day in Berkeley—this is where the coincidences begin—I spotted her in a gallery on Shattuck Avenue. I had not known she was in America, yet there was no sense of surprise. This is one of the things about Anna, she belongs exactly wherever she happens to be. I stood in the street for a moment watching her—admiring her, I suppose. The gallery was a large high white room with a glass front. She was leaning against a desk with a sheaf of papers in her hand, reading. She wore a white dress. Her hair, bleached silver by the sun, was done in a complicated fashion, with a single heavy braid hanging down at her shoulder. She might have been a piece on show, standing there so still in that tall, shadowless light behind sun-reflecting glass. I went in and spoke to her, admiring again that long, slightly off-centre, melancholy face with its close-set grey eyes and florentine mouth. I remembered the two tiny white spots on the bridge of her nose where the skin was stretched tight over the bone. She was friendly, in her distant way. She watched my lips as I talked. On the walls there were two or three vast canvases, done in the joky, minimalist style of the time, hardly distinguishable in their pastel bareness from the blank spaces surrounding them. I asked her if she was thinking of buying something. This amused her. I work here, she said, pushing back the blonde braid from her shoulder. I invited her to lunch, but she shook her head. She gave me her telephone number. When I stepped out into the sunlit street a jet plane was passing low over-head, its engines making the air rattle, and there was a smell of cypresses and car exhaust, and a faint whiff of tear gas from the direction of the campus. All this was fifteen years ago. I crumpled the file card on which she had written her phone number, and started to throw it away. But I kept it.

She lived in the hills, in a mock-Tyrolean, shingled wooden house which she rented from a mad widow. More than once on the way there I stood up to get off the bus and go home, bored and half-annoyed already at the thought of Anna's amused, appraising glance, that impenetrable smile. When I called her she had spoken hardly a dozen words, and twice she put a hand over the phone and talked to someone with her in the room. Yet that morning I had shaved with particular care, and put on a new shirt, and selected an impressive volume on mathematical theory to carry with me. Now, as the bus threaded its way up these narrow roads, I was assailed by a sense of revulsion, I seemed to myself an obscurely shameful, lewd object, exposed and cringing, with my palped and powdered flesh, my baby-blue shirt, the floppy book clutched in my hand like a parcel of meat. The day was overcast, and there was mist in the pines. I climbed a zigzag of damp steps to the door, looking about me with an expression of bland interest, trying to appear blameless, as I always seem to do when I am on unfamiliar territory. Anna wore shorts, and her hair was loose. The sight of her there suddenly in the doorway, ash-blonde, at ease, her long legs bare, caused an ache at the root of my tongue. The house was dim inside. A few books, prints on the wall, a straw hat on a hook. The widow's cats had left a trace of themselves on the carpets and the chairs, a sharp, citrus stink, not wholly unpleasant.

Daphne was sitting cross-legged in a canvas chair, shelling peas into a nickel bowl. She wore a bathrobe, and her hair was wrapped in a towel. Another coincidence, you see.

What did we talk about that day, the three of us? What did I do? Sat down, I suppose, drank a beer, stretched out my legs and leaned back, playing at being relaxed. I cannot see myself. I am a sort of floating eye, watching, noting, scheming. Anna came and went between the living room and the kitchen, bringing cheese and oranges and sliced avocados. It was Sunday. The place was quiet. I watched through the window the mist moving among the trees. The telephone rang and Anna answered it, turning away and murmuring into the receiver. Daphne smiled at me. Her glance was unfocused, a kind of soft groping among the objects around her. She rose and handed me the bowl and the remaining unshelled peas, and went away upstairs. When she came back in a while she was dressed, her hair was dried and she was wearing her spectacles, and at first I did not recognise her, and thought she was yet another tenant of the house. It was only then that I realised it was she I had seen on the lawn that day at Professor Something's party. I started to tell her about it, about having seen her, but I changed my mind, for the same, unknown reason that I had turned away that first time without speaking to her. She took the bowl of peas from me and sat down again. Anna answered another phonecall, murmuring, quietly laughing. It occurred to me that my presence was hardly impinging on their day, that they would have done just these same things if I were not there. It was a soothing thought. I had not been invited to dinner, but it seemed accepted that I would stay. After we had eaten we sat on at the table for a long time. The fog thickened, pressing against the windows. I see the two of them opposite me there in that milky twilight, the dark one and the fair: they have an air of complicity, of secret amusement, as if they are sharing a mild, not very unkind joke at my expense. How distant it all seems, an age away, when we were still innocent, if that is the word, which I doubt.

I was, I confess it, captivated by them, their looks, their composure, their casual selfishness. They embodied an ideal that I had not known I harboured until now. I was still working at my science in those days, I was going to be one of those great, cold technicians, the secret masters of the world. Now suddenly another future had opened up, as if these two had caused a whole rockface before me to fall away and reveal beyond the swirling dust a vast, radiant distance. They were splendid, at once languorous and dashing. They reminded me of a pair of adventuresses out of the last century. They had arrived in New York the previous winter, and drifted by stages across the country to this tawny, sunlit shore, where they were poised now, as if on tiptoe, hands joined and arms extended, with the Pacific all before them. Though they had been in this house nearly half a year their impress was so light, so fleeting, that the rooms had barely registered their presence. They seemed to have no belongings—even the straw hat hanging on the door had been left behind by a previous tenant. There must have been friends, or acquaintances at least—I'm thinking of those phone-calls—but I never met them. Once in a while their landlady would descend on them, a darkly dramatic person with soulful eyes and very black hair twisted tight into a bun and skewered with a carved wooden pin. She dressed like an Indian squaw, festooning herself with beads and brightly coloured scarves. She would surge about the house distractedly, talking over her shoulder and trailing a dense, musky perfume, then fling herself with a balletic leap on to the couch in the living room and sit for an hour telling of her woes—the result mostly of what with a throb in her voice she referred to as *man trouble*—meanwhile getting steadily, tearfully drunk on Calvados, a supply of which she kept in a locked cupboard in the kitchen. A ghastly woman, I could not abide her, that leathery skin and daubed mouth, all that hysteria, that messy loneliness. The girls, however, found her greatly entertaining. They liked to do imitations of her, and made catchphrases of things she said. Sometimes, listening to them mimicking her, I wondered if perhaps, when I was not there, they treated *me* like this, lobbing remarks at each other in a comically solemn version of my voice and laughing softly, in that jaded way they had, as if the joke were not really funny, just ridiculous.

They thought the country, too, was a scream, especially California. We had a lot of fun together laughing at the Americans, who just then were entering that stage of doomed hedonistic gaiety through which we, the gilded children of poor old raddled Europe, had already passed, or so we believed. How innocent they seemed to us, with their flowers and their joss sticks and their muddled religiosity. Of course, I felt a secret twinge of guilt, sneering at them like this. I had been captivated by the country when I first came there, now it was as if I had joined in mocking some happy, good-hearted creature, the fat girl at the party against whom only a moment ago I had been pressing myself, under cover of the general romp, in wordless, swollen ecstasy.

Perhaps contempt was for us a form of nostalgia, of homesickness, even? Living there, amid those gentle, paintbox colours, under that dome of flawless blue, was like living in another world, a place out of a storybook. (I used to dream of rain—real, daylong, Irish rain—as if it were something I had been told about but had never seen.) Or perhaps laughing at America was a means of defence? It's true, at times it crossed our minds, or it crossed *my* mind, at least, that we might be just the teeniest bit laughable ourselves. Was there not a touch of the preposterous about us, with our tweeds and our sensible shoes, our extravagant accents, our insolently polite manners? More than once I thought I detected a suppressed smile twitching the lips of some person who was supposed to be the unknowing butt of our ridicule. Even among ourselves there were moments of silence, of awkwardness, when a half-formed admission hovered between us, like a bad, embarrassing smell. A trio of expatriates meeting in this mellow playground—what could be more novelettish? We were a triangle, for God's sake!

We were a triangle. It happened, the inevitable, one afternoon a month or so after we met. We had been sitting on the porch at the back of the house drinking gin and smoking something with a horrid taste and the oddest effects. The day was hot and hazy. Above us a coin-coloured sun was stuck in the middle of a white sky. I was watching a cloud of hummingbirds sipping at a honeysuckle bush beside the porch steps. Daphne, in shorts and halter and high-heeled sandals, stood up, a little unsteadily, blinking, and wandered into the house. I followed her. I was not thinking of anything—I was fetching more ice, something like that. After the glare outside I could hardly see indoors, everywhere I turned the air had a huge dark hole in it. Idly I looked about for Daphne, following the sound of the ice tinkling in her glass, from the kitchen through the living room to the bedroom. The blind was drawn. She was sitting on the side of the bed, gazing before her in the amber half-light. My head suddenly began to ache. She drained her drink in one long gulp, and was still holding the glass when we lay down together, and a bead of ice slid out of it and dropped into the hollow of my shoulder. Her lips were chill and wet. She began to say something, and laughed softly into my mouth. Our clothes seemed tight as bandages, I clawed at them, snorting. Then abruptly we were naked. There was a startled pause. Somewhere nearby children were playing. Daphne laid her hand on my hip. Her eyes were closed, and she was smiling with her eyebrows raised, as if she were listening to a distant, dreamy, and slightly funny melody. I heard a sound, and looked over my shoulder. Anna was standing in the doorway. I had a glimpse of myself as she would see me, my glimmering flanks and pale backside, my fish-mouth agape. She hesitated a moment, and then walked to the bed with her eyes on the ground, as if deep in thought, and sat down beside us and began to undress. Daphne and I lay quietly in each other's arms and watched her. She pulled her blouse over her head, and surfaced like a swimmer, tossing her hair. A metal clasp left its mauve imprint in the centre of her back. Why did she seem to me so much older now than us, world-weary, a little used, an adult joining tolerantly in a children's not quite permissible game? Daphne hardly breathed, her fingers steadily tightening on my hip. Her lips were parted, and she frowned a little, gazing at Anna's bared flesh, lost in a sort of vague amazement. I could feel her heartbeat, and my own. We might have been attending a ritual disrobing.

A ritual, yes, that's how it was. We strove together slowly on the bed, the three of us, as if engaged in an archaic ceremonial of toil and worship, miming the fashioning and raising of something, a shrine, say, or a domed temple. How grave we were, how pensive, with what attentiveness we handled each other's flesh. No one spoke a word. The women had begun by exchanging a chaste kiss. They smiled, a little bashfully. My hands were trembling. I had felt this choking sense of transgression once before, long ago, when as a child I tussled with two girl cousins in the dark on the stairs one winter evening at Coolgrange—the same dread and incredulity, the same voluptuous, aching, infantile glee. Dreamily we delved and nuzzled, shivering, sighing. Now and then one of us would clutch at the other two with a child's impatient, greedy fervour and cry out softly, tinily, as if in pain or helpless sorrow. It seemed to me at times that there were not two women but one, a strange, remote creature, many-armed, absorbed behind an enamelled mask in something I could not begin to know. At the end, the final spasm gathering itself inside me, I raised myself up on trembling arms, with Daphne's heels pressed in the small of my back, and looked down at the two of them gnawing at each other with tender avidity, mouth on open mouth, and for a second, as the blood welled up in my eyes, I saw their heads merge, the fair one and the dark, the tawny and the panther-sleek. At once the shudder started in my groin, and I fell upon them, exultant and afraid.

But afterwards it was Daphne alone who lay in my arms, still holding me inside her, while Anna got up and walked to the window, and lifted the canvas blind at the side with one finger and stood gazing out into the hazy glare of afternoon. The children were still at play. There's a school, Anna murmured, up the hill. She laughed quietly and said, *But what do I know, I ask you?* It was one of the mad widow's catchphrases. Suddenly everything was sad and grey and waste. Daphne put her face against my shoulder and began to weep silently. I will always remember those children's voices.

It was a strange encounter, never to be repeated. I brood on it now, not for the obvious reasons, but because it puzzles me. The act itself, the troilism, was not so remarkable: in those days everyone was doing that sort of thing. No, what struck me then, and strikes me still, is the curious passiveness of my role in that afternoon's doings. I was the man among the three of us, yet I felt that it was I who was being softly, irresistibly penetrated. The wise will say that I was only the link along which the two of them had negotiated their way, hand over hand, into each other's arms. It may be true, but it is not of much significance, and certainly not the central thing. I could not rid myself of the feeling that a rite was being performed, in which Anna Behrens was the priestess and Daphne the sacrificial offering, while I was a mere prop. They wielded me like a stone phallus, bowing and writhing about me, with incantatory sighs. They were—

They were saying goodbye. Of course. It's just occurred to me. They were not finding each other, but parting. Hence the sadness and the sense of waste, hence Daphne's bitter tears. It was nothing to do with me, at all.

Well well. That's the advantage of jail, one has the time and leisure really to get to the heart of things.

The illusion of their melting into each other which I had experienced at the end of our bout on the bed that day was to last for a long time. Even yet when I think of them together it is a kind of double-headed coin that I see, on which are stamped their twin profiles, serene, emblematic, looking away, a stylised representation of paired virtues—Calm and Fortitude, let's say, or, better still, Silence and Sacrifice. I am remembering a certain moment, when Anna lifted her bruised, glistening mouth from between Daphne's legs and, glancing back at me with a complicitous, wry little smile, leaned aside so that I might see the sprawled girl's lap lying open there, intricate and innocent as a halved fruit. Everything was present, I see now, in that brief passage of renunciation and discovery. A whole future began just there.

I do not recall proposing to Daphne. Her hand, so to speak, had already been granted me. We were married one misty, hot afternoon in August. The ceremony was quick and squalid. I had a headache all through it. Anna and a colleague of mine from the university acted as witnesses. Afterwards the four of us went back to the house in the hills and drank cheap champagne. The occasion was not a success. My colleague made a limp excuse and departed after half an hour, leaving the three of us together in a restless, swirling silence. All sorts of unspoken things swam in the air between us like slithery, dangerous fish. Then Anna, with that smile, said she supposed we young things would want to be alone, and left. Suddenly I was prey to an absurd embarrassment. I jumped up and began collecting the empty bottles and the glasses, avoiding Daphne's eye. There was sun and mist in the kitchen window. I stood at the sink looking out at the blue-black ghosts of trees on the hillside, and two great, fat, inexplicable tears gathered on the rims of my eyelids, but would not fall.

I do not know that I loved Daphne in the manner that the world understands by that word, but I do know that I loved her ways. Will it seem strange, cold, perhaps even inhuman, if I say that I was only interested really in what she was on the surface? Pah, what do I care how it seems. This is the only way another creature can be known: on the surface, that's where there is depth. Daphne walking through a room searching for her spectacles, touching things gently, quickly, reading things with her fingertips. The way she had of turning aside and peering into her purse, frowning, lips compressed, like a maiden aunt fetching up a shilling for sweets. Her stinginess, her sudden rushes of greed, childish and endearing. That time, years ago, I can't remember where, when I came upon her at the end of a party, standing by a window in a blue dress in the half-light of an April dawn, lost in a dream—a dream from which I, tipsy and in a temper, unceremoniously woke her, when I could—dear Christ!—when I could have hung back in the shadows and painted her, down to the tiniest, tenderest detail, on the blank inner wall of my heart, where she would be still, vivid as in that dawn, my dark, mysterious darling.

We quickly agreed—tacitly, as always—to leave America. I gave up my studies, the university, my academic career, everything, with hardly a second thought, and before the year was out we had sailed for Europe.

Maolseachlainn Mac Giolla Gunna, my counsel and, he insists, my friend, has a trick of seizing on the apparently trivial in the elaboration of his cases. Anecdotes of his methods circulate in the corridors of chancery, and around the catwalks in here. Details, details are his obsession. He is a large, lumbering, unhandy man— yards, literally yards of pinstripe—with a big square head and raggedy hair and tiny, haunted eyes. I think a life spent poking in the crevices of other people's nasty little tragedies has damaged something in him. He exudes an air of injured longing. They say he is a terror in court, but when he sits at the scarred table in the counsel room here, with his half-glasses hooked on that big head, crouched over his papers and writing out notes in a laborious, minute hand, panting a little and muttering to himself, I am reminded irresistibly of a certain fat boy from my schooldays, who was disconsolately in love with me, and whom I used to get to do my homework for me.

At present Maolseachlainn is deeply interested in why I went to Whitewater in the first place. But why should I not have gone there? I knew the Behrenses—or God knows I knew Anna, anyway. I had been away for ten years, I was paying a social call, as a friend of the family. This, however, is not good enough, it seems. Maolseachlainn frowns, slowly shaking his great head, and without realising it goes into his court routine. Is it not true that I left my mother's house in anger only a day after my arrival there? Is it not the case that I was in a state of high indignation because I had heard my father's collection of pictures had been sold to Helmut Behrens for what I considered a paltry sum? And is it not further the case that I had reason already to feel resentment against the man Behrens, who had attempted to cuckold my father in—But hold on there, old man, I said: that last bit only came to light later on. He always looks so crestfallen when I stop him in his tracks like this. All the same, facts are facts.

It is true, I did fight with my mother again, I did storm out of the house (with the dog after me, of course, trying to bite my heels). However, Binkie Behrens was not the cause of the row, or not directly, anyway. As far as I remember it was the same old squabble: money, betrayal, my going to the States, my leaving the States, my marriage, my abandoned career, all that, the usual— and, yes, the fact that she had flogged my birthright for the price of a string of plug-ugly ponies out of which she had imagined she would make a fortune to provide for herself in the decrepitude of her old age, the deluded bloody bitch. There was as well the business of the girl Joanne. As I was leaving I paused and said, measuring my words, that I thought it hardly appropriate for a woman of my mother's position in society—her position!—in society!—to be so chummy with a stable-girl. I confess I had intended to cause outrage, but I am afraid I was the one who ended up goggle-eyed. My mother, after a moment's silence, stared me straight in the face, with brazen insouciance, and said that Joanne was not a child, that she was in fact twenty-seven years of age. She is—with a pause here for effect—she is like a son to me, the son I never had. Well, I said, swallowing hard, I'm happy for you both, I'm sure! and flounced out of the house. On the drive, though, I had to stop and wait for my indignation and resentment to subside a little before I could get my breath back. Sometimes I think I am an utter sentimentalist.

*

I got to Whitewater that evening. The last leg of the journey I made by taxi from the village. The driver was an immensely tall, emaciated man in a flat cap and an antique, blue-flannel suit. He studied me with interest in the driving-mirror, hardly bothering to watch the road ahead of us. I tried staring back at him balefully, but he was unabashed, and only grinned a little on one side of his thin face with a peculiarly friendly air of knowing. Why do I remember people like this so vividly? They clutter my mind, when I look up from the page they are thronged around me in the shadows, silent, mildly curious—even, it might be, solicitous. They are witnesses, I suppose, the innocent bystanders who have come, without malice, to testify against me.

I can never approach Whitewater without a small, involuntary gasp of admiration. The drive leads up from the road in a long, deep, treeless curve, so that the house seems to turn, slowly, dreamily, opening wide its Palladian colonnades. The taxi drew to a stop on the gravel below the great front steps, and with the sudden silence came the realisation—yes, Maolseachlainn, I admit it—that I had no reasonable cause to be there. I sat for a moment looking about me in groggy consternation, like a wakened sleepwalker, but the driver was watching me in the mirror now with rapt expectancy, and I had to pretend to know what I was about. I got out of the car and stood patting my pockets and frowning, but I could not fool him, his lopsided grin grew slyer still, for a second I thought he was going to wink at me. I told him brusquely to wait, and mounted the steps pursued by an unshakeable sensation of general mockery.

After a long time the door was opened by a wizened little angry man in what appeared at first to be a bus conductor's uniform. A few long strands of very black hair were plastered across his skull like streaks of boot polish. He looked at me with deep disgust. Not open today, he said, and was starting to shut the door in my face when I stepped smartly past him into the hall. I gazed about me, rubbing my hands slowly and smiling, playing the returned expatriate. Ah, I said, the old place! The great Tintoretto on the stairs, swarming with angels and mad-eyed martyrs, blazed at me its vast chromatic chord. The doorman or whatever he was danced about anxiously behind me. I turned and loomed at him, still grinning, and said no, I wasn't a tripper, but a friend of the family—was Miss Behrens at home, by any chance? He dithered, distrustful still, then told me to wait, and scuttled off down the hall, splaying one flat foot as he went and carefully smoothing the oiled hairs on his pate.

I waited. All was silent save for the ticking of a tall, seventeenth-century German clock. On the wall beside me there was a set of six exquisite little Bonington watercolours, I could have put a couple of them under my arm there and then and walked out. The clock took a laboured breath and pinged the half-hour, and then, all about me, in farther and farther rooms, other clocks too let fall their single, silvery chimes, and it was as if a tiny tremor had passed through the house. I looked again at the Tintoretto. There was a Fragonard, too, and a Watteau. And this was only the hall-way. What was going on, what had happened, that it was all left unattended like this? I heard the taximan outside sounding his horn, a tentative, apologetic little toot. He must have thought I had forgotten about him. (I had.) Somewhere at the back of the house a door banged shut, and a second later a breath of cool air brushed past my face. I advanced creakingly along the hall, a hot, almost sensuous thrill of apprehensiveness pulsing behind my breast-bone. I am at heart a timid man, and large deserted places make me nervous. One of the figures in the Fragonard, a silken lady with blue eyes and a plump lower lip, was watching me sidelong with what seemed an expression of appalled but lively speculation. Cautiously I opened a door. The fat knob turned under my hand with a wonderful, confiding smoothness. I entered a long, high, narrow, many-windowed room. The wallpaper was the colour of tarnished gold. The air was golden too, suffused with the heavy soft light of evening. I felt as if I had stepped straight into the eighteenth century. The furnishings were sparse, there were no more than five or six pieces—some delicate, lyre-backed chairs, an ornate sideboard, a small ormolu table—placed just so, in such a way that not the things but the space around them, the light itself, seemed arranged. I stood quite still, listening, I did not know for what. On the low table there was a large and complicated jigsaw puzzle, half-assembled. Some of the pieces had fallen to the floor. I gazed at them, sprinkled on the parquet like puddles of something that had spilled, and once again a faint shiver seemed to pass through the house. At the far end of the room a french window stood wide-open, and a gauze curtain billowed in the breeze. Outside there was a long slope of lawn, whereon, in the middle distance, a lone, heraldic horse was prancing. Farther off was the river bend, the water whitening in the shallows, and beyond that there were trees, and then vague mountains, and then the limitless, gilded blue of summer. It struck me that the perspective of this scene was wrong somehow. Things seemed not to recede as they should, but to be arrayed before me—the furniture, the open window, the lawn and river and far-off mountains—as if they were not being looked at but were themselves looking, intent upon a vanishing point here, inside the room. I turned then, and saw myself turning as I turned, as I seem to myself to be turning still, as I sometimes imagine I shall be turning always, as if this might be my punishment, my damnation, just this breathless, blurred, eternal turning towards her.

You have seen the picture in the papers, you know what she looks like. A youngish woman in a black dress with a broad white collar, standing with her hands folded in front of her, one gloved, the other hidden except for the fingers, which are flexed, ringless. She is wearing something on her head, a cap or clasp of some sort, which holds her hair drawn tightly back from her brow. Her prominent black eyes have a faintly oriental slant. The nose is large, the lips full. She is not beautiful. In her right hand she holds a folded fan, or it might be a book. She is standing in what I take to be the lighted doorway of a room. Part of a couch can be seen, or maybe a bed, with a brocade cover. The darkness behind her is dense and yet mysteriously weightless. Her gaze is calm, inexpectant, though there is a trace of challenge, of hostility, even, in the set of her mouth. She does not want to be here, and yet cannot be elsewhere. The gold brooch that secures the wings of her wide collar is expensive and ugly. All this you have seen, all this you know. Yet I put it to you, gentle connoisseurs of the jury, that even knowing all this you still know nothing, next to nothing. You do not know the fortitude and pathos of her presence. You have not come upon her suddenly in a golden room on a summer eve, as I have. You have not held her in your arms, you have not seen her asprawl in a ditch. You have not—ah no!—you have not killed for her.

I stood there, staring, for what seemed a long time, and gradually a kind of embarrassment took hold of me, a hot, shamefaced awareness of myself, as if somehow I, this soiled sack of flesh, were the one who was being scrutinised, with careful, cold attention. It was not just the woman's painted stare that watched me. Everything in the picture, that brooch, those gloves, the flocculent darkness at her back, every spot on the canvas was an eye fixed on me unblinkingly. I retreated a pace, faintly aghast. The silence was fraying at the edges. I heard cows lowing, a car starting up. I remembered the taxi, and turned to go. A maid was standing in the open french window. She must have come in just then and seen me there and started back in alarm. Her eyes were wide, and one knee was flexed and one hand lifted, as if to ward off a blow. For a moment neither of us stirred. Behind her a sudden breeze burnished the grassy slope. We did not speak. Then slowly, with her hand still raised, she stepped backwards carefully through the window, teetering a little as her heels blindly sought the level of the paved pathway outside. I felt an inexplicable, brief rush of annoyance—a presentiment, perhaps, a stray zephyr sent ahead of the storm that was to come. A telephone was ringing somewhere. I turned quickly and left the room.

There was no one in the hall. The telephone rang and rang, with peevish insistence. I could still hear it going as I descended the front steps. The taxi had left, of course. I swore, and set off down the drive, hobbling over the stony ground in my thin-soled Spanish shoes. The low sun glared in my face. When I looked back at the house the windows were ablaze, and seemed to be laughing fatly in derision. I began to perspire, and that brought on the midges. I asked myself again what had possessed me to come to White-water. I knew the answer, of course. It was the smell of money that had attracted me, as the smell of sweat was attracting these damned flies. I saw myself, as if from one of those sunstruck windows, skulking along here in the dust, hot, disgruntled, over-weight, head bowed and fat back bent, my white suit rucked at the armpits and sagging in the arse, a figure of fun, the punchline of a bad joke, and at once I was awash with self-pity. Christ! was there no one who would help me? I halted, and cast a troubled glance around me, as if there might be a benefactor lurking among the trees. The silence had a sense of muffled gloating. I plunged on again, and heard the sound of engines, and presently an enormous black limousine came around the bend, followed by a sleek red sportscar. They were going at a stately pace, the limousine bouncing gently on its springs, and for a second I thought it was a funeral. I stepped on to the grass verge but kept on walking. The driver of the limousine, a large, crop-headed man, sat erect and vigilant, his hands lightly cupped on the rim of the steering wheel, as if it were a projectile he might pluck from its moorings and throw with deadly aim. Beside him there was a stooped, shrunken figure, as the car swished past I glimpsed a dark eye and a liver-spotted skull, and huge hands resting one upon the other on the crook of a stick. A blonde woman wearing dark glasses was driving the sportscar. We gazed at each other with blank interest, like strangers, as she went by. I recognised her, of course.

Ten minutes later I was trudging along the road with my thumb stuck out when I heard her pull up behind me. I knew it would be she. I stopped, turned. She remained in the car, her wrists folded before her on the steering wheel. There was a brief, wordless tussle to see which one of us would make the first move. We compromised. I walked back to the car and she got out to meet me. I *thought* it was you, she said. We smiled, and were silent. She wore a cream suit and a white blouse. There was blood on her shoes. Her hair was yellower than I remembered, I wondered if she was dyeing it now. I told her she looked marvellous. I meant it, but the words sounded hollow, and I blushed. Anna, I said. I remembered, with a soft shock, how one day long ago I stole the envelope of one of her letters to Daphne, and took it into the lavatory and prised open the flap, my heart pounding, so that I might lick the gum where she had licked. The thought came to me: I loved her! and I gave a sort of wild, astonished laugh. She took off her sunglasses and looked at me quizzically. My hands were trembling. Come and see Father, she said, he needs cheering up.

She drove very fast, working the controls probingly, as if she were trying to locate a pattern, a secret formula, hidden in this mesh of small, deft actions. I was impressed, even a little cowed. She was full of the impatient assurance of the rich. We did not speak. In a moment we were at the house, and pulled up in a spray of gravel. She opened her door, then paused and looked at me for a moment in silence and shook her head. Freddie Montgomery, she said. Well!

As we went up the steps to the front door she linked her arm lightly in mine. I was surprised. When I knew her, all those years ago, she was not one for easy intimacies—intimacies, yes, but not easy ones. She laughed and said, God, I'm a little drunk, I think. She had been to the hospital in the city—Behrens had suffered some sort of mild attack. The hospital was in an uproar. A bomb had gone off in a car in a crowded shopping street, quite a small device, apparently, but remarkably effective. She had wandered unchallenged into the casualty ward. There were bodies lying everywhere. She walked among the dead and dying, feeling like a survivor herself. Good God, Anna, I said. She gave a tense little laugh. What an experience, she said—luckily Flynn keeps a flask of something in the glove compartment. She had taken a few good swigs, and was beginning to regret it now.

We went into the house. The uniformed doorman was nowhere to be seen. I told Anna how he had gone off and left me to wander at will about the place. She shrugged. She supposed everyone had been downstairs watching the news of the bombing on television. All the same, I said, anyone could have got in. Why, she asked, do you think someone might come and plant a bomb here? And she looked at me with a peculiar, bitter smile.

She led the way into the gold salon. The french window was still open. There was no sign of the maid. A sort of shyness made me keep my eyes averted from the other end of the room, where the picture leaned out a little from the wall, as if listening intently. I sat down gingerly on one of the Louis Quinze chairs while Anna opened the carved and curlicued sideboard and poured out two whopping measures of gin. There was no ice, and the tonic was flat, but I didn't care, I needed a drink. I was still breathless with the notion of having been in love with her. I felt excited and bemused, and ridiculously pleased, like a child who has been given something precious to play with. I said it to myself again—*I loved her!*—trying it out for the sound of it. The thought, lofty, grand, and slightly mad, fitted well with the surroundings. She was pacing between me and the window, clutching her glass tightly in both hands. The gauze curtain bellied lazily at the edge of my vision. Something in the air itself seemed to be shaking. Suddenly the telephone on the low table beside me sprang to life with a crashing noise. Anna snatched it up and cried yes, yes, what? She laughed. It's some taximan, she said to me, looking for his fare. I took the phone and spoke harshly to the fellow. She watched me intently, with a kind of avid amusement. When I put down the receiver she said gaily, Oh, Freddie, you've got so pompous! I frowned. I was not sure how to respond. Her laughter, her glazed stare, were tinged with hysteria. But then, I too was less than calm. Look at that, she said. She was peering in annoyance at her bloodstained shoes. She clicked her tongue, and putting down her glass she quickly left the room. I waited. All this had happened before. I went and stood in the open window, a hand in my pocket, swigging my gin. Pompous, indeed—what did she mean? The sun was almost down, the light was gathering in bundles above the river. I stepped out on to the terrace. A balm of soft air breathed on my face. I thought how strange it was to be here like this, glass in hand, in the silence and calm of a summer evening, while there was so much darkness in my heart. I turned and looked up at the house. It seemed to be flying swiftly against the sky. I wanted my share of this richness, this gilded ease. From the depths of the room a pair of eyes looked out, dark, calm, unseeing.

Flynn, the crop-headed chauffeur, approached me from the side of the house with an air of tight-lipped politeness which was somehow menacing, rolling on the balls of his disproportionately dainty feet. He sported a bandit's drooping blue-black moustache, trimmed close and squared off at the ends, so that it looked as if it had been painted on to his large, pasty face. I do not like moustaches, have I mentioned that? There is something lewd about them which repels me. I have no doubt the prison shrink could explain what such an aversion signifies—and I've no doubt, too, that in my case he would be wrong. Flynn's was a particularly offensive specimen. The sight of it gave me heart suddenly, cheered me up, I don't know why. I followed him eagerly into the house. The dining room was a great dim cavern full of the glint and gleam of precious things. Behrens came in leaning on Anna's arm, a tall, delicate figure in rich tweeds and a bow-tie. He moved slowly, measuring his steps. His head, trembling a little, was smooth and steeply domed, like a marvellous, desiccated egg. It must have been twenty years since I had seen him last. I confess I was greatly taken with him now. He had the fine high patina of something lovingly crafted, like one of those exquisite and temptingly pocket-sized jade figurines which I had been eyeing only a moment ago on the mantelpiece. He took my hand and squeezed it slowly in his strangler's grip, looking deep into my eyes as if he were trying to catch a glimpse of someone else in there. Frederick, he said, in his breathy voice. So like your mother.

We dined at a rickety table in the bay of a tall window overlooking the garden. The cutlery was cheap, the plates mismatched. It was something I remembered about Whitewater, the makeshift way that life was lived in odd corners, at the edge of things. The house was not meant for people, all that magnificence would not tolerate their shoddy doings in its midst. I watched Behrens cutting up a piece of bleeding meat. Those enormous hands fascinated me. I was always convinced that at some time in the past he had killed someone. I tried to imagine him young, in flannels and a blazer, carrying a tennis racquet—*Oh look, here's Binkie!*—but it was impossible. He talked about the bombing. Five dead—or was it six by now?—from a mere two pounds of explosive! He sighed and shook his head. He seemed more impressed than shocked. Anna hardly spoke. She was pale, and looked tired and distracted. I noticed for the first time how she had aged. The woman I knew fifteen years ago was still there, but fixed inside a coarser outline, like one of Klimt's gem-encrusted lovers. I looked out into the luminous grey twilight, aghast and in an obscure way proud at the thought of what I had lost, of what might have been. Piled clouds, a last, bright strip of sky. A blackbird whistled suddenly. Someday I would lose all this too, I would die, and it would all be gone, this moment at this window, in summer, on the tender brink of night. It was amazing, and yet it was true, it would happen. Anna struck a match and lighted a candle on the table between us, and for a moment there was a sense of hovering, of swaying, in the soft, dark air.

My mother, I said to Behrens, and had to stop and clear my throat—my mother gave you some pictures, I believe. He turned his raptor's gaze on me. *Sold*, he said, and it was almost a whisper, sold, not gave. He smiled. There was a brief silence. He was quite at ease. He was sorry, he said, if I had come in the hope of seeing the pictures again. He could understand that I might be attached to them. But he had got rid of them almost at once. He smiled again, gently. There were one or two quite nice things, he said, but they would not have been comfortable, here, at Whitewater.

There you are, father, I thought, so much for your connoisseur's eye.

I wanted to do something for your mother, you see, Behrens was saying. She had been ill, you know. I gave her much more than the market value—you mustn't tell her that, of course. She wanted to set up in business of some kind, I think. He laughed. Such a spirited woman! he said. There was another silence. He fiddled with his knife, amused, waiting. I realised, with some astonishment, that he must have thought I had come to demand the return of the collection. Then, of course, I began to wonder if despite his protestations he had cheated on the price. The notion bucked me up immensely. Why, you old scoundrel, I thought, laughing to myself, you're just like all the rest of us. I looked at Anna's profile faintly reflected in the window before me. What was she, too, but an ageing spinster, with her wrinkles and her dyed hair—probably Flynn serviced her once a month or so, between hosing down the car and taking his moustache to the barber's for a trim. Damn you all! I poured myself a brimming glass of wine, and spilled some on the tablecloth, and was glad. Oh dark, dark.

I expected to be asked to stay the night, but when we had drunk our coffee Anna excused herself, and came back in a minute and said she had phoned for a taxi. I was offended. I had come all this way to see them and they would not even offer me a bed. An ugly silence fell. Behrens at my prompting had been talking about Dutch painters. Did I imagine it, or did he glance at me with a sly smile when he asked if I had been into the garden room? Before I realised it was the gilded salon that he meant he had passed on. Now he sat, head trembling, his mouth open a little, staring dully at the candle-flame. He lifted a hand, as if he were about to speak again, but let it fall slowly. The lights of a car swept the window and a horn tooted. Behrens did not get up. So good to see you, he murmured, giving me his left hand. So good.

Anna walked with me to the front door. I felt I had somehow made a fool of myself, but could not think how, exactly. In the hall our footsteps sounded very loud, a confused and faintly absurd racket. It's Flynn's night off, Anna said, or I would have had him drive you. I said stiffly that was quite all right. I was asking myself if we could be the same two people who had rolled with Daphne naked on a bed one hot Sunday afternoon on the other side of the world, on the other side of time. How could I have imagined I had ever loved her. Your father seems well, I said. She shrugged. Oh, she said, he's dying. At the door, I don't know what I was thinking of, but I fumbled for her hand and tried to kiss her. She stepped back quickly, and I almost fell over. The taxi tooted again. Anna! I said, and then could think of nothing to add. She laughed bleakly. Go home, Freddie, she said, with a wan smile, and shut the door slowly in my face.

I knew who would be driving the taxi, of course. Don't say anything, I said to him sternly, not a word! He looked at me in the mirror with a mournful, accusing eye, and we lumbered off down the drive. I realised I had nowhere to go.

It is September. I have been here now for two months. It seems longer than that. The tree that I can glimpse from the window of my cell has a drab, dusty look, it will soon begin to turn. It trembles, as if in anticipation, at night I fancy I can hear it, rustling excitedly out there in the dark. The skies in the morning are splendid, immensely high and clear. I like to watch the clouds building and dispersing. Such huge, delicate labour. Today there was a rainbow, when I saw it I laughed out loud, as at a wonderful, absurd joke. Now and then people pass by, under the tree. It must be a shortcut, that way. At nine come the office girls with cigarettes and fancy hairdos, and, a little later, dreamy housewives lugging shopping bags and babies. At four every afternoon a schoolboy straggles by, bearing an enormous satchel on his back like a hump. Dogs come too, trotting very fast with an air of determination, stop, give the tree a quick squirt, pass on. Other lives, other lives. Lately, since the season began to change, they all seem to move, even the boy, with a lighter tread, borne up, as if they are flying, somehow, through the glassy blue autumnal air.

At this time of year I often dream about my father. It is always the same dream, though the circumstances vary. The person in it is indeed my father, but not as I ever knew him. He is younger, sturdier, he is cheerful, he has a droll sense of humour. I arrive at a hospital, or some such large institution, and, after much searching and confusion, find him sitting up in bed with a steaming mug of tea in his hand. His hair is boyishly rumpled, he is wearing someone else's pyjamas. He greets me with a sheepish smile. On impulse, because I am flustered and have been so worried, I embrace him fervently. He suffers this unaccustomed display of emotion with equanimity, patting my shoulder and laughing a little. Then I sit down on a chair beside the bed and we are silent for a moment, not quite knowing what to do, or where to look. I understand that he has survived something, an accident, or a shipwreck, or a hectic illness. Somehow it is his own foolhardiness, his recklessness (my father, reckless!), that has got him into danger, and now he is feeling silly, and comically ashamed of himself. In the dream it is always I who have been responsible for his lucky escape, by raising the alarm, calling for an ambulance, getting the lifeboat out, something like that. My deed sits between us, enormous, unmanageable, like love itself, proof at last of a son's true regard. I wake up smiling, my heart swollen with tenderness. I used to believe that in the dream it was death I was rescuing him from, but lately I have begun to think that it is, instead, the long calamity of his life I am undoing at a stroke. Now perhaps I'll have another, similar task to perform. For they told me today my mother has died.

By the time the taxi got me to the village the last bus to the city had left, as my driver, with melancholy enjoyment, had assured me would be the case. We sat in the darkened main street, beside a hardware shop, the engine purring. The driver turned around in his seat, lifting his cap for a rapid, one-finger scratch, and settled down to see what I would do next. Once again I was struck by the way these people stare, the dull, brute candour of their interest. I had better give him a name—it is Reck, I'm afraid—for I shall be stuck with him for a while yet. He would be happy, he said, to drive me into the city himself. I shook my head: it was a good thirty miles, and I already owed him money. Otherwise, he said, with an awful, ingratiating smile, his mother might put me up—Mrs Reck, it seemed, ran a public house with a room upstairs. The idea did not appeal to me, but the street was dark and grimly silent, and there was something very depressing about those tools in that shop window, and yes, I said faintly, with a hand to my forehead, yes, take me to your mother.

But she was not there, or asleep or something, and he led me up the back stairs himself, going on tiptoe like a large, shaky spider. The room had a little low window, one chair, and a bed with a hollow in the middle, as if a cadaver had lately been removed from it. There was a smell of piss and porter. Reck stood smiling at me shyly, kneading his cap in his hands. I bade him a firm goodnight, and he withdrew, lingeringly. The last I saw of him was a bony hand slowly pulling the door closed behind him. I walked back and forth once or twice gingerly, the floorboards creaking. Did I wring my hands, I wonder? The low window and the sagging bed gave me a vertiginous sense of disproportion, I seemed too tall, my feet too big. I sat on the side of the bed. A faint radiance lingered in the window. If I leaned down sideways I could see a crooked chimney pot and a silhouette of trees. I felt like the gloomy hero in a Russian novel, brooding in my bolthole above the dramshop in the village of Dash, in the year Dot, with my story all before me, waiting to be told.

I did not sleep. The sheets were clammy and somehow slippery, and I was convinced I was not the first to have tossed and turned between them since their last laundering. I tried to lie, tensed like a spring, in such a way that as little of me as possible came in contact with them. The hours were marked by a distant churchbell with a peculiarly dull note. There was the usual barking of dogs and bellowing of cattle. The sound of my own fretful sighs infuriated me. Now and then a car or a lorry passed by, and a box of lighted geometry slid rapidly over the ceiling and down the walls and poured away into a corner. I had a raging thirst. Waking dreams assailed me with grotesque and bawdy visions. Once, on the point of sleep, I had a sudden, dreadful sense of falling, and I sprang awake with a jerk. Though I tried to put her out of my mind I kept returning to the thought of Anna Behrens. What had happened to her, that she should lock herself away in that drear museum, with only a dying old man for company? But perhaps nothing had happened, perhaps that was it. Perhaps the days just went by, one by one, without a sound, until at last it was too late, and she woke up one morning and found herself stuck fast in the middle of her life. I imagined her there, sad and solitary, bewitched in her magic castle, year after year, and—oh, all sorts of mad notions came into my head, I am too embarrassed to speak of them. And as I was thinking these things, another thought, on another, murkier level, was winding and winding its dark skein. So it was out of a muddled conflation of ideas of knight errantry and rescue and reward that my plan originated. I assure you, your Honour, this is no sly attempt at exoneration: I only wish to explain my motives, I mean the deepest ones, if such a thing is possible. As the hours went on, and stars flared in the little window and then slowly faded again, Anna Behrens merged in my mind with the other women who were in some way in my care—Daphne, of course, and even my mother, even the stable-girl, too—but in the end, when the dawn came, it was that Dutch figure in the picture in the garden room who hovered over the bed and gazed at me, sceptical, inquisitive and calm. I got up and dressed, and sat on the chair by the window and watched the ashen light of day descend upon the rooftops and seep into the trees. My mind was racing, my blood fizzled in my veins. I knew now what I would do. I was excited, and at the same time I had a deep sense of dread. There were stirrings downstairs. I wanted to be out, out, being and doing. I started to leave the room, but paused and lay on the bed for a moment to calm myself, and fell at once into a profound and terrible sleep. It was as if I had been struck down. I cannot describe it. It lasted no more than a minute or two. I woke up shaking. It was as if the very heart of things had skipped a beat. So it was that the day began, as it would continue, in the horrors.

Mrs Reck was tall and thin. No, she was short and fat. I do not remember her clearly. I do not wish to remember her clearly. For God's sake, how many of these grotesques am I expected to invent? I'll call her for a witness, and you can do the job yourselves. At first I thought she was in pain, but it was only a terrible, tongue-tied shyness that was making her duck and flinch. She fed me sausages and rashers and black pudding in the parlour behind the bar (it was the executioner who ate a hearty breakfast). An intricate silence filled the room, I could hear myself swallow. Shadows hung down the walls like fronds of cobweb. There was a picture of Jesus with his dripping heart on show, done in thick shades of crimson and cream, and a photograph of some pope or other blessing the multitudes from a Vatican balcony. A feeling of gloom settled like heartburn in my breast. Reck appeared, in his braces and shirtsleeves, and asked coyly if everything was all right. Grand, I said stoutly, grand! He stood and gazed at me, smiling tenderly, with a sort of happy pride. I might have been something he had left to propagate overnight. Ah, these poor, simple lives, so many, across which I have dragged my trail of slime. He had not once mentioned the monies I owed him—even on the phone he had apologised for not waiting for me. I rose and edged past him in the doorway. Just popping out for a moment, I said, get a breath of air. I could feel my horrible smile, like something sticky that had spread over my face. He nodded, and a little flicker of sadness passed across his brow and down his sheep's muzzle. You knew I was going to do a flit, didn't you? Why did you not stop me? I don't details. In the night, when the egg hatched and the thing first flexed its sticky, brittle wings, I had told myself that when morning came and real life started up again I would laugh at such a preposterous notion. And I did laugh, even if it was in a thoughtful sort of way, and I believe, I really do, that if I had not been stranded in that hole, with nothing to pass the time except my own dark thoughts, none of this would have happened. I would have gone to Charlie French and borrowed some money from him, and returned to the island and paid my debt to Señor Aguirre, and then I would have taken my wife and child and come home, to Coolgrange, to make my peace with my mother, and settle down, and become a squireen like my father, and live, and be happy. Ah—

What was I saying? My plan, yes. Your Lordship, I am no mastermind. The newspapers, which from the start have been quite beside themselves—it was the silly season, after all, and I gave them a glorious, running story—have portrayed me both as a reckless thug and a meticulous, ice-cool, iron-willed blond beast. But I swear, it was all just drift, like everything else. I suppose at first I played with the idea, telling it to myself as a sort of story, as I lay there, the sleepless prince, in Mother Reck's gingerbread house, while the innocent stars crowded silently in the window. In the morning I rose and held it up to the light, and already it had begun to harden, to set. Strangely, it was like the work of someone else, which had been given to me to measure and to test. This process of distancing seems to have been an essential preliminary to action. Perhaps this accounts for the peculiar sensation which came over me there on the bridge above that gurgling river. It's hard to describe. I felt that I was utterly unlike myself. That is to say, I was perfectly familiar with this large, somewhat overweight, fair-haired man in a wrinkled suit sitting here fretfully twiddling his thumbs, yet at the same time it was as if I—the real, thinking, sentient I—had somehow got myself trapped inside a body not my shopcoat such as I had not seen since I was a child. He smiled and nodded at me, and put aside his brush. He would not speak, however—professional etiquette, no doubt—until he had taken up position behind the counter, leaning forward on his arms with his head cocked to one side. Wire-rimmed glasses, I thought, would have completed the effect. I liked him straight away. Good day to you, sir, he said, in a cheery, hand-rubbing sort of voice. I felt better already. He was polite to just the correct degree, without undue subservience, or any hint of nosiness. I bought a ball of twine and a roll of brown wrapping paper. Also a hank of rope—coiled, I recall, in a tight cylinder, very like a hangman's knot—good hard smooth hemp, not that modern plastic stuff. I had little notion of what I intended to do with these things. The rope, for instance, was pure indulgence. I didn't care. It was years—decades!—since I had experienced such simple, greedy pleasure. The shopman placed my purchases lovingly before me on the counter, crooning a little under his breath, smiling, pursing his lips approvingly. It was playtime. In this pretend-world I could have anything I wanted. A tenon saw, for instance, with rosewood stock. A set of brass fire irons, their handles made in the shape of crouching monkeys. That white enamelled bucket, with a delicate, flesh-blue shadow down one side. Oh, anything! Then I spotted the hammer. One moulded, polished piece of stainless steel, like a bone from the thigh of some swift animal, with a velvety, black rubber grip and a blued head and claw. I am utterly unhandy, I do not think I could drive a nail straight, but I confess I had always harboured a secret desire to have a hammer like that. More laughter in court, of course, more ribald guffaws from the wiseacres in the gallery. But I insist, your Honour, gentle handymen of the jury, I insist it was an innocent desire, a wish, an ache, on the part of the deprived child inside me—not Bunter, not him, but the true, lost ghost of my boyhood—to possess this marvellous toy. For the first time my fairy-godfather hesitated. There are other models, he ventured, less—a hurried, breathy whisper—less expensive, sir. But no, no, I could not resist it. I must have it. That one. Yes, that one, there, with the tag on it. Exhibit A, in other words.

I stumbled out of the shop with my parcel under my arm, bleared and grinning, happy as a drunken schoolboy. The shopkeeper came to the door to watch me go. He had shaken hands with me in an odd, cryptic manner. Perhaps he was a mason, and was testing to see if I too might be a member of the brotherhood?—but no, I prefer to think he was merely a decent, kindly, well-meaning man. There are not many such, in this testimony.

I felt by now that I knew the village. I felt in fact that I had been here before, and even that I had done all these things before, walked about aimlessly in the early morning, and sat on the bridge, and gone into a shop and purchased things. I have no explanation: I only felt it. It was as if I had dreamed a prophetic dream and then forgotten it, and this was the prophecy coming true. But then, something of that sense of inevitability infected everything I did that day—inevitable, mind you, does not mean excusable, in my vocabulary. No indeed, a strong mixture of Catholic and Calvinist blood courses in my veins.

It came to me suddenly, with happy inconsequentiality, that it was midsummer day.

This is a wonderful country, a man with a decent accent can do almost anything. I thought I was heading for the bus stop, to see if there was a bus to the city, but instead—more inevitability— I found myself outside a tumbledown garage in the village square. A boy in filthy overalls a number of sizes too small for him was heaving tyres and whistling tunelessly out of the side of his face. A rusty tin sign nailed to the wall above his head proclaimed: *Melmoth's ar Hire*. The boy paused and looked at me blankly. He had stopped whistling, but kept his lips puckered. Car? I said, pointing to the sign, for hire, yes? I jiggled an invisible steering wheel. He said nothing, only frowned in deep puzzlement, as if I had asked for something utterly outlandish. Then a stout, big-bosomed woman came out of the cash office and spoke to him sharply. She wore a crimson blouse and tight black trousers and high-heeled, toeless sandals. Her hair, black as a crow's wing, was piled up in a brioche shape, with ringlets trailing down at the sides. She reminded me of someone, I could not think who. She led me into the office, where with a lurch I spied, among a cluster of gaudy postcards tacked to the wall behind her desk, a view of the island, and the harbour, and the very bar where I had first encountered Randolph the American. It was unnerving, an omen, even a warning, perhaps. The woman was studying me up and down with a sort of smouldering surmise. With another shock I realised who it was she reminded me of: the mother of the squalling baby in Señor Aguirre's apartment.

The car was a Humber, a great, heavy, high model, not old enough to be what they call vintage, just hopelessly out of fashion. It seemed to have been built for a simpler, more innocent age than this, one peopled by a species of big children. The upholstery had a vaguely fecal smell. I drove sedately through the village in third gear, perched high above the road as if I were being borne along on a palanquin. The engine made a noise like muffled cheering. I had paid a deposit of five pounds, and signed a document in the name of Smyth (I thought the y a fiendishly clever touch). The woman had not even asked to see a driving licence. As I say, this is a wonderful country. I felt extraordinarily light-hearted.

Speaking of jaunts: I went to my mother's funeral today. Three plain-clothes men took me in a closed car, I was very impressed. We sped through the city with the siren hee-hawing, it was like my arrest all over again, but in reverse. A lovely, sunny, crisp morning, pale smoke in the air, a few leaves down already on the pavements. I felt such a strange mingling of emotions—a certain rawness, of course, a certain pain, but elation, too, and something like grief that yet was not without sweetness. I was grieving not for my mother only, perhaps not for her at all, but for things in general. Maybe it was just the usual September melancholy, made unfamiliar by the circumstances. We drove by the river under a sky piled high with bundles of luminous Dutch clouds, then south through leafy suburbs. The sea surprised me, as it always does, a bowl of blue, moving metal, light rising in flakes off the surface. All three detectives were chain-smokers, they worked at it grimly, as if it were a part of their duties. One of them offered me a cigarette. Not one of my vices, I said, and they laughed politely. They seemed embarrassed, and kept glancing warily out of the windows, as if they had been forced to come on an outing with a famous and disreputable relative and were afraid of being spotted by someone they knew. Now we were in the country, and there was mist on the fields still, and the hedges were drenched. She was buried in the family plot in the old cemetery at Coolgrange. I was not allowed to leave the car, or even to open a window. I was secretly glad, for somehow I could not conceive of myself stepping out suddenly just like that, into the world. The driver parked as near as possible to the graveside, and I sat in a fug of cigarette smoke and watched the brief, hackneyed little drama unfold beyond the fogged glass, among the leaning headstones. There were few mourners: an aunt or two, and an old man who had worked years ago for my father in the stables. The girl Joanne was there, of course, red-eyed, her poor face blotched and swollen, dressed in a lumpy pullover and a crooked skirt. Charlie French stood a little apart from the rest, with his hands awkwardly clasped. I was surprised to see him there. Decent of him to come, courageous, too. Neither he nor the girl looked in my direction,

So I am driving away from the village, in the Humber Hawk, with a foolish grin on my face. I felt, for no good reason, that I was escaping all my problems, I pictured them dwindling in space and time like the village itself, a quaint jumble of things getting steadily smaller and smaller. If I had stopped for a moment to think, of course, I would have realised that what I was leaving behind me was not my tangled troubles, as I fondly imagined, but, on the contrary, a mass of evidence, obvious and unmistakable as a swatch of matted hair and blood. I had skipped Ma Reck's without paying for my lodgings, I had bought a burglar's kit in the village shop, and now I had as good as stolen a car—and all this not five miles from what would soon come to be known as the scene of the crime. The court will agree, these are hardly the marks of careful premeditation. (Why is it that every other thing I say sounds like the sly preamble to a plea of mitigation?) The fact is, I was not thinking at all, not what could really be called thinking. I was content to sail through sun and shade along these dappled back roads, one hand on the wheel and an elbow out of the window, with the scents of the countryside in my nostrils and the breeze whipping my hair. Everything would be well, everything would work itself out. I do not know why I felt so elated, perhaps it was a form of delirium. Anyway, I told myself, it was only a madcap game I was playing, I could call it off whenever I wished.

Meanwhile here was Whitewater, rising above the trees.

An empty tour bus was parked at the gate. The driver's door

was open, and the driver was lounging in the stepwell, sunning himself. He watched me as I swung past him into the drive. I waved to him. He wore tinted glasses. He did not smile. He would remember me.

Afterwards the police could not understand why I showed so little circumspection, driving up brazenly like that, in broad daylight, in that unmistakable motor car. But I believed, you see, that the matter would be entirely between Behrens and me, with Anna perhaps as go-between. I never imagined there would be anything so vulgar as a police investigation, and headlines in the papers, and all the rest of it. A simple business transaction between civilised people, that's what I intended. I would be polite but firm, no more than that. I was not thinking in terms of threats and ransom demands, certainly not. When later I read what those reporters wrote—the Midsummer Manhunt, they called it—I could not recognise myself in their depiction of me as a steely, ruthless character. Ruthless—me! No, as I drove up to Whitewater it was not police I was thinking of, but only the chauffeur Flynn, with his little pig eyes and his boxer's meaty paws. Yes, Flynn was a man to avoid.

Halfway up the drive there was

God, these tedious details.

Halfway up there was a fork in the drive. A wooden arrow with HOUSE written on it in white paint pointed to the right, while to the left a sign said STRICTLY PRIVATE. I stopped the car. See me there, a big blurred face behind the windscreen peering first this way, then that. It is like an illustration from a cautionary tract: the sinner hesitates at the parting of the ways. I drove off to the left, and my heart gave an apprehensive wallop. Behold, the wretch forsakes the path of righteousness.

I rounded the south wing of the house, and parked on the grass and walked across the lawn to the garden room. The french (tobacco, spices, and, in secret, slaves). She keeps house for him since her mother's death. She did not like her mother. Her father dotes on her, his only child. She is, he proclaims, his treasure. She devises menus—Father has a delicate stomach—inspects the kitchen, she even supervises his wine cellar. She keeps an inventory of the household linen in a little notebook attached to her belt by a fine gold chain, using a code of her own devising, for she has never learned to read or write. She is strict with the servants, and will permit no familiarities. Their dislike she takes for respect. The house is not enough to absorb her energies, she does good works besides: she visits the sick, and is on the board of visitors of the town's almshouse. She is brisk, sometimes impatient, and there are mutterings against her among the almsfolk, especially the old women. At times, usually in spring and at the beginning of winter, everything becomes too much for her. Notice the clammy pallor of her skin: she is prey to obscure ailments. She takes to her bed and lies for days without speaking, hardly breathing, while outside in the silvery northern light the world goes about its busy way. She tries to pray, but God is distant. Her father comes to visit her at evening, walking on tiptoe. These periods of prostration frighten him, he remembers his wife dying, her terrible silence in the last weeks. If he were to lose his daughter too—But she gets up, wills herself to it, and very soon the servants are feeling the edge of her tongue again, and he cannot contain his relief, it comes out in little laughs, roguish endearments, a kind of clumsy skittishness. She considers him wryly, then turns back to her tasks. She cannot understand this notion he has got into his head: he wants to have her portrait painted. I'm old, is all he will say to her, I am an old man, look at me! And he laughs, awkwardly, and avoids her eye. My portrait? she says, mine?—I am no fit subject for a painter. He shrugs, at which she is first startled, then grimly amused: he might at least have attempted to contradict her. He seems to realise what is going through her mind, and tries to mend matters, but he becomes flustered, and, watching him fuss and fret and pluck at his cuffs, she realises with a pang that it's true, he has aged. Her father, an old man. The thought has a touch of bleak comedy, which she cannot account for. You have fine hands, he says, growing testy, annoyed both at himself and her, your mother's hands—we'll tell him to make the hands prominent. And so, to humour him, but also because she is secretly curious, she goes along one morning to the studio. The squalor is what strikes her first of all. Dirt and daubs of paint everywhere, gnawed chicken bones on a smeared plate, a chamber pot on the floor in the corner. The painter matches the place, with that filthy smock, and those fingernails. He has a drinker's squashed and pitted nose. She thinks the general smell is bad until she catches a whiff of his breath. She discovers that she is relieved: she had expected someone young, dissolute, threatening, not this pot-bellied old soak. But then he fixes his little wet eyes on her, briefly, with a kind of impersonal intensity, and she flinches, as if caught in a burst of strong light. No one has ever looked at her like this before. So this is what it is to be known! It is almost indecent. First he puts her standing by the window, but it does not suit, the light is wrong, he says. He shifts her about, grasping her by the upper arms and walking her backwards from one place to another. She feels she should be indignant, but the usual responses do not seem to function here. He is shorter than her by a head. He makes some sketches, scribbles a colour note or two, then tells her to come tomorrow at the same time. And wear a darker dress, he says. Well! She is about to give him a piece of her mind, but already he has turned aside to another task. Her maid, sitting by the door, is biting her lips and smirking. She lets the next day pass, and the next, just to show him. When she does return he says nothing about the broken appointment, only looks at her black dress—pure silk, with a broad collar of Spanish lace—and was rattled. There was a knot in the pit of my stomach and my palms were damp. All the elation I had felt on the way here had evaporated, leaving behind it a stark sense of foreboding. I was struck, for the first time, really, by the enormity of what I was embarked on. I felt like a child whose game has led him far into the forest, and now it is nightfall, and there are shadowy figures among the trees. The guide had finished her account of the treasures in the room—the picture, *my* picture, was given two sentences, and a misattribution—and walked out now with one arm raised stiffly above her head, still talking, shepherding the party behind her. When they had gone I waited, staring fixedly at the doorknob, expecting her to come back and haul me out briskly by the scruff of the neck. Somewhere inside me a voice was moaning softly in panic and fright. This is something that does not seem to be appreciated—I have remarked on it before—I mean how timorous I am, how easily daunted. But she did not return, and I heard them tramping away up the stairs. I set to work again feverishly. I see myself, like the villain in an old three-reeler, all twitches and scowls and wriggling eyebrows. I got the picture off the wall, not without difficulty, and laid it flat on the floor—shying away from that black stare—and began to tear off lengths of wrapping paper. I would not have thought that paper would make so much noise, such scuffling and rattling and ripping, it must have sounded as if some large animal were being flayed in here. And it was no good, my hands shook, I was all thumbs, and the sheets of paper kept rolling back on themselves, and I had nothing to cut the twine with, and anyway the picture, with its thick, heavy frame, was much too big to be wrapped. I scampered about on my knees, talking to myself and uttering little squeaks of distress. Everything was going wrong. Give it up, I told myself, oh please, please, give it up now, while there's still time! but another part of me gritted its teeth and said, no you don't, you coward, get up, get on your feet, do it! So I looked into them I felt I was seeing clear through her head. Why did she not run away? Behind her, in one of the great upstairs windows, a dozen heads were crowded, goggling at us. I could make out the guide-woman's glasses and the American's appalling shirt. I think I must have cried aloud in rage, an old lion roaring at the whip and chair, for the maid flinched and stepped back a pace. I caught her wrist in an iron claw and, wrenching open the car door, fairly flung her into the back seat. Oh, why did she not run away! When I got behind the wheel, fumbling and snarling, I caught a whiff of something, a faint, sharp, metallic smell, like the smell of worn pennies. I could see her in the mirror, crouched behind me as in a deep glass box, braced between the door and the back of the seat, with her elbows stuck out and fingers splayed and her face thrust forward, like the cornered heroine in a melodrama. A fierce, choking gust of impatience surged up inside me. Impatience, yes, that was what I felt most strongly—that, and a grievous sense of embarrassment. I was mortified. I had never been so exposed in all my life. People were looking at me—she in the back seat, and the tourists up there jostling at the window, but also, it seemed, a host of others, of phantom spectators, who must have been, I suppose, an intimation of all that horde who would soon be crowding around me in fascination and horror. I started the engine. The gears shrieked. In my agitation I kept getting ahead of myself and having to go back and repeat the simplest actions. When I had got the car off the grass and on to the drive I let the clutch out too quickly, and the machine sprang forward in a series of bone-shaking lurches, the bonnet going up and down like the prow of a boat caught in a wash and the shock absorbers grunting. The watchers at the window must have been in fits by now. A bead of sweat ran down my cheek. The sun had made the steering wheel almost too hot to hold, and there was a blinding glare on the windscreen. The maid was scrabbling at the door handle, I roared at her and she stopped at once, and looked at me wide-eyed, like a rebuked child. Outside the gate the bus driver was still sitting in the sun. When she saw him she tried to get the window open, but in vain, the mechanism must have been broken. She pounded on the glass with her fists. I spun the wheel and the car lumbered out into the road, the tyres squealing. We were shouting at each other now, like a married couple having a fight. She pummelled me on the shoulder, got a hand around in front of my face and tried to claw my eyes. Her thumb went up my nose, I thought she would tear off the nostril. The car was going all over the road. I trod with both feet on the brake pedal, and we sailed in a slow, dragging curve into the hedge. She fell back. I turned to her. I had the hammer in my hand. I looked at it, startled. The silence rose around us like water. Don't, she said. She was crouched as before, with her arms bent and her back pressed into the corner. I could not speak, I was filled with a kind of wonder. I had never felt another's presence so immediately and with such raw force. I saw her now, really saw her, for the first time, her mousy hair and bad skin, that bruised look around her eyes. She was quite ordinary, and yet, somehow, I don't know—somehow radiant. She cleared her throat and sat up, and detached a strand of hair that had caught at the corner of her mouth.

You must let me go, she said, or you will be in trouble.

It's not easy to wield a hammer in a motor car. When I struck her the first time I expected to feel the sharp, clean smack of steel on bone, but it was more like hitting clay, or hard putty. The word *fontanel* sprang into my mind. I thought one good bash would do it, but, as the autopsy would show, she had a remarkably strong skull—even in that, you see, she was unlucky. The first blow fell just at the hairline, above her left eye. There was not much blood, only a dark-red glistening dent with hair matted in it. She shuddered, but remained sitting upright, swaying a little, looking at me with eyes that would not focus properly. Perhaps I would have stopped then, if she had not suddenly launched herself at me across the back of the seat, flailing and screaming. I was dismayed. How could this be happening to me—it was all so *unfair*. Bitter tears of self-pity squeezed into my eyes. I pushed her away from me and swung the hammer in a wide, backhand curve. The force of the blow flung her against the door, and her head struck the window, and a fine thread of blood ran out of her nostril and across her cheek. There was blood on the window, too, a fan-shaped spray of tiny drops. She closed her eyes and turned her face away from me, making a low, guttural noise at the back of her throat. She put a hand up to her head just as I was swinging at her again, and when the blow landed on her temple her fingers were in the way, and I heard one of them crack, and I winced, and almost apologised. Oh! she said, and suddenly, as if everything inside her had collapsed, she slithered down the seat on to the floor.

There was silence again, clear and startling. I got out of the car and stood a moment, breathing. I was dizzy. Something seemed to have happened to the sunlight, everywhere I looked there was an underwater gloom. I thought I had driven only a little way, and expected to see the gates of Whitewater, and the tour bus, and the driver running towards me, but to my astonishment the road in both directions was empty, and I had no idea where I was. On one side a hill rose steeply, and on the other I could see over the tops of pine trees to far-off, rolling downs. It all looked distinctly improbable. It was like a hastily painted backdrop, especially that smudged, shimmering distance, and the road winding innocently away. I found I was still clutching the hammer. With a grand sweep of my arm I flung it from me, and watched it as it flew, tumbling slowly end over end, in a long, thrilling arc, far, far out over the blue pine-tops. Then abruptly I bent forward and vomited up houses, and housing estates, and straggling factories, and super-markets big as aircraft hangars. I stared through the windscreen in dreamy amazement. I might have been a visitor from another part of the world altogether, hardly able to believe how much like home everything looked and yet how different it was. I did not know where I was going, I mean I was not going anywhere, just driving. It was almost restful, sailing along like that, turning the wheel with one finger, shut off from everything. It was as if all my life I had been clambering up a steep and difficult slope, and now had reached the peak and leaped out blithely into the blue. I felt so free. At the first red traffic light the car drifted gently to a stop as if it were subsiding into air. I was at the junction of two suburban roads. On the left there was a little green rise with a chestnut tree and a neat row of new houses. Children were playing on the grassy bank. Dogs gambolled. The sun shone. I have always harboured a secret fondness for quiet places such as this, unremarked yet cherished domains of building and doing and tending. I leaned my head back on the seat and smiled, watching the youngsters at play. The lights changed to green, but I did not stir. I was not really there, but lost somewhere, in some sunlit corner of my past. There was a sudden rapping on the window beside my ear. I jumped. A woman with a large, broad, horsy face—she reminded me, dear God, of my mother!—was peering in at me and saying something. I rolled down the window. She had a loud voice, it sounded very loud to me, at any rate. I could not understand her, she was talking about an accident, and asking me if I was all right. Then she pressed her face forward and squinnied over my shoulder, and opened her mouth and groaned. Oh, she said, the poor child! I turned my head. There was blood all over the back seat now, far too much, surely, for just one person to have shed. For a mad instant, in which a crafty spark of hope flared and died, I wondered if there *had* been a crash, which somehow I had not noticed, or had forgotten, if some overloaded vehicle had ploughed into the back of us, flinging bodies and all this blood in through the rear window. I could not speak. I had thought she was dead, but there she was, kneeling between the seats and groping at the window beside her, I could hear her fingers squeaking on the glass. Her hair hung down in bloodied ropes, her face was a clay mask streaked with copper and crimson. The woman outside was gabbling into my ear about telephones and ambulances and the police—the police! I turned to her with a terrible glare. Madam! I said sternly (she would later describe my voice as *cultured* and *authoritative*), will you please get on about your business! She stepped back, staring in shock. I confess I was myself impressed, I would not have thought I could muster such a commanding tone. I rolled up the window and jammed the car into gear and shot away, noticing, too late, that the lights had turned to red. A tradesman's van coming from the left braked sharply and let out an indignant squawk. I drove on. However, I had not gone more than a street or two when suddenly an ambulance reared up in my wake, its siren yowling and blue light flashing. I was astonished. How could it have arrived so promptly? In fact, this was another of those appalling co-incidences in which this case abounds. The ambulance, as I would later learn, was not looking for me, but was returning from—yes—from the scene of a car crash, with—I'm sorry, but, yes—with a dying woman in the back. I kept going, haring along with my head down, my nose almost touching the rim of the wheel. I do not think I could have stopped, locked in fright as I was. The ambulance drew alongside, swaying dangerously and trumpeting like a frenzied big beast. The attendant in the passenger seat, a burly young fellow in shirtsleeves, with a red face and narrow sideburns, looked at the blood-streaked window behind me with mild, professional interest. He conferred briefly with the driver, then signalled to me, with complicated gestures, nodding and mouthing, to of rope and threw that away too. Then I lifted out the picture and walked with it to where there was a sagging barbed-wire fence and a ditch with a trickle of water at the bottom, and there I dumped it. What was I thinking of, I don't know. Perhaps it was a gesture of renunciation or something. Renunciation! How do I dare use such words. The woman with the gloves gave me a last, dismissive stare. She had expected no better of me. I went back to the car, trying not to look at it, the smeared windows. Something was falling on me: a delicate, silent fall of rain. I peered upwards in the glistening sunlight and saw a cloud directly overhead, the merest smudge of grey against the summer blue. I thought: I am not human. Then I turned and walked away.

All my adult life I have had a recurring dream (yes, yes, dreams again!), it comes once or twice a year and leaves me feeling disturbed for days afterwards. As usual it is not a dream in the ordinary sense, for not much happens in it, really, and nothing is explicit. There is mainly an undefined but profound and mounting sensation of unease, which rises at the end to full-fledged panic. A long time ago, it seems, I have committed a crime. No, that is too strong. I have done something, it is never clear what, precisely. Perhaps I stumbled upon something, it may even have been a corpse, and covered it up, and almost forgot about it. Now, years later, the evidence has been found, and they have come to question me. As yet there is nothing to suggest that I was directly involved, not a hint of suspicion attaches to me. I am merely another name on a list. They are mild, soft-spoken, stolidly deferential, a little bored. The young one fidgets. I respond to their questions politely, with a certain irony, smiling, lifting an eyebrow. It is, I tell myself smugly, the performance of my life, a masterpiece of dissembling. Yet the older one, I notice, is regarding me with deepening interest, his shrewd eyes narrowing. I must have said something. What have I said? I begin to blush, I cannot help it. A horrible constriction takes hold of me. I babble, what is intended as a relaxed little laugh turns into a strangled gasp. At length I run down, like a clockwork toy, and sit and gape at them helplessly, panting. Even the younger one, the Sergeant, is interested now. An appalling silence descends, it stretches on and on, until at last my sleeping self makes a bolt for it and I start awake, aghast and sweating. What is peculiarly awful in all this is not the prospect of being dragged before the courts and put in jail for a crime I am not even sure I have committed, but the simple, terrible fact of having been found out. This is what makes me sweat, what fills my mouth with ashes and my heart with shame.

And now, as I hurried along the cement road, with the railway track beside me and the sea beyond, I had that same feeling of ignominy. What a fool I had been. What trouble there would be in the days, the weeks, the years ahead. Yet also there was a sensation of lightness, of buoyancy, as if I had thrown off an awkward burden. Ever since I had reached what they call the use of reason I had been doing one thing and thinking another, because the weight of things seemed so much greater than that of thoughts. What I said was never exactly what I felt, what I felt was never what it seemed I should feel, though the feelings were what felt genuine, and right, and inescapable. Now I had struck a blow for the inner man, that guffawing, fat foulmouth who had been telling me all along I was living a lie. And he had burst out at last, it was he, the ogre, who was pounding along in this lemon-coloured light, with blood on his pelt, and me slung helpless over his back. Everything was gone, the past, Coolgrange, Daphne, all my previous life, gone, abandoned, drained of its essence, its significance. To do the worst thing, the very worst thing, that's the way to be free. I would never again need to pretend to myself to be what I was not. The thought made my head spin and my empty stomach heave.

I was prey to a host of niggling worries. This pullover was smelly, and too tight for me. The knee of my left trouser-leg had a small rip in it. People would notice that I had not shaved today. And I needed, I positively longed, to wash my hands, to plunge up to the elbows in scalding suds, to sluice myself, to drench, rinse,

How blue the sea was, how gay the little flags fluttering and snapping on the hotel battlements. All was quiet, save for the sea-breeze crooning in the telegraph wires, and something somewhere that creaked and knocked, creaked and knocked. I smiled. I might have been a child again, daydreaming here, in these toy surroundings. I could smell the sea, and the sea-wrack on the beach, and the cat-smell of the sand. A train was on the way, yes, a puff-puff, the rails were humming and shivering in anticipation. Not a soul to be seen, not a grown-up anywhere, except, away down the beach, a few felled sunbathers on their towels. I wonder why the place was so deserted? Perhaps it wasn't, perhaps there were seaside crowds all about, and I didn't notice, with my inveterate yearning towards backgrounds. I closed my eyes, and something swam up dreamily, a memory, an image, and sank again without breaking the surface. I tried to catch it before it was gone, but there was only that one glimpse: a doorway, I think, opening on to a darkened room, and a mysterious sense of expectancy, of something or someone about to appear. Then the train came through, a slow, rolling thunder that made my diaphragm shake. The passengers were propped up in the wide windows like manikins, they gazed at me blankly as they were borne slowly past. It occurred to me I should have turned my face away: everyone was a potential witness now. But I thought it did not matter. I thought I would be in jail within hours. I looked about me, taking great breaths, drinking my fill of the world that I would soon be losing. A gang of boys, three or four, had appeared in the grounds of the hotel. They straggled across the unkempt lawns, and stopped to throw stones at a For Sale sign. I rose, with a leaden sigh, and left the station and set off along the road again.

I took a bus into the city. It was a single-decker, on an infrequent route, coming from far out. The people on it all seemed to know concerned. I seemed to float, bemused, in dreamy detachment, as if I had been given a great dose of local anaesthetic. Perhaps this is what it means to be in shock? No: I think it was just the certainty that at any moment a hand would grasp me by the shoulder while a terrible voice boomed out an official caution. By now they would have my name, a description would be in circulation, hard-eyed men in bulging jackets would be cruising the streets on the look-out for me. That none of this was so is still a puzzle to me. The Behrenses must have known at once who it was that had taken that particular picture, yet they said nothing. And what about the trail of evidence I left behind me? What about the people who saw me, the Recks, the señorita at the garage, the man in the hardware shop, that woman who looked like my mother who came upon me sitting like a waxwork model of myself at the traffic lights? Your Lordship, I would not wish to encourage potential wrongdoers, but I must say, it is easier to get away with wrongdoing, for a time at least, than is generally acknowledged. Vital days—how easily one slips into the lingo!—*vital days* were to pass before they even began to know who it was they were after. If I had not continued to be as rash as I was at the start, if I had stopped and taken stock, and considered carefully, I believe I might not be here now, but in some sunnier clime, tending my guilt under an open sky. But I did not stop, did not consider. I got off the bus and set off at once in the direction in which I happened to be facing, since my fate, I was convinced, awaited me all around, in the open arms of the law. Capture! I nursed the word in my heart. It comforted me. It was the promise of rest. I dodged along through the crowds like a drunk, surprised that they did not part before me in horror. All round me was an inferno of haste and noise. A gang of men stripped to the waist was gouging a hole in the road with pneumatic drills. The traffic snarled and bellowed, sunlight flashing like knives off the windshields and the throbbing roofs of cars. The air giggled wanly. I retreated, simpering, and went back to the pub and pounded on the door with renewed force. After some time there were dragging footsteps inside and the sound of locks being undone. What do you want, Wally said crossly, blinking in the harsh sunlight slanting down from the street. He was wearing a purple silk dressing-gown and shapeless slippers. He looked me up and down with distaste, noting the stubble and the filthy pullover. I told him my car had broken down, and that I needed to make a phonecall. He gave a sardonic snort and said, A phonecall! as if it were the richest thing he had heard in ages. He shrugged. It was nearly opening time anyway. I followed him inside. His calves were plump and white and hairless, I wondered where I had seen others like them recently. He switched on a pink-shaded lamp behind the bar. There's the phone, he said with a wave, pursing his lips derisively. I asked if I could have a gin first. He sniffed, his sceptic's heart gratified, and permitted himself a thin little smile. Have a smash-up, did you? he said. For a second I did not know what he was talking about. Oh, the car, I said, no, no it just—stopped. And I thought, with bleak amusement: There's the first question answered and I haven't lied. He turned away to make my drink, priest-like in his purple robe, then set it before me and propped himself on the edge of his stool with his fat arms folded. He knew I had been up to something, I could see it from the look in his eye, at once eager and disdainful, but he could not bring himself to ask. I grinned at him and drank my drink, and gleaned a grain of enjoyment from his dilemma. I said it was a good idea, wasn't it, the siesta. He raised an eyebrow. I pointed a finger at his dressing-gown. A nap, I said, in the middle of the day: good idea. He did not think that was funny. From somewhere in the shadowy reaches behind me a tousle-haired young man appeared, clad only in a drooping pair of underpants. He gave me a bored glance and asked Wally if the paper was in yet. Here, I said, take mine, go ahead. I must have been twisting it in my hands, it was rolled into a tight baton. He prised it open and read the headlines, his lips moving. Fucking bombers, he said, fucking lunatics. Wally had fixed him with a terrible glare. He threw the paper aside and wandered off, scratching his rump. I held out my glass for a refill. We still charge for drinks, you know, Wally said. We'll accept money. I gave him my last fiver. A thin blade of light had got in through a chink in a shutter somewhere and stood at a slant beside me, embedded in the floor. I watched Wally's plump back as he refilled my glass. I wondered if I might tell him what I had done. It seemed perfectly possible. Nothing, I told myself, nothing shocks Wally, after all. I could almost believe it. I imagined him looking at me with a twist of the mouth and one eyebrow arched, trying not to laugh as I recounted my horrid tale. The thought of confessing gave me a little lift, it was so splendidly irresponsible. It made the whole thing seem no more than a spot of high jinks, a jape that had gone wrong. I chuckled mournfully into my glass. You look like shit, Wally said complacently. I asked for another gin, a double this time.

Distinctly in my head her voice again said: Don't.

The boy with the curls came back, now wearing tight jeans and a shiny tight green shirt. He was called Sonny. Wally left him in charge of the bar and waddled off to his quarters, his dressing-gown billowing behind him. Sonny poured a generous measure of crème de menthe into a tumbler and filled it up with ice cubes, then perched himself on the stool, squirming his narrow little nates, and examined me without much enthusiasm. You're new, he said, making it sound like an accusation. No I'm not, I said, you are, and I smirked, pleased with myself. He made a wide-eyed face. Well excuse me, he said, I'm sure. Wally came back, dressed and coiffed and reeking of pomade. I had another double. My face was growing taut, it felt like a mud mask. I had reached that stage of inebriation where everything was settling into another version of reality. It seemed not drunkenness, but a form of enlightenment, almost a sobering-up. A crowd of theatre people came in, prancing and squawking. They looked at my appearance and then at each other, brimming with merriment. Talk about rough trade, one said, and Sonny tittered. And I thought, that's what I'll do, I'll get one of them to take me home and hide me, Lady Macbeth there with the mascara and the blood-red nails, or that laughing fellow in the harlequin shirt—why not? Yes, that's what I should do, I should live henceforth among actors, practise among them, study their craft, the grand gesture and the fine nuance. Perhaps in time I would learn to play my part sufficiently well, with enough conviction, to take my place among the others, the naturals, those people on the bus, and all the rest of them.

It was only when Charlie French came in that I realised it was for him I had been waiting. Good old Charlie. My heart flooded with fondness, I felt like embracing him. He was in his chalkstripes, carrying a battered, important-looking briefcase. Although he had seen me three days ago he tried at first not to know me. Or perhaps he really didn't recognise me, in my dishevelled, wild-eyed state. He said he had thought I was going down to Coolgrange. I said I had been there, and he asked after my mother. I told him about her stroke. I laid it on a bit, I think—I may even have shed a tear. He nodded, looking past my left ear and jingling the coins in his trousers pocket. There was a pause, during which I snuffled and sighed. So, he said brightly, you're off on your travels again, are you? I shrugged. His car's broke down, isn't it, Wally said, and expelled an unpleasant little chuckle. Charlie assumed a sympathetic frown. Is that right? he said slowly, with a dreamy lack of emphasis. The crowd of actors behind us suddenly shrieked, so piercingly that glasses chimed, but he might not have heard them, he did not even blink. He had perfected a pose for places and occasions such as this, by which he managed to be at once here and not here. He stood very straight, his black brogues planted firmly together and his briefcase leaning against his leg, with one fist on the bar—oh, I can see him!—and the other hand holding his whiskey glass suspended halfway to his lips, just as if he had stumbled in here by mistake and was too much the gentleman to cut and run before partaking of a snifter and exchanging a few civilities with the frantic denizens of the place. He could maintain this air of being just about to leave throughout a whole night's drinking. Oh yes, Charlie could act them all into a cocked hat.

The more I drank the fonder I became of him, especially as he kept paying for gins as fast as I could drink them. But it was not just that. I was—I am—genuinely fond of him, I think I have said so already. Did I mention that he got me my job at the Institute? We had kept in touch during my years in college—or at least *he* had kept in touch with *me*. He liked to think of himself as the wise old family friend watching over with an avuncular eye the brilliant only son of the house. He took me out for treats. There were teas at the Hibernian, the odd jaunt to the Curragh, the dinner at Jammet's every year on my birthday. They never quite worked, these occasions, they smacked too much of contrivance. I was always afraid that someone would see me with him, and while I squirmed and scowled he would sink into a state of restless melancholy. When we were ready to part there would be a sudden burst of hearty chatter which was nothing but relief badly disguised, then we would each turn and slink away guiltily. Yet he was not deterred, and the day after my return with Daphne from America he took me for a drink in the Shelbourne and suggested that, as he put it, I might like to give the chaps at the Institute a hand. I was still feeling groggy—we had made a hideous winter crossing, on what was hardly more than a tramp steamer—and he was so diffident, and employed such elaborate depreciations, that it was a with no fixed duties, people embarked furtively on projects of their own. There was an economist, a tall, emaciated person with a greenish face and unruly hair, who was devising a foolproof system for betting on the horses. He offered one day to let me in on it, clutching my wrist in a trembling claw and hissing urgently into my ear, but then something happened, I don't know what, he grew suspicious, and in the end would not speak to me, and avoided me in the corridors. This was awkward, for he was one of a select band of savants with whom I had to treat in order to gain access to the computer. This machine was at the centre of all our activities. Time on it was strictly rationed, and to get an un-interrupted hour at it was a rare privilege. It ran all day and through the night, whirring and crunching in its vast white room in the basement. At night it was tended by a mysterious and sinister trio, a war criminal, I think, and two strange boys, one with a damaged face. Three years I spent there. I was not violently unhappy. I just felt, and feel, as I say, a little ridiculous, a little em-barrassed. And I never quite forgave Charlie French.

It was late when we left the pub. The night was made of glass. I was very drunk. Charlie helped me along. He was worrying about his briefcase, and clutched it tightly under his arm. Every few yards I had to stop and tell him how good he was. No, I said, holding up a hand commandingly, no, I want to say it, you're a good man, Charles, a good man. I wept copiously, of course, and retched drily a few times. It was all a sort of glorious, grief-stricken, staggering rapture. I remembered that Charlie lived with his mother, and wept for that, too. But how is she, I shouted sorrowfully, tell me, Charlie, how is she, that sainted woman? He would not answer, pretended not to hear, but I kept at it and at last he shook his head irritably and said, She's dead! I tried to embrace him, but he walked away from me. We came upon a hole in the street with a

I woke in splintered sunlight with a shriek fading in my ears. Big sagging bed, brown walls, a smell of damp. I thought I must be at Coolgrange, in my parents' room. For a moment I lay without moving, staring at sliding waterlights on the ceiling. Then I remembered, and shut my eyes tight and hid my head in my arms. The darkness drummed. I got up and dragged myself to the window, and stood amazed at the blue innocence of sea and sky. Far out in the bay white sailboats were tacking into the wind. Below the window was a little stone harbour, and beyond that the curve of the coast road. An enormous seagull appeared and flung itself on flailing pinions at the glass, shrieking. They must think you are Mammy, Charlie said behind me. He was standing in the doorway. He wore a soiled apron, and held a frying pan in his hand. The gulls, he said, she used to feed them. At his back a white, impenetrable glare. This was the world I must live in from now on, in this searing, inescapable light. I looked at myself and found I was naked.

I sat in the vast kitchen, under a vast, grimy window, and watched Charlie making breakfast in a cloud of fat-smoke. He did not look too good in daylight, he was hollow and grey, with flakes of dried shaving soap on his jaw and bruised bags under his phlegm-coloured eyes. Besides the apron he wore a woollen cardigan over a soiled string vest, and sagging flannel trousers. Used to wait till I was gone, he said, then throw the food out of the window. He shook his head and laughed. A terrible woman, he said, terrible. He brought a plate of rashers and fried bread and a swimming egg and set it down in front of me. There, he said, only thing for a sore head. I looked up at him quickly. *A sore head?* Had I blurted something out to him last night, some drunken confession? But no, Charlie would not make that kind of joke. He went back to the stove and lit a cigarette, fumbling with the matches.

Look, Charlie, I said, I may as well tell you, I've got into a bit of a scrape.

I thought at first he had not heard me. He went slack, and a dreamy vacancy came over him, his mouth open and drooping a little on one side and his eyebrows mildly lifted. Then I realised that he was being tactful. Well, if he didn't want to know, that was all right. But I wish to have it in the record, m'lud, that I would have told him, if he had been prepared to listen. As it was I merely let a silence pass, and then asked if I might borrow a razor, and perhaps a shirt and tie. Of course, he said, of course, but he would not look me in the eye. In fact, he had not looked at me at all since I had got up, but edged around me with averted gaze, busying himself with the teapot and the pan, as if afraid that if he paused some awful awkward thing would arise which he would not know how to deal with. He suspected something, I suppose. He was no fool. (Or not a great fool, anyway.) But I think too it was simply that he did not quite know how to accommodate my presence. He fidgeted, moving things about, putting things away in drawers and cupboards and then taking them out again, murmuring to himself distractedly. People did not come often to this house. Some of the weepy regard I had felt for him last night returned. He seemed almost maternal, in his apron and his old felt slippers. He would take care of me. I gulped my tea and gloomed at my untouched fry congealing on its plate. A car horn tooted outside, and Charlie with an exclamation whipped off his apron and hurried out of the kitchen. I listened to him blundering about the house. In a surprisingly short time he appeared again, in his suit, with his briefcase under his arm, and sporting a raffish little hat that made him look like a harassed bookie. Where are you based, he said, frowning at a spot beside my left shoulder, Coolgrange, or—? I said nothing, only looked at him appealingly, and he said, Ah, and nodded slowly, and slowly withdrew. Suddenly, though, I did not want him to go—alone, I would be alone!—and I rushed after him and made him come back and tell me how the stove worked, and where to find a key, and what to say if the milkman called. He was puzzled by my vehemence, I could see, and faintly alarmed. I followed him into the hall, and was still talking to him as he backed out at the front door, nodding at me warily, with a fixed smile, as if I were—ha! I was going to say, a dangerous criminal. I scampered up the stairs to the bedroom, and watched as he came out on the footpath below, a clownishly foreshortened figure in his hat and his baggy suit. A large black car was waiting at the kerb, its twin exhaust pipes discreetly puffing a pale-blue mist. The driver, a burly, dark-suited fellow with no neck, hopped out smartly and held open the rear door. Charlie looked up at the window where I stood, and the driver followed his glance. I saw myself as they would see me, a blurred face floating behind the glass, blear-eyed, unshaven, the very picture of a fugitive. The car slid away smoothly and passed along the harbour road and turned a corner and was gone. I did not stir. I wanted to stay like this, with my forehead against the glass and the summer day out there before me. How quaint it all seemed, the white-tipped sea, and the white and pink houses, and the blurred headland in the distance, quaint and happy, like a little toy world laid out in a shop window. I closed my eyes, and again that fragment of memory swam up out of the depths—the doorway, and the darkened room, and the sense of something imminent—but this time it seemed to be not my own past I was remembering.

The silence was swelling like a tumour at my back.

Hurriedly I fetched my plate with the fried egg and greying rashers from the kitchen, taking the stairs three at a time, and came back and opened the window and clambered on to the narrow, wrought-iron balcony outside. A strong, warm wind was blowing, it startled me, and left me breathless for a moment. I picked up the pieces of food and flung them into the air, and watched the gulls swooping after the rich tidbits, crying harshly in surprise and greed. From behind the headland a white ship glided soundlessly into view, shimmering in the haze. When the food was gone I threw the plate away too, I don't know why, skimmed it like a discus out over the road and the harbour wall. It slid into the water with hardly a splash. There were strings of lukewarm fat between my fingers and egg-yolk under my nails. I climbed back into the room and wiped my hands on the bedclothes, my heart pounding in excitement and disgust. I did not know what I was doing, or what I would do next. I did not know myself. I had become a stranger, unpredictable and untrustworthy.

I explored the house. I had never been here before. It was a great gaunt shadowy place with dark drapes and big brown furniture and bald spots in the carpets. It was not exactly dirty, but there was a sense of staleness, of things left standing for too long in the same spot, and the air had a grey, dull feel to it, as if a vital essence in it had been used up long ago. There was a smell of must and stewed tea and old newspapers, and, everywhere, a flattish, faintly sweet something which I took to be the afterglow of Mammy French. I suppose there will be guffaws if I say I am a fastidious man, but it's true. I was already in some distress before I started poking among Charlie's things, and I feared what I might find. His sad little secrets were no nastier than mine, or anyone else's, yet when here and there I turned over a stone and they came scuttling out, I shivered, and was ashamed for him and for myself. I steeled myself, though, and persevered, and was rewarded in the end. There was a rolltop desk in his bedroom, which took me ten minutes of hard work with a kitchen knife to break into, squatting on my heels and sweating beads of pure alcohol. Inside I found some banknotes and a plastic wallet of credit cards. There were letters, too—from my mother, of all people, written thirty, forty years before. I did not read them, I don't know why, but put them back carefully, along with the credit cards, and even the cash, and locked the desk again. As I was going out I exchanged a shamefaced little grin with my reflection in the wardrobe mirror. That German, what's his name, was right: money is abstract happiness.

The bathroom was on the first-floor return, a sort of wooden lean-to with a gas geyser and a gigantic, clawfooted bath. I crouched over the handbasin and scraped off two days' growth of stubble with Charlie's soap-encrusted razor. I had thought of growing a beard, for disguise, but I had lost enough of myself already, I did not want half of my face to disappear as well. The shaving-glass had a concave, silvery surface in which my magnified features—a broad, pitted jaw, one black nose-hole with hairs, a single, rolling eyeball—bobbed and swayed alarmingly, like things looming in the window of a bathysphere. When I had finished I got into the tub and lay with my eyes shut while the water cascaded down on me from the geyser. It was good, at once a solace and a scalding chastisement, and if the gas had not eventually gone out I might have stayed there all day, lost to myself and everything else in that roaring, steamy darkness. When I opened my eyes tiny stars were whizzing and popping in front of me. I padded, dripping, into Charlie's room, and spent a long time deciding what to wear. In the end I chose a dark-blue silk shirt and a somewhat louche, flowered bow-tie to go with it. Black socks, of course—silk again: Charlie is not one to stint himself—and a pair of dark trousers, baggy but well cut, of a style which was antique enough to have come back into fashion. For the present I would do without underwear: even a killer on the run has his principles, and mine precluded getting into another man's drawers. My own clothes—how odd they looked, thrown on the bedroom floor, as if waiting to be outlined in chalk—I gathered in a bundle, and with my face averted carried them to the kitchen and stuffed them into a plastic rubbish bag. Then I washed and dried the breakfast things, and was standing in the middle of the floor with a soiled tea-towel in my hand when the image of her bloodied face shot up in front of me like something in a fairground stall, and I had to sit down, winded and shaking. For I kept forgetting, you see, forgetting all about it, for quite long periods. I suppose my mind needed respite, in order to cope. Wearily I looked about the big dank kitchen. I wondered if Charlie would notice there was a plate missing. Why did I throw it into the sea, why did I do that? It was not yet noon. Time opened its black maw in my face. I went into one of the front rooms—net curtains, vast dining table, a stuffed owl under glass—and stood at the window looking out at the sea. All that blue out there was daunting. I paced the floor, stopped, stood listening, my heart in my mouth. What did I expect to hear? There was nothing, only the distant noise of other lives, a tiny ticking and plinking, like the noise of an engine cooling down. I remembered days like this in my childhood, strange, empty days when I would wander softly about the silent house and seem to myself a kind of ghost, hardly there at all, a memory, a shadow of some more solid version of myself living, oh, living marvellously, elsewhere.

I must stop. I'm sick of myself, all this.

Time. The days.

Go on, go on.

Disgust, now, that is something I know about. Let me say a word or two about disgust. Here I sit, naked under my prison garb, wads of pallid flesh trussed and bagged like badly packaged meat. I get up and walk around on my hind legs, a belted animal, shedding an invisible snow of scurf everywhere I move. Mites live on me, they lap my sweat, stick their snouts into my pores and gobble up the glop they find there. Then the split skin, the cracks, the crevices. Hair: just think of hair. And this is only the surface. Imagine what is going on inside, the purple pump shuddering and squelching, lungs fluttering, and, down in the dark, the glue factory at its ceaseless work. Animate carrion, slick with gleet, not ripe enough yet for the worms. Ach, I should—

Calm, Frederick. Calm.

My wife came to see me today. This is not unusual, she comes every week. As a remand prisoner I have the right to unrestricted visiting, but I have not told her this, and if she knows it she has said nothing. We prefer it this way. Even at its most uneventful the Thursday visiting hour is a bizarre, not to say uncanny ritual. It is conducted in a large square lofty room with small windows set high up under the ceiling. A partition of plywood and glass, an ugly contraption, separates us from our loved ones, with whom we converse as best we can by way of a disinfected plastic grille. This state of virtual quarantine is a recent imposition. It is meant to keep out drugs, we're told, but I think it is really a way of keeping *in* those interesting viruses which lately we have begun to incubate in here. The room has a touch of the aquarium about it, with that wall of greenish glass, and the tall light drifting down from above, and the voices that come to us out of the plastic lattices as if bubbled through water. We inmates sit with shoulders hunched, leaning grimly on folded arms, wan, bloated, vague-eyed, like unhoused crustaceans crouching at the bottom of a tank. Our visitors exist in a different element from ours, they seem more sharply defined than we, more intensely present in their world.

Sometimes we catch a look in their eyes, a mixture of curiosity and compassion, and faint repugnance, too, which strikes us to the heart. They must feel the force of our longing, must hear it, almost, the mermen's song, a high needle-note of pure woe buzzing in the glass that separates us from them. Their concern for our plight is not a comfort, but distresses us, rather. This is the tenderest time of our week, we desire tranquillity, decorum, muted voices. We are constantly on edge, worried that someone's wife or girlfriend out there will make a scene, jump up and shout, pound her fists on the partition, weep. When such a thing does happen it is awful, just awful, and afterwards the one that it happened to is an object of sympathy and awe amongst us, as if he had suffered a bereavement.

No fear of Daphne making a scene. She maintains an admirable poise at all times. Today, for instance, when she told me about the child, she spoke quietly, looking away from me with her usual air of faint abstraction. I confess I was annoyed at her, I couldn't hide it. She should have told me she was having him tested, instead of just presenting me with the diagnosis out of the blue like this. She gave me a quizzical look, tilting her head to one side and almost smiling. Are you surprised? she said. I turned my face away crossly and did not answer. Of course I was not surprised. I knew there was something wrong with him, I always knew—I told her so, long before she was ready to admit it. From the start there was the way he moved, warily, quaking, on his scrawny little legs, as if trying not to drop some large, unmanageable thing that had been dumped into his arms, looking up at us in bewilderment and supplication, like a creature looking up out of a hole in the ground. Where did you take him, I said, what hospital, and what did they say exactly? She shrugged. They were very nice, she said, very sympathetic. The doctor had talked to her for a long time. It is a very rare condition, somebody's syndrome, I have forgotten the name already, some damn Swiss or Swede—what does it matter. He will never speak properly. He'll never do anything properly, it seems. There is something wrong with his brain, something is missing, some vital bit. She explained it all to me, repeating what the doctor told her, but I was only half-listening. A sort of weariness had come over me, a sort of lethargy. Van is his name, have I mentioned that? Van. He's seven. When I get out he will probably be, what, thirty-something? Jesus, almost as old as I am now. A big child, that's what the country people will call him, not without fondness, at Coolgrange. A big child.

I will not, I will not weep. If I start now I'll never stop.

In the afternoon I broke into Charlie's desk again, and took some cash and ventured out to the newsagent's on the harbour. What a strange, hot thrill of excitement I felt, stepping into the shop. My stomach wobbled, and I seemed to be treading slowly through some thick, resistant medium. I think a part of me hoped—no, expected—that somehow I would be saved, that as in a fairy-tale everything would be magically reversed, that the wicked witch would disappear, that the spell would be lifted, that the maid would wake from her enchanted sleep. And when I picked up the papers it seemed for a moment as if some magic had indeed been worked, for at first I could see nothing in them except more stuff about the bombing and its aftermath. I bought three mornings, and an early-evening edition, noting (is this only hindsight?) the hard look that the pimpled girl behind the counter gave me. Then I hurried back to the house, my heart going at a gallop, as if it were some choice erotica I was clutching under my arm. Indoors again, I left the papers on the kitchen table and ran to the bathroom, where in my agitation I managed to pee on my foot. After a lengthy, feverish search I found a quarter-full bottle of gin and took a good slug from the neck. I tried to find something else to do, but it was no good, and with leaden steps I returned to the kitchen and sat down slowly at the table and spread out the papers in front of me. There it was, a few paragraphs in one of the mornings, squeezed under a photograph of a bandaged survivor of the bombing sitting up in a hospital bed. In the evening edition there was a bigger story, with a photograph of the boys I had seen playing in the hotel grounds. It was they who had found her. There was a photograph of her, too, gazing out solemn-eyed from a blurred background, it must have been lifted from a group shot of a wedding, or a dance, for she was wearing a long, ugly dress with an elaborate collar, and was clutching something, flowers, perhaps, in her hands. Her name was Josephine Bell. There was more inside, a file picture of Behrens and a view of Whitewater House, and an article on the Behrens collection, littered with misspellings and garbled dates. A reporter had been sent down to the country to talk to Mrs Brigid Bell, the mother. She was a widow. There was a photograph of her standing awkwardly in front of her cottage, a big, raw-faced woman in an apron and an old cardigan, peering at the camera in a kind of stolid dismay. Her Josie, she said, was a good girl, a decent girl, why would anyone want to kill her. And suddenly I was back there, I saw her sitting in the mess of her own blood, looking at me, a bleb of pink spittle bursting on her lips. *Mammy* was what she said, that was the word, not Tommy, I've just this moment realised it. *Mammy*, and then: *Love*.

first I would know of it. But still I stood there, watching and watching, more like a pining lover than a man on the run.

Everything was changed, everything. I was estranged from myself and all that I had once supposed I was. My life up to now had only the weightless density of a dream. When I thought about my past it was like thinking of what someone else had been, someone I had never met but whose history I knew by heart. It all seemed no more than a vivid fiction. Nor was the present any more solid. I felt light-headed, volatile, poised at an angle to everything. The ground under me was stretched tight as a trampoline, I must keep still for fear of unexpected surges, dangerous leaps and bounces. And all around me was this blue and empty air.

I could not think directly about what I had done. It would have been like trying to stare steadily into a blinding light. It was too big, too bright, to contemplate. It was incomprehensible. Even still, when I say *I did it*, I am not sure I know what I mean. Oh, do not mistake me. I have no wish to vacillate, to hum and haw and kick dead leaves over the evidence. I killed her, I admit it freely. And I know that if I were back there today I would do it again, not because I would want to, but because I would have no choice. It would be just as it was then, this spider, and this moonlight between the trees, and all, all the rest of it. Nor can I say I did not mean to kill her—only, I am not clear as to when I began to mean it. I was flustered, impatient, angry, she attacked me, I swiped at her, the swipe became a blow, which became the prelude to a second blow—its apogee, so to speak, or perhaps I mean perigee—and so on. There is no moment in this process of which I can confidently say, there, that is when I decided she should die. Decided?—I do not think it was a matter of deciding. I do not think it was a matter of thinking, even. That fat monster inside me just saw his chance and leaped out, frothing and flailing. He had scores to settle with the world, and Josie Bell, at that moment, was world enough for him. I could not stop him. Or could I? He is me, after all, and I am he. But no, things were too far gone for stopping. Perhaps that is the essence of my crime, of my culpability, that I let things get to that stage, that I had not been vigilant enough, had not been enough of a dissembler, that I left Bunter to his own devices, and thus allowed him, fatally, to understand that he was free, that the cage door was open, that nothing was forbidden, that everything was possible.

After my first appearance in court the newspapers said I showed no sign of remorse when the charges were read out. (What did they expect, that I would weep, rend my garments?) They were on to something, in their dim-witted way. Remorse implies the expectation of forgiveness, and I knew that what I had done was unforgivable. I could have feigned regret and sorrow, guilt, all that, but to what end? Even if I had felt such things, truly, in the deepest depths of my heart, would it have altered anything? The deed was done, and would not be cancelled by cries of anguish and repentance. Done, yes, finished, as nothing ever before in my life had been finished and done—and yet there would be no end to it, I saw that straight away. I was, I told myself, responsible, with all the weight that word implied. In killing Josie Bell I had destroyed a part of the world. Those hammer-blows had shattered a complex of memories and sensations and possibilities—a life, in short— which was irreplaceable, but which, somehow, must be replaced. For the crime of murder I would be caught and put away, I knew this with the calmness and certainty which only an irrelevance could inspire, and then they would say I had paid my debt, in the belief that by walling me up alive they had struck a sort of balance. They would be right, according to the laws of retribution and revenge: such balance, however, would be at best a negative thing. No, no. What was required was not my symbolic death—I recognised this, though I did not understand what it meant—but for her to be brought back to life. That, and nothing less.

That evening when Charlie returned he put his head cautiously around the door as if he feared there might be a bucket of water balanced on it. I leered at him, swaying. I had finished the gin, and moved on, reluctantly, to whiskey. I was not drunk, exactly, but in a kind of numbed euphoria, as if I had just come back from a lengthy and exquisitely agonising visit to the dentist. Under the new buzz the old hangover lurked, biding its time. My skin was hot and dry all over, and my eyes felt scorched. Cheers! I cried, with a fatuous laugh, and the ice cubes chuckled in my glass. Charlie was darting sidelong looks at my outfit. Hope you don't mind, I said. Didn't think we'd be the same size. Ah, he said, yes, well, I've shrunk in my old age, you see. And he gave a graveyard laugh. I could see he had been hoping I would be gone when he came home. I followed him out to the hall, where he took off his bookie's titfer and put it with his briefcase on the bog-oak hall-stand. He went into the dining room and poured himself a modest whiskey, adding a go of flattish soda from a screw-top bottle. He took a sip, and stood for a little while as if stalled, with a hand in his pocket, frowning at his feet. My presence was interfering with his evening rituals. He put away the whiskey bottle without offering me a refill. We traipsed back to the kitchen, where Charles donned his apron and rooted about in cupboards and on murky shelves for the makings of a stew. While he worked he talked distractedly over his shoulder, with a cigarette hanging from a corner of his lopsided mouth and one eye screwed shut against the smoke. He was telling me about a sale he had made, or a picture he had bought, or something like that. I think he only spoke for fear of the prospect of silence. Anyway I was not really listening. I watched him glugging the better half of a fifty-pound bottle of

Pomerol into the stew. An inch of cigarette ash went into the pot as well, he tried vainly to fish it out with a spoon, clucking in annoyance. You can imagine what it's like for me, he said, actually parting with pictures! I nodded solemnly. In fact, what I was imagining was Charlie in his poky gallery, bowing and scraping and wringing his hands in front of some fur-coated bitch reeking of face-powder and perspiration, whose hubby had given her the money to bag a bauble for her birthday. I was depressed suddenly, and suddenly tired.

He served up the stew, spilling some on the floor. He was not good with implements, they tended to turn treacherous in his hands, to wobble and veer and let things slither off. We carried our plates into the dining room and sat down at the table under the stuffed owl's virulent, glassy stare. We drank the rest of the Pomerol, and Charles fetched another bottle. He continued to make an elaborate business of avoiding my eye, smiling about him at the floor, the furniture, the fire irons in the grate, as if the commonplace had suddenly presented itself to his attention with a new and unexpected charm. The lowering sun was shining full upon me through the tall window at my back. The stew tasted of burnt fur. I pushed my plate aside and turned and looked out at the harbour. There was a shimmering flaw in the window-pane. Something made me think of California, something about the light, the little yachts, the gilded evening sea. I was so tired, so tired, I could have given up then and there, could have drifted out into that summer dusk as easily as a breeze, unknown, planless, free. Charlie squashed out a sodden fag-end on the rim of his plate. Did you see that thing about Binkie Behrens in the paper? he said. I poured myself another fill of wine. No, I said, what was that, Charles?

By the by, what would I have done in all this affair without the solace of drink and its deadening effect? I seem to have got over those days in a series of quaking lunges from one brief state of drunken equilibrium to another, like a fugitive fleeing across a zigzag of slimed stepping-stones. Even the colours, gin-blue and claret-red, are they not the very emblems of my case, the court-colours of my testimony? Now that I have sobered up forever I look back not only on that time but on all my life as a sort of tipsy but not particularly happy spree, from which I knew I would have to emerge sooner or later, with a bad headache. This, ah yes, this is hangover time with a vengeance.

The rest of that evening, as I recall it, was a succession of distinct, muffled shocks, like falling downstairs slowly in a dream. That was when I learned that my father had kept a mistress. I was first astonished, then indignant. I had been his alibi, his camouflage! While I sat for hours in the back of the car above the yacht club in Dun Laoghaire on Sunday afternoons, he was off fucking his fancy-woman. Penelope was her name—Penelope, for God's sake! Where did they meet, I wanted to know, was there a secret love nest where he kept her, a bijou little hideaway with roses round the door and a mirror on the bedroom ceiling? Charlie shrugged. Oh, he said, they used to come here. At first I could not take it in. Here? I cried. Here? But what about—? He shrugged again, and gave a sort of grin. Mammy French, it seems, did not mind. On occasion she even had the lovers join her for tea. She and Penelope exchanged knitting patterns. You see, she knew—Charlie said, but stopped, and a spot of colour appeared in the cracked skin over each cheekbone, and he ran a finger quickly around the inside of his shirt collar. I waited. She knew I was fond of your—of Dolly, he said at last. By now I was fairly reeling. Before I could speak he went on to tell me how Binkie Behrens too had been after my mother, how he would invite her and my father to Whitewater and ply my father with drink so he would not notice Binkie's gamy eye and wandering hands. And then my mother would come and tell Charlie all about it, and they would laugh together. Now he shook his head and sighed. Poor Binkie, he said. I sat aghast; lost in wonderment and trying to hold my wine glass straight. I felt like a child hearing for the first time of the doings of the gods: they crowded in my buzzing head, these tremendous, archaic, flawed figures with their plots and rivalries and impossible loves. Charlie was so matter-of-fact about it all, half wistful and half amused. He spoke mostly as if I were not there, looking up now and then in mild surprise at my squeaks and snorts of astonishment. And you, I said, what about you and my—? I could not put it into words. He gave me a look at once arch and sly.

Here, he said, finish the bottle.

I think he told me something more about my mother, but I don't remember what it was. I do remember phoning her later that night, sitting cross-legged in the dark on the floor in the hall, with tears in my eyes and the telephone squatting in my lap like a frog. She seemed immensely far away, a miniature voice booming at me tinily out of a thrumming void. Freddie, she said, you're drunk. She asked why had I not come back, to collect my bag if for nothing else. I wanted to say to her, Mother, how could I go home, now? We were silent for a moment, then she said Daphne had called her, wondering where I was, what I was doing. Daphne! I had not thought of her for days. Through the doorway at the end of the hall I watched Charlie pottering about in the kitchen, rattling the pots and pans and pretending he was not trying to hear what I was saying. I sighed, and the sigh turned into a thin little moan. Ma, I said, I've got myself into such trouble. There was a noise on the line, or maybe it was in my head, like a great rushing of many wings. What? she said, I can't hear you—what? I laughed, and two big tears ran down the sides of my nose. Nothing, I shouted, nothing, forget it! Then I said, Listen, do you know who Penelope is—was—do you know about her? I was shocked at myself. Why did I say such a thing, why did I want to wound her? She was silent for a moment, and then she laughed. That bitch? she said, of course I knew about her. Charlie had come to the doorway, and stood, with a rag in one hand and a plate in the other, watching me. The light was behind him, I could not see his face. There was another pause. You're too hard on yourself, Freddie, my mother said at last, in that reverberant, faraway voice, you make things too hard on yourself. I did not know what she meant. I still don't. I waited a moment, but she said nothing more, and I could not speak. Those were the last words we would ever exchange. I put down the receiver gently, and got to my feet, not without difficulty. One of my knees was asleep. I limped into the kitchen. Charlie was bent over the sink doing the washing-up, with yet another cigarette dangling from his lip, sleeves rolled, his waist-coat unbuckled at the back. The sky in the window in front of him was a pale shade of indigo, I thought I had never seen anything so lovely in my life.

Charlie, I said, swaying, I need a loan.

I had always been a weeper, but now any hint of kindness could make me blub like a babe. When there and then he sat down at the kitchen table and wrote out a cheque—I have it still: spidery black scrawl, an illegible signature, a stewy thumb-print in one corner— I tried to seize his liver-spotted hand, I think I meant to kiss it. He made a little speech, I don't remember it well. My mother figured in it, Daphne too. I think even Penelope's name was mentioned. I wonder if he was drunk? He kept looming into focus and fading out again, yet I felt this was less an effect of my blurred vision than of a sort of tentativeness on his part. Oh, Charlie, you should have heeded that niggle of suspicion, you should have thrown me out that night, fuddled and defenceless though I was.

The next thing I recall is being on my knees in the lavatory, puking up a ferruginous torrent of wine mixed with fibrous strands of meat and bits of carrot. The look of this stuff gushing out filled me with wonder, as if it were not vomit, but something rich and strange, a dark stream of ore from the deep mine of my innards. Then there is an impression of everything swaying, of glistening darkness and things in it spinning past me, as though I were being whirled round and round slowly on a wobbly carousel made of glass. Next I was lying on my back on the big, disordered bed upstairs, shivering and sweating. There was a light on, and the window was a box of deep, gleaming darkness. I fell asleep, and after what seemed a moment woke again with the sun in my face. The house was silent around me, but there was a thin, continuous ringing which I seemed to feel rather than hear. The sheets were a sodden tangle. I did not want to move, I felt as fragile as crystal. Even my hair felt breakable, a shock of erect, minute filaments bristling with static. I could feel the blood rushing along my veins, quick and heavy as mercury. My face was swollen and hot, and strangely smooth to the touch: a doll's face. When I closed my eyes a crimson shape pulsed and faded and pulsed again on the inside of my lids, like the repeated afterimage of a shell bursting in black-ness. When I swallowed, the ringing in my ears changed pitch. I dozed, and dreamed I was adrift in a hot lake. When I woke it was afternoon. The light in the window, dense, calm, unshadowed, was a light shining straight out of the past. My mouth was dry and swollen, my head seemed packed with air. Not since childhood had I known this particular state of voluptuous distress. It was not really illness, more a kind of respite. I lay for a long time, hardly stirring, watching the day change, listening to the little noises of the world. The brazen sunlight slowly faded, and the sky turned from lilac to mauve, and a single star appeared. Then suddenly it was late, and I lay in a sleepy daze in the soft summer darkness and would not have been surprised if my mother had appeared, young and smiling, in a rustle of silk, with a finger to her lips, to say interviewed. Did they remember me, that pallid stranger dreaming on the bench in the deserted station? They did, they gave a description of me: an elderly man with black hair and a bushy beard. The woman at the traffic lights was sure I was in my early twenties, well-dressed, with a moustache and piercing eyes. Then there were the tourists at Whitewater who saw me make off with the painting, and Reck and his ma, of course, and the idiot boy and the woman at the garage where I hired the car: from each of their accounts another and more fantastic version of me emerged, until I became multiplied into a band of moustachioed cutthroats, rushing about glaring and making threatening noises, like a chorus of brigands in an Italian opera. I nearly laughed. And yet I was disappointed. Yes, it's true, I was disappointed. Did I want to be found out, did I hope to see my name splashed in monster type across every front page? I think I did. I think I longed deep down to be made to stand in front of a jury and reveal all my squalid little secrets. Yes, to be found out, to be suddenly pounced upon, beaten, stripped, and set before the howling multitude, that was my deepest, most ardent desire. I hear the court catching its breath in surprise and disbelief. But ah, do you not also long for this, in your hearts, gentlepersons of the jury? To be rumbled. To feel that heavy hand fall upon your shoulder, and hear the booming voice of authority telling you the game is up at last. In short, to be unmasked. Ask yourselves. I confess (I confess!), those days that passed while I waited for them to find me were the most exciting I have ever known, or ever hope to know. Terrible, yes, but exciting too. Never had the world appeared so unstable, or my place in it so thrillingly precarious. I had a raw, lascivious awareness of myself, a big warm damp thing parcelled up in someone else's clothes. At any moment they might catch me, they might be watching me even now, murmuring into their handsets and signalling to the marksmen on the roof. First there would be panic, then pain. And when everything was gone, every shred of dignity and pretence, what freedom there would be, what lightness! No, what am I saying, not lightness, but its opposite: weight, gravity, the sense at last of being firmly grounded. Then finally I would be me, no longer that poor impersonation of myself I had been doing all my life. I would be real. I would be, of all things, human.

I took the bus to town, and got off at a street where I used to live years ago, when I was a student, and walked along by the railings of the park in the warm wind under the seething trees, my heart filled with nostalgia. A man in a cap, with terrible, soiled eyes, stood on the pavement shaking a fist in the air and roaring obscene abuse at the cars passing by. I envied him. I would have liked to stand and shout like that, to pour out all that rage and pain and indignation. I walked on. A trio of light-clad girls came tripping out of a bookshop, laughing, and for a second I was caught up in their midst, my side-teeth bared in a frightful grin, a beast among the graces. In a bright new shop I bought a jacket and trousers, two shirts, some ties, underwear, and, in a flourish of defiance, a handsome but not altogether unostentatious hat. I thought I detected a slight stiffening of attention when I produced Charlie's credit cards—my God, did they know him, did he shop here?—but I turned up my accent to full force and dashed off his signature with aplomb, and everyone relaxed. I was not really worried. In fact, I felt ridiculously excited and happy, like a boy on a birthday spree. (What is it about the mere act of buying things, that it can afford me so much simple pleasure?) I seemed to swim along the street, upright as a seahorse, breasting the air. I think I must have been feverish still. The people among whom I moved were strange to me, stranger than usual, I mean. I felt I was no longer of their species, that something had happened since I had last encountered a crowd of them together, that an adjustment had occurred in me, a tiny, amazingly swift and momentous evolutionary event. I passed through their midst like a changeling, a sport of nature. They were beyond me, they could not touch me—could they see me, even, or was I now outside the spectrum of their vision? And yet how avidly I observed them, in hunger and wonderment. They surged around me at a sort of stumble, dull-eyed and confused, like refugees. I saw myself, bobbing head and shoulders above them, disguised, solitary, nursing my huge secret. I was their unrecognised and their unacknowledged dream—I was their Moosbrugger. I came to the river, and dawdled on the bridge, among the beggars and the fruit-sellers and the hawkers of cheap jewellery, admiring the wind-blurred light above the water and tasting the salt air on my lips. The sea! To be away, out there, out over countless fathoms, lost in all that blue!

I went—everything was so simple—I went into a bar and bought a drink. Each sip was like a sliver of precious metal, chill and smooth. It was a cavernous place, very dark. The light from the street glared whitely in the open doorway. I might have been somewhere in the south, in one of those dank, tired ports I used to know so well. At the back, in a lighted place like a stage, some youths with shaven heads and outsize lace-up boots were playing a game of billiards. The balls whirred and clacked, the young men softly swore. It was like something out of Hogarth, a group of wigless surgeons, say, intent over the dissecting table. The barman, arms folded and mouth open, was watching a horse race on the television set perched high up on a shelf in a corner above him. A tubercular young man in a black shortie overcoat came in and stood beside me, breathing and fidgeting. I could tell from the tension coming off him that he was working himself up to something, and for a moment I was pleasurably alarmed. He might do anything, anything. But he only spoke. *I've lived here thirty-three years*, he said, in a tone of bitter indignation, *and everyone is afraid*. The barman glanced at him with weary contempt and turned back to the television. Blue horses galloped in silence over bright-green turf. *I am afraid*, the young man said, resentful now. He gave a tremendous twitch, hunching his shoulders and ducking his head and throwing up one arm, as if something had bitten him on the neck. Then he turned and went out hurriedly, clutching his coat about him. I followed, leaving my drink half-finished. It was blindingly bright outside. I spotted him, a good way off already, dodging along through the crowds with his elbows pressed to his sides, taking tight, swift little steps, nimble as a dancer. Nothing could stop him. In the thickest surge of bodies he would find a chink at once, and swivel deftly from the waist up and dive through without altering his pace. What a pair we would have made, if anyone had thought to link us, he in his tight shabby coat and I with my fancy hat and expensive clutch of carrier bags. I could hardly keep up with him, and after a minute or two I was puffing and in a sweat. I had an unaccountable sense of elation. Once he paused, and stood glaring into the window of a chemist's shop. I waited, loitering at a bus stop, keeping him in the corner of my eye. He was so intent, and seemed to quiver so, that I thought he was going to do something violent, turn and attack someone, maybe, or kick in the window and stamp about among the cameras and the cosmetic displays. But he was only waiting for another shudder to pass through him. This time when he flung up his arm his leg shot up as well, as if elbow and knee were connected by an invisible string, and a second later his heel came down on the pavement with a ringing crack. He cast a quick look up and down the street, to see if anyone had noticed, and gave himself a casual little shake, as if by that he would make the previous spasm appear to have been intentional too, and then he was off again like a whippet. I wanted to catch up with him, I wanted to speak to him. I did not know what I would say. I would not offer him sympathy, certainly not. I did not pity him, I saw nothing in him to merit my from the pavement, ignoring the looks of the passers-by, who appeared to find my merriment unseemly. I did not care about the jacket—in fact, the loss of it chimed in a mysteriously apt way with that of its discarded predecessor—but I would have liked to see where those girls would go. I imagined a lean-to made of rags and bits of galvanised iron on a dusty patch of waste ground, with a starving dog and snot-nosed infants, and a drunken hag crouched over a steaming pot. Or perhaps there was a Fagin somewhere waiting for them, skulking in the shadows in some derelict tenement, where the light of summer fingered the shutters, and dust motes drifted under lofty ceilings, and the rat's claw in the wainscoting scratched at the silence, scratched, stopped, and scratched again. So I went along happily for a little while, dreaming up other lives, until I spotted a whey-faced giant with rubber legs clomping ahead of me on two sticks, and I set off after him in eager pursuit.

What was I doing, why was I following these people—what enlightenment was I looking for? I did not know, nor care. I was puzzled and happy, like a child who has been allowed to join in an adults' game. I kept at it for hours, criss-crossing the streets and the squares with a drunkard's dazed single-mindedness, as if I were tracing out a huge, intricate sign on the face of the city for someone in the sky to read. I found myself in places I had not known were there, crooked alleyways and sudden, broad, deserted spaces, and dead-end streets under railway bridges where parked cars basked fatly in the evening sun, their toy-coloured roofs agleam. I ate a hamburger in a glass-walled café with moulded plastic chairs and tinfoil ashtrays, where people sat alone and gnawed at their food like frightened children abandoned by their parents. The daylight died slowly, leaving a barred, red and gold sunset trembling in the sky, and as I walked along it was like walking under the surface of a broad, burning river. The evening crowds were out, girls in tight trousers and high heels, and brawny young men with

I have had a shock. My counsel has been to see me today, bringing an extraordinary piece of news. Usually I enjoy our little conferences, in a lugubrious sort of way. We sit at a square table in a small airless room with no windows. The walls are painted filing-cabinet grey. Light from a strip of neon tubing above our heads sifts down upon us like a fine-grained mist. The bulb makes a tiny, continuous buzzing. Maolseachlainn at first is full of energy, rooting in his bag, shuffling his papers, muttering. He is like a big, worried bear. He works at finding things to talk to me about, new aspects of the case, obscure points of law he might bring up, the chances of our getting a sympathetic judge, that sort of thing. He speaks too fast, stumbling over his words as if they were so many stones. Gradually the atmosphere of the place gets in at him, like damp, and he falls silent. He takes off his specs and sits and blinks at me. He has a way of squeezing the bridge of his nose between two fingers and a thumb which is peculiarly endearing. I feel sorry for him. I think he truly does like me. This puzzles him, and, I suspect, disturbs him too. He believes he is letting me down when he runs out of steam like this, but really, there is nothing left to say. We both know I will get life. He cannot understand my equanimity in the face of my fate. I tell him I have taken up Buddhism. He smiles carefully, unsure that it is a joke. I divert him with tales of prison life, fleshing them out with impersonations—I do our governor here very convincingly. When Maolseachlainn laughs there is no sound, only a slow heaving of the shoulders and a stretched, shiny grin.

By the way, what an odd formulation that is: to get life. Words so rarely mean what they mean.

Today I saw straight away he was in a state about something. He kept clawing at the collar of his shirt and clearing his throat, and taking off his half-glasses and putting them back on again. Also there was a smeary look in his eye. He hummed and hawed, and mumbled about the concept of justice, and the discretion of the courts, and other such folderol, I hardly listened to him. He was so mournful and ill at ease, shifting his big backside on the prison chair and looking everywhere except at me, that I could hardly keep from laughing. I pricked up my ears, though, when he started to mutter something about the possibility of my making a guilty plea—and this after all the time and effort he expended at the beginning in convincing me I should plead not guilty. Now when I caught him up on it, rather sharply, I confess, he veered off at once, with an alarmed look. I wonder what he's up to? I should have kept at it, and got it out of him. As a diversionary measure he dived into his briefcase and brought out a copy of my mother's will. I had not yet heard the contents, and was, I need hardly say, keenly interested. Maolseachlainn, I noticed, found this subject not much easier than the previous one. He coughed a lot, and frowned, and read out stuff about gifts and covenants and minor bequests, and was a long time getting to the point. I still cannot credit it. The old bitch has left Coolgrange to that stable-girl, what's-her-name, Joanne. There is some money for Daphne, and for Van's schooling, but for me, nothing. I suppose I should not be surprised, but I am. I was not a good son, but I was the only one she had. Maolseachlainn was watching me with compassion. I'm sorry, he said. I smiled and shrugged, though it was not easy. I wished he would go away now. Oh, I said, it's understandable, after all, that she would make a new will. He said nothing. There was a peculiar silence. Then, almost tenderly, he handed me the document, and I looked at the date. The thing was seven, nearly eight years old. She had cut me out long ago, before ever I came back to disgrace her and the family name. I recalled, with shocking clarity, the way she looked at me that day in the kitchen at Coolgrange, and heard again that cackle of raucous laughter. Well, I'm glad she enjoyed her joke. It's a good one. I find a surprising lack of bitterness in my heart. I am smiling, though probably it seems more as if I am wincing. This is her contribution to the long course of lessons I must learn.

Maolseachlainn stood up, assuming his heartiest manner, as always, in an attempt to disguise his relief at the prospect of getting away. I watched him struggle into his navy-blue overcoat and knot his red woollen muffler around his neck. Sometimes, when he first arrives, his clothes give off little wafts and slivers of the air of outdoors. I snuff them up with surreptitious pleasure, as if they were the most precious of perfumes. What's it like, outside? I said now. He paused, and blinked at me in some alarm. I think he thought I was asking him for an overall picture, as if I might have forgotten what the world looked like. The day, I said, the weather. His brow cleared. He shrugged. Oh, he said, grey, just grey, you know. And I saw it at once, with a pang, the late November afternoon, the dull shine on the wet roads, and the children straggling home from school, and rooks tossing and wheeling high up against ragged clouds, and the tarnished glow in the sky off behind bare, blackened branches. These were the times I used to love, the weather's unconsidered moments, when the vast business of the world just goes on quietly by itself, as if there were no one to notice, or care. I see myself as a boy out there, dawdling along that wet road, kicking a stone ahead of me and dreaming the enormous dream of the future. There was a path, I remember, that cut off through an oak wood a mile or so from home, which I knew must lead to Coolgrange eventually. How green the shadows, and deep the track, how restless the silence seemed, that way. Every time I passed by there, coming up from the cross, I said to myself, Next time, next time. But always when the next time came I was in a rush, or the light was fading, or I was just not in the mood to break new ground, and so I kept to the ordinary route, along the road. In the end I never took that secret path, and now, of course, it is too late.

I have been doing calculations in my head—it keeps my mind off other things—and I find to my surprise that I spent no more than ten days in all at Charlie's house, from midsummer day, or night, rather, until the last, momentous day of June. That *is* ten, isn't it? Thirty days hath September, April, June—yes, ten. Or is it nine. It's nine nights, certainly. But where does the day end and the night start, and vice versa? And why do I find the night a more easily quantifiable entity than day? I have never been any good at this kind of thing. The simpler the figures the more they fox me. Anyway. Ten days, thereabouts, more or less, is the length of my stay with Charlie French, whose hospitality and kindness I did not mean to betray. It seemed a longer time than that. It seemed weeks and weeks. I was not unhappy there. That's to say, I was no more unhappy there than I would have been somewhere else. Unhappy! What a word! As the days went on I grew increasingly restless. My nerves seethed, and there was a permanent knot of pain in my guts. I suffered sudden, furious attacks of impatience. Why didn't they come for me, what were they doing? In particular I resented the Behrenses' silence, I was convinced they were playing a cruel game with me. But all the time, behind all these agitations, there was that abiding, dull, flat sensation. I felt disappointed. I felt let down. The least I had expected from the enormities of which I was guilty was that they would change my life, that they would make things happen, however awful, that there would be a constant succession of heart-stopping events, of alarms and sudden frights and hairbreadth escapes. I do not know how I got through the days. I awoke each morning with an anguished start, as if a pure, distilled drop of pain had plopped on to my forehead. That big old house with its smells and cobwebs was oppressive. I drank a lot, of course, but not enough to make myself insensible. I tried to achieve oblivion, God knows, I poured in the booze until my lips went numb and my knees would hardly bend, but it was no good, I could not escape myself. I waited with a lover's rapt expectancy for the evenings, when I would put on my hat and my new clothes—my new mask!—and step forth gingerly, a quavering Dr Jekyll, inside whom that other, terrible creature chafed and struggled, lusting for experience. I felt I had never until now looked at the ordinary world around me, the people, places, things. How innocent it all seemed, innocent, and doomed. How can I express the tangle of emotions that thrashed inside me as I prowled the city streets, letting my monstrous heart feed its fill on the sights and sounds of the commonplace? The feeling of power, for instance, how can I communicate that? It sprang not from what I had done, but from the fact that I had done it and *no one knew*. It was the secret, the secret itself, *that* was what set me above the dull-eyed ones among whom I moved as the long day died, and the streetlights came on, and the traffic slid away homeward, leaving a blue haze hanging like the smoke of gunfire in the darkening air. And then there was that constant, hot excitement, like a fever in the blood, that was half the fear of being unmasked and half the longing for it. Somewhere, I knew, in dayrooms and in smoke-filled, shabby offices, faceless men were even now painstakingly assembling the evidence against me. I thought about them at night, as I lay in Charlie's mother's big lumpy bed. It was strange to be the object of so much meticulous attention, strange, and not entirely unpleasant. Does that seem perverse? But I was in another country now, where the old rules did not apply.

It was hard to sleep, of course. I suppose I did not want to sleep, afraid of what I would encounter in my dreams. At best I would manage a fitful hour or two in the darkness before dawn, and wake up exhausted, with an ache in my chest and my eyes scalding. Charlie too was sleepless, I would hear at all hours his creaking step on the stair, the rattle of the teapot in the kitchen, the laborious, spasmodic tinkle as he emptied his old man's bladder in the bathroom. We saw little of each other. The house was big enough for us both to be in it at the same time and yet feel we were alone. Since that first, drunken night he had been avoiding me. He seemed to have no friends. The phone never rang, no one came to the house. I was surprised, then, and horribly alarmed, to return early one evening from my rambles in town and find three big black cars parked on the road, and a uniformed Guard loitering in the company of two watchful men in anoraks at the harbour wall. I made myself walk past slowly, an honest citizen out for a stroll at end of day, though my heart was hammering and my palms were damp, and then skipped around the back way and got in through the mews. Halfway up the jungly garden I tripped and fell, and tore my left hand on a rose bush that had run wild. I crouched in the long grass, listening. Smell of loam, smell of leaves, the thick feel of blood on my wounded hand. The yellow light in the kitchen window turned the dusk around me to tenderest blue. There was a strange woman inside, in a white apron, working at the stove. When I opened the back door she turned quickly and gave a little shriek. Holy God, she said, who are you? She was an elderly person with a henna wig and ill-fitting dentures and a scattered air. Her name, as we shall discover presently, was

Madge. They're all upstairs, she said, dismissing me, and turned back to her steaming saucepans.

There were five of them, or six, counting Charlie, though at first it seemed to me there must be twice that number. They were in the big gaunt drawing room on the first floor, standing under the windows with drinks in their hands, ducking and bobbing at each other like nervous storks and chattering as if their lives depended on it. Behind them the lights of the harbour glimmered, and in the far sky a huge bank of slate-blue cloud was shutting down like a lid on the last, smouldering streak of sunset fire. At my entrance the chattering stopped. Only one of them was a woman, tall, thin, with foxy red hair and an extraordinary stark white face. Charlie, who was standing with his back to me, saw me first reflected in their swivelling glances. He turned with a pained smile. Ah, he said, there you are. His winged hair gleamed like a polished helm. He was wearing a bow-tie. Well, I heard myself saying to him, in a tone of cheery truculence, well, you might have told me! My hands were trembling. There was a moment of uncertain silence, then the talk abruptly started up again. The woman went on watching me. Her pale colouring and vivid hair and long, slender neck gave her a permanently startled look, as if at some time in the past she had been told a shocking secret and had never quite absorbed it. Charlie, mumbling apologetically, had put a shaky old hand under my elbow and was gently but firmly steering me backwards out of the room. The fear I had felt earlier had turned into annoyance. I felt like giving him a clout, and putting a dent in that ridiculous praetorian helmet of hair. Tell Madge, he was saying, tell Madge to give you something to eat, and I'll be down presently. He was so worried I thought he was going to weep. He stood on the top step and watched me make my way downstairs, as if he were afraid I would come scampering back up again if he took his eye off me, and only when I had safely reached the bottom and was heading for the kitchen did he turn back to the drawing room and his guests.

The kitchen was filled with steam, and Madge, her wig awry, looked even hotter and more harassed than before. This place, she said bitterly, honest to God! She was, as she picturesquely put it, Mr French's occasional woman, and came in when there were dinner parties, and that. This was interesting. Dinner parties, indeed! I helped her by opening the wine, and sat down at the table with a bottle for myself. I had drunk half of it when there was a loud knock at the front door that set my heart thumping again. I went into the hall, but Charlie was already rattling hurriedly down the stairs. When he opened the door I could see the two anoraks outside, guarding the way for a burly man and a tall, sleek woman, as they advanced at a regal pace into the hall. Ah, Max, Charlie said, and stepped forward with clumsy eagerness. The woman he ignored. Max shook hands with him briefly, and then took back his hand and ran it upwards quickly over his low, truculent brow. Christ, he said, you're far enough out, I thought we were never going to get here. They moved towards the stairs, Charlie and Max in front and the woman behind them. She wore an ugly blue gown and a triple rope of pearls. She glanced along the hall and caught my eye, and held it until I looked away. Madge had come out of the kitchen, and hovered at my shoulder. There's his nibs, she whispered, and the missus too.

I waited a while after they had gone up, and when Madge returned to her cooking I followed them, and slipped into the drawing room again. Charlie and Max and Mrs Max were standing at one of the windows admiring the view, while the others bobbed and ducked and tried not to stare too openly in their direction. I seized an armful of bottles from the mantelpiece and passed among them, topping up their glasses. The men had an eager, slightly anxious air, like that of big, blue-suited schoolboys on their first adult outing, except for one old chap with a nose like a blood-orange and stains down the front of his waistcoat, who stood to one side all on his own, glazed and dejected. The others carefully looked through me, but he brightened up at once, and was ready for a chat. What do you think, anyway, he said loudly, will we win, will we? I understood it to be a rhetorical question. We will, I said stoutly, and gave him a broad wink. He raised his eyebrows and stepped back a pace, however, peering at me doubtfully. By God, he said, I don't know, now. I shrugged, and passed on blandly. Charlie had caught sight of me, and was smiling fixedly in alarm. Mine was a vodka, Mrs Max said coldly when I offered her gin. My attention was on her husband. He had a raw, scrubbed look to him, as if he had been exposed for a long time to some far rougher form of light and weather than the others in the room had ever known. His movements, too, the way he held himself, the slow, deliberate way he turned his glance or lifted his hand to his brow, all these bore a unique stamp, and were weighted with a kind of theatrical awareness. His voice was slow and guttural, and he had a violent manner of speaking that was impressive, and even, in an odd way, seductive. It was the voice of a man moving inexorably forward through a forest of small obstacles. I imagined him carelessly crunching things underfoot, flowers, or snails, or the insteps of his enemies. Well, Charlie, he was saying, still buying cheap and selling dear? Charlie blushed, and glanced at me. That's right, Mrs Max said, embarrass everyone. She spoke loudly, with a dull emphasis, and did not look at him. It was as if she were lobbing remarks past his shoulder at a sardonic ally listening there. Nor did he look at her, it might have been a disembodied voice that had spoken. He laughed harshly. Have you acquired that Dutch job for me yet? he said. Charlie, grinning in anguish, shook his head, speechless. His left eyelid began to flutter, as if a moth had suddenly come to life under it. I proffered the whiskey bottle but he among themselves, but no, they decided, Charlie was not that way inclined: remember that horsy woman down the country, the lost love of his life?) Really, we were like father and son, except that no son would be so steadfast, and no father so forgiving of my little ways. At times it was hard to tell which was master and which the man. Tonight, for instance, when the main course was finished, I sat myself down among the guests and poured a glass of wine as if it were the most natural thing in the world. A silence fell, and Charlie frowned, and rolled a breadcrumb about on the tablecloth, pretending he was thinking about something else, and Max stared balefully out of the window at the harbour lights while his henchmen around him fidgeted and glanced at each other nervously, and at last I took up my glass, and rose and said, Well! I suppose us ladies better withdraw, and fairly flounced out of the room. In the hall, of course, I leaned against the wall and laughed. All the same, my hands were shaking. Stage fright, I suppose. What an actor the world has lost in me!

Now what shall I do?

I went upstairs to the drawing room. No, I went into the kitchen. Madge: wig, false teeth, white apron, I have done all that. Out again. In the hall I found Foxy. She had wandered out of the dining room. Under the stairs was a dark place, there we met. I could see her face in the gloom, her eyes watching me, so solemn and fearful. Why are you sad? I said, and for a moment she did not know what to do with her hands, then she put them behind her back, and flexed one knee and briefly swayed her shoulders and her hips, like a schoolgirl playing the coquette. Who says I'm sad? she said. I'm not sad. And I thought she was going to cry. Did she see it in me, the terror and the shame, had she seen it from the first? For she had sought me out, I knew that. I reached behind her and opened a door, and we stepped suddenly on to bare floorboards in an empty room. There was a smell, dry and oniony, that was the smell of a certain attic room at Coolgrange. A parallelogram of moonlight was propped against one wall like a broken mirror. I am still holding these damned plates. I put them on the floor at our feet, and while I was still bending she touched my shoulder and said something which I did not catch. She laughed softly, in surprise, it seemed, as if the sound of her own voice were unexpected. Nothing, she said, nothing. She shook in my arms. She was all teeth, breath, clutching fingers. She held my head between her hands as if she would crush it. She had kicked off her shoes, they clattered where they fell. She raised one foot behind her and pressed it against the door, pressed, and pressed. Her thighs were cold. She wept, her tears fell on my hands. I bit her throat. We were like—I don't know. We were like two messengers, meeting in the dark to exchange our terrible news. O God, she said, O God. She put her forehead against my shoulder. Our hands were smeared with each other. The room came back, the moonlight, the oniony smell. No thought, except: her white face, her hair. Forgive me, I said. I don't know why I laughed. Anyway, it wasn't really a laugh.

How peaceful the days are now, here at the dead end of the year. Sitting in the fastness of this grey room I sometimes imagine I am utterly alone, that there is no one around me for miles and miles. It is like being in the deep hold of a great grey ship. The air is heavy and still, it presses in my ears, on my eyes, on the base of my skull. A trial date has been fixed at last. I know this should concentrate my mind, give me a purpose and so on, make me excited, or afraid, but it does not. Something has happened to my sense of time, I think in aeons now. The days, the weeks of this banal little courtroom drama will register as no more than a pinprick. I have become a lifer.

Again today Maolseachlainn brought up the topic of how I

should plead. I let him maunder on for a while, then I got fed up and told him I would dispense with his services if he did not come straight out and say whatever it was he had on his mind. This was disingenuous of me, for I had realised, of course, since his last visit, that he was hinting at the possibility of an arrangement—I understand, from the conversations I have had in here, that there is hardly a sentence handed down that has not been prearranged among counsel. I was curious to know what the court could want from me. Now, as I watched poor old Mac squirm and sweat, I thought I had it: Charlie, of course—they were trying to salvage something of Charlie's reputation. (How could I have imagined they would care a fig for Charlie, or his reputation?) I would do all I could for him, that went without saying, though it seemed to me a bit late now. All right, Mac, I said, holding up a hand, I'll plead guilty—and what then? He gave me one of his over-the-spectacles looks. Then it'll be an open-and-shut case, won't it? he said. This, I realised after a moment, was intended as a witticism. He grinned dolefully. What he meant was that the trial would open, I would deny the charges as stated, plead guilty to manslaughter or something, the judge would pass sentence, with a bit lopped off in return for my co-operation, and then, presto, it would all be over, the hearing would end, the case would be closed. He could guarantee nothing, he said, but he had a duty to his client to try to secure the best judgment that was possible within the law. He is very charming when he waxes pompous like this. What's the point, I said, what's the trick? He shrugged. The trick is that no evidence will be heard. Simple as that. For a moment we were silent. And will that work, I said, will that save him? He frowned in puzzlement, and at once I saw I had been wrong, that Charlie and his embarrassment were not the subject here. I laughed. I've said it before, sometimes I think I am hopelessly innocent. Maolseach-lainn glanced over his shoulder—he did, he really did—and leaned

In fact, her name was Marian. Not that it matters.

They stayed very late, all except Mrs Max, who left directly dinner was over. I watched as she was driven away, sitting up very straight in the back of one of the black limousines, a ravaged Nefertiti. Max and his pals went upstairs again, and caroused until the dawn was breaking. I spent the night in the kitchen playing cards with Madge. Where was Marian? I don't know—I got blotto, as usual. Anyway, our moment was over, if we were to encounter each other now we would only be embarrassed. Yet I think I must have gone to look for her, for I recall blundering about upstairs, in the bedrooms, and falling over repeatedly in the dark. I remember, too, standing at a wide-open window, very high up, listening to the strains of music outside on the air, a mysterious belling and blaring, that seemed to move, to fade, as if a clamorous cavalcade were departing into the night. I suppose it came from some dance-hall, or some nightclub on the harbour. I think of it, however, as the noise of the god and his retinue, abandoning me.

Next day the weather broke. At mid-morning, when my hangover and I got up, the sun was shining as gaily and as heartlessly as it had all week, and the houses along the coast shimmered in a pale-blue haze, as if the sky had crumbled into airy geometry there. I stood at the window in my drawers, scratching and yawning. It struck me that I had become almost accustomed to this strange way of life. It was as if I were adapting to an illness, after the initial phase of frights and fevers. A churchbell was ringing. Sunday. The strollers were out already, with their dogs and children. Across the road, at the harbour wall, a man in a raincoat stood with his hands clasped behind his back, gazing out to sea. I could hear voices downstairs. Madge was in the kitchen doing last night's washing-up. She gave me a peculiar glance. I was wearing Charlie's dressing-gown. How is it, I wonder, that I did not catch it then, that new, speculative note in Madge's voice, which should have alerted me? She had a helper with her this morning, her niece, a dim-looking child of twelve or so with—with what, what does it matter what she had, what she was like. All these minor witnesses, none of whom will ever be called now. I sat at the table drinking tea and watched them as they worked. The child I could see was fright-ened of me. Fe fi fo fum. He's gone out, you know, Madge said, her arms plunged in suds, Mr French, he went out as I was coming in. Her tone was unaccountably accusing, as if Charlie had fled the house because of me. But then, he had.

In the afternoon a huge cloud grew up on the horizon, grey and scampered away up the street with their coats over their heads. I laughed to see them go, the child leaping the puddles and Madge wallowing in her wake. Then I spotted the car, parked a little way up the road, on the other side, with two dim, large, motionless figures seated in the front, their faces blurred behind the streaming windscreen.

I sat in a chair in the drawing room, gazing before me, my hands gripping the armrests and my feet placed squarely side by side on the floor. I do not know how long I stayed like that, in that glimmering, grey space. I have an impression of hours passing, but surely that cannot be. There was a smell of cigarettes and stale drink left over from last night. The rain made a soothing noise. I sank into a kind of trance, a waking sleep. I saw myself, as a boy, walking across a wooded hill near Coolgrange. It was in March, I think, one of those blustery, Dutch days with china-blue sky and tumbling, cindery clouds. The trees above me swayed and groaned in the wind. Suddenly there was a great quick rushing noise, and the air darkened, and something like a bird's vast wing crashed down around me, thrashing and whipping. It was a branch that had fallen. I was not hurt, yet I could not move, and stood as if stunned, aghast and shaking. The force and swiftness of the thing had appalled me. It was not fright I felt, but a profound sense of shock at how little my presence had mattered. I might have been no more than a flaw in the air. Ground, branch, wind, sky, world, all these were the precise and necessary co-ordinates of the event. Only I was misplaced, only I had no part to play. And nothing cared. If I had been killed I would have fallen there, face down in the dead leaves, and the day would have gone on as before, as if nothing had happened. For what would have happened would have been nothing, or nothing extraordinary, anyway. Adjustments would have been made. Things would have had to squirm out from under me. A stray ant, perhaps, would explore the bloody chamber of my ear. But the light would have been the same, and the wind would have blown as it had blown, and time's arrow would not have faltered for an instant in its flight. I was amazed. I never forgot that moment. And now another branch was about to fall, I could hear that same rushing noise above me, and feel that same dark wing descending.

The telephone rang, with a sound like glass breaking. There was a hubbub of static on the line. Someone seemed to be asking for Charlie. No, I shouted, no, he's not here! and threw down the receiver. Almost at once the thing began to shrill again. Wait, wait, don't hang up, the voice said, this *is* Charlie. I laughed, of course. I'm down the road, he said, just down the road. I was still laughing. Then there was a silence. The Guards are here, Freddie, he said, they want to speak to you, there's been some sort of misunderstanding. I closed my eyes. Part of me, I realised, had been hoping against hope, unable quite to believe that the game was up. The hum in the wires seemed the very sound of Charlie's anxiety and embarrassment. Charlie, I said, Charlie, Charlie, why are you hiding in a phone box, what did you think I would do to you? I hung up before he could answer.

I was hungry. I went down to the kitchen and made an enormous omelette, and devoured half a loaf of bread and drank a pint of milk. I sat hunched over the table with my elbows planted on either side of the plate and my head hanging, stuffing the food into myself with animal indifference. The rain-light made a kind of dusk in the room. I heard Charlie as soon as he entered the house—he never was very good at negotiating his way around the furniture of life. He put his head in at the kitchen door and essayed a smile, without much success. I motioned to the chair opposite me and he sat down gingerly. I had started on the cold remains of last night's boiled potatoes. I was ravenous, I could not get enough to eat. Charles, I said, you look terrible. He did. He was grey and shrunken, with livid hollows under his eyes. The collar of his shirt was buttoned though he wore no tie. He ran a hand over his jaw and I heard the bristles scrape. He had been up early, he said, they had got him up and asked him to go to the station. For a second I did not understand, I thought he meant the train station. He kept his eyes on my plate, the mess of spuds there. Something had happened to the silence around us. I realised that the rain had stopped. God almighty, Freddie, he said softly, what have you done? He seemed more bemused than shocked. I fetched another, half-full bottle of milk from the back of the fridge. Remember, Charlie, I said, those treats you used to stand me in Jammet's and the Paradiso? He shrugged. It was not clear if he was listening. The milk had turned. I drank it anyway. I enjoyed them, you know, those occasions, I said, even if I didn't always show it. I frowned. Something wrong there, something off, like the milk. Mendacity always makes my voice sound curiously dull, a flat blaring at the back of the throat. And why resurrect now an ancient, unimportant lie? Was I just keeping my hand in, getting a bit of practice for the big tourney that lay ahead? No, that's too hard. I was trying to apologise, I mean in general, and how was I supposed to do that without lying? He looked so old, sitting slumped there with his head drooping on its stringy neck and his mouth all down at one side and his bleared eyes fixed vaguely before him. Oh, fuck it, Charlie, I said, I'm sorry.

Was it coincidence, I wonder, that the policeman made his move just at that moment, or had he been listening outside the door? In films, I have noticed, the chap with the gun always waits in the corridor, back pressed to the wall, the whites of his eyes gleaming, until the people inside have had their say. And this one was, I suspect, a keen student of the cinema. He had a hatchet face and lank black hair and wore a sort of padded military jacket. The sub-machine gun he was holding, a blunt squarish model with only about an inch of barrel, looked remarkably like a toy. Of the three of us he seemed the most surprised. I could not help admiring the deft way he had kicked in the back door. It hung quivering on its hinges, the broken latch lolling like a hound's tongue. Charlie stood up. It's all right, officer, he said. The policeman advanced into the doorway. He was glaring at me. You're fucking under arrest, you are, he said. Behind him, in the yard, the sun came out suddenly, and everything shone and glittered wetly.

More policemen came in then by the front way, there seemed to be a large crowd of them, though they were in fact only four. One of them was the fellow I had seen standing at the harbour wall that morning, I recognised the raincoat. All were carrying guns, of assorted shapes and sizes. I was impressed. They ranged themselves around the walls, looking at me with a kind of bridling curiosity. The door to the hall stood open. Charlie made a move in that direction and one of the policemen in a flat voice said: Hang on. There was silence except for the faint, metallic pattering of police radios outside. We might have been awaiting the entrance of a sovereign. The person who came in at last was a surprise. He was a slight, boyish man of thirty or so, with sandy hair and transparent blue eyes. I noticed at once his hands and feet, which were small, almost dainty. He approached me at an angle somehow, looking at the floor with a peculiar little smile. His name, he said, was Haslet, Detective Inspector Haslet. (Hello, Gerry, hope you don't mind my mentioning your dainty hands—it's true, you know, they are.) The oddness of his manner—that smile, the oblique glance—was due, I realised, to shyness. A shy policeman! It was not what I had expected. He looked about him. There was a moment of awkwardness. No one seemed to know quite what to do next. He turned his downcast eyes in my direction again. Well, he said to no one in particular, are we right? Then all was briskness suddenly. The one with the machine gun—Sergeant Hogg, let's call him—stepped forward and, laying his weapon down on the table, deftly clapped a pair of handcuffs on my wrists. (By the way, they are not as uncomfortable as they might seem—in fact, there was something about being manacled that I found almost soothing, as if it were a more natural state than that of untrammelled freedom.) Charlie frowned. Is that necessary, Inspector? he said. It was such a grand old line, and so splendidly delivered, with just the right degree of solemn hauteur, that for a second I thought it might elicit a small round of applause. I looked at him with renewed admiration. He had thrown off that infirm air of a minute or two ago, and looked, really, quite impressive there in his dark suit and silver wings of hair. Even his unshaven cheeks and tieless collar only served to give him the appearance of a statesman roused from his bed to deal with some grave crisis in the affairs of the nation. Believe me, I am sincere when I say I admire his expertise as a quick-change artist. To place all faith in the mask, that seems to me now the true stamp of refined humanity. Did I say that, or someone else? No matter. I caught his eye, to show him my appreciation, and to ask him—oh, to ask some sort of pardon, I suppose. Afterwards I worried that my glance might have seemed to him more derisive than apologetic, for I think I must have worn a smirk throughout that grotesque kitchen comedy. His mouth was set grimly, and a nerve was twitching in his jaw—he had every right to be furious—but in his eyes all I could see was a sort of dreamy sadness. Then Hogg prodded me in the back, and I was marched quickly down the hall and out into the dazzling light of afternoon.

There was a moment of confusion as the policemen milled on the pavement, craning their stumpy necks and peering sharply this way and that about the harbour. What did they expect, a rescue party? I noticed that they all wore running shoes, except Haslet, the good country boy, in his stout brown brogues. One of his men bumped into him. Too many cops spoil the capture, I said brightly. No one laughed, and Haslet pretended he had not heard. I thought it was awfully witty, of course. I was still in that mood of mad elation, I cannot explain it. I seemed not to walk but bound along, brimful of tigerish energy. Everything sparkled in the rinsed sea-air. The sunlight had a flickering, hallucinatory quality, and I felt I was seeing somehow into the very process of it, catching the photons themselves in flight. We crossed the road. The car I had seen from the upstairs window was still there, the windscreen stippled with raindrops. The two figures sitting in the front watched us with cautious curiosity as we went past. I laughed— they were not police, but a large man and his large missus, out for a Sunday spin. The woman, chewing slowly on a sweet, goggled at the handcuffs, and I raised my wrists to her in a friendly salute. Hogg poked me again between the shoulder blades and I almost stumbled. I could see I was going to have trouble with him.

There were two cars, unmarked and nondescript, a blue one and a black. The comedy of car doors opening, like beetles' wings. I was put into the back seat with Sergeant Hogg on one side of me and a big, baby-faced bruiser with red hair on the other. Haslet leaned on the door. Did you caution him? he enquired mildly. There was silence. The two detectives in the front seats went very still, as if afraid to stir for fear of laughing. Hogg stared grimly before him, his mouth set in a thin line. Haslet sighed and walked away. The driver carefully started up the engine. You have the right to remain silent blah blah blah, Hogg said venomously, without looking at me. Thank you, Sergeant, I said. I thought this another splendid bit of repartee. We took off from the kerb with a squeal, leaving a puff of tyre-smoke behind us on the air. I wondered if Charlie was watching from the window. I did not look back.

*

I pause to record that Helmut Behrens has died. Heart. Dear me, this is turning into the Book of the Dead.

How well I remember that journey. I had never travelled so fast in a car. We fairly flew along, weaving through the sluggish Sunday traffic, roaring down the inside lanes, taking corners on two wheels. It was very hot, with all the windows shut, and there was a musky, animal stink. The atmosphere bristled. I was entranced, filled with terror and a kind of glee, hurtling along like this, packed in with these big, sweating, silent men, who sat staring at the road ahead with their arms tightly folded, clasping to them their excitement and their pent-up rage. I could feel them breathing. Speed soothed them: speed was violence. The sun shone in our eyes, a great, dense glare. I knew that at the slightest provocation they would set on me and beat me half to death, they were just waiting for the chance. Even this knowledge, though, was bracing. I had never in my life been so entirely the centre of attention. From now on I would be watched over, I would be tended and fed and listened to, like a big, dangerous baby. No more running, no more hiding and waiting, no more decisions. I snuggled down between my captors, enjoying the hot chafe of metal on my wrists. Yet all the while another part of my mind was registering another version of things—was thinking, for instance, of all that I was losing. I looked at the streets, the buildings, the people, as if for the last time. I, who am a countryman at heart—yes, yes, it's true—and never really knew or cared for the city, even when I lived here, had come to love it now. Love? That is not a word I use very often. Perhaps I mean something else. It was the loss, yes, the imminent loss of—of what, I don't know. I was going to say, *of the community of men*, something solemn and grand like that, but when was I ever a part of *that* gathering? All the same, as we travelled along, some deep cavern of my heart was filling up with the grief of crowding the hallways to get a look at me, but hardly a soul was about, and the few who passed me by hardly looked at me, and I could not help feeling a little offended. We stopped in a gaunt, unpleasant room, and had to wait some minutes for Inspector Haslet to arrive. Two tall windows, extremely grimy, their lower panes reinforced with wire mesh, gave on to the yard. There was a scarred desk, and a number of wooden chairs. No one sat. We shuffled our feet and looked at the ceiling. Someone cleared his throat. An elderly Guard in shirtsleeves came in. He was bald, and had a sweet, almost childlike smile. I noticed he was wearing a pair of thick black boots, tightly laced and buffed to a high shine. They were a comforting sight, those boots. In the coming days I was to measure my captors by their footwear. Brogues and boots I felt I could trust, running shoes were sinister. Inspector Haslet's car arrived in the yard. Once again we stood about awaiting his entrance. He came in as before, with the same diffident half-smile. I stood in front of the desk while he read out the charges. It was an oddly formal little ceremony. I was reminded of my wedding day, and had to suppress a grin. The bald old Guard typed out the charge sheet on an ancient upright black machine, as if he were laboriously picking out a tune on a piano, the tip of his tongue wedged into a corner of his mouth. When Inspector Haslet asked if I had anything to say I shook my head. I would not have known where to begin. Then the ritual was over. There was a kind of general relaxing, and the other detectives, except Hogg, shuffled out. It was like the end of Mass. Hogg produced cigarettes, and offered the grinning packet to Haslet and the Guard at the typewriter, and even, after a brief hesitation, to me. I felt I could not refuse. I tried not to cough. Tell me, I said to Haslet, how did you find me? He shrugged. He had the air of a schoolboy who has scored an embarrassingly high mark in his exams. The girl in the paper shop, he said. You never read only the one story, every day. Ah, I said, yes, of faraway frown and drumming his fingers on a jumble of papers. He indicated the chair beside him. I sat down gingerly. When he turned sideways to face me our knees were almost touching. He studied a far corner of the ceiling. Well, he said, do you want to talk to me? Oh, I did, I did, I wanted to talk and talk, to confide in him, to pour out all my poor secrets. But what could I say? What secrets? The bald Guard was at his typewriter again, blunt fingers poised over the keys, his eyes fixed on my lips in lively expectation. Hogg too was waiting, standing by the window and jingling the coins in his trousers pocket. I would not have cared what I said to them, they meant nothing to me. The Inspector was a different matter. He kept reminding me of someone I might have known at school, one of those modest, inarticulate heroes who were not only good at sport but at maths as well, yet who shrugged off praise, made shy by their own success and popularity. I had not the heart to confess to him that there was nothing to confess, that there had been no plan worthy of the name, that I had acted almost without thinking from the start. So I made up a rigmarole about having intended to make the robbery seem the work of terrorists, and a lot of other stuff that I am ashamed to repeat here. And then the girl, I said, the woman—for a second I could not think of her name!—and then *Josie*, I said, had ruined everything by trying to stop me taking the picture, by attacking me, by threatening to to to—I ran out of words, and sat and peered at him helplessly, wringing my hands. I so much wanted him to believe me. At that moment his credence seemed to me almost as desirable as forgiveness. There was a silence. He was still considering the corner of the ceiling. He might not have been listening to me at all. Jesus, Hogg said quietly, with no particular emphasis, and the Guard behind the desk cleared his throat. Then Haslet stood up, wincing a little and flexing one knee, and ambled out of the room, and shut the door softly behind him. I could hear him walk away along the corridor at the same leisurely pace. There were voices faintly, his and others. Hogg was looking at me over his shoulder in disgust. You're a right joker, aren't you, he said. I thought of answering him, but decided on prudence instead. Time passed. Someone laughed in a nearby room. A motorcycle started up in the yard. I studied a yellowed notice on the wall dealing with the threat of rabies. I smiled, Mad-dog Montgomery, captured at last.

Inspector Haslet came back then, and held open the door and ushered in a large, red-faced, sweating man in a striped shirt, and another, younger, dangerous-looking fellow, one of Hogg's breed. They gathered round and looked at me, leaning forward intently, breathing, their hands flat on the desk. I told my story again, trying to remember the details so as not to contradict myself. It sounded even more improbable this time. When I finished there was another silence. I was becoming accustomed already to these interrogative and, as it seemed to me, deeply sceptical pauses. The red-faced man, a person of large authority, I surmised, appeared to be in a rage which he was controlling only with great difficulty. His name will be—Barker. He looked at me hard for a long moment. Come on, Freddie, he said, why did you kill her? I stared back at him. I did not like his contemptuously familiar tone—*Freddie*, indeed!—but decided to let it go. I recognised in him one of my own kind, the big, short-tempered, heavy-breathing people of this world. And anyway, I was getting tired of all this. I killed her because I could, I said, what more can I say? We were all startled by that, I as much as they. The younger one, Hickey—no, Kickham, gave a sort of laugh. He had a thin, piping, almost musical voice that was peculiarly at odds with his menacing look and manner. What's-his-name, he said, he's a queer, is he? I looked at him helplessly. I did not know what he was talking about. Pardon? I said. French, he said impatiently, is he a fairy? I laughed, I could not help it. I did not know whether it was more comic or preposterous, the idea of Charlie prancing into Wally's and pinching the bottoms of his boys. (It appears that Wally's creature, Sonny of the emerald hues, had been telling scurrilous lies about poor Charlie's predilections. Truly, what a wicked world this is.) Oh no, I said, no—he has an occasional woman. It was just nervousness and surprise that made me say it, I had not meant to attempt a joke. No one laughed. They all just went on looking at me, while the silence tightened and tightened like something being screwed shut, and then, as if at a signal, they turned on their heels and trooped out and the door slammed behind them, and I was left alone with the elderly Guard, who smiled his sweet smile at me and shrugged. I told him I was feeling nauseous again, and he went off and fetched me a mug of sticky-sweet tea and a lump of bread. Why is it that tea, just the look of it, always makes me feel miserable, like an abandoned waif? And how lost and lonely everything seemed, this stale room, and the vague noises of people elsewhere going about their lives, and the sunlight in the yard, that same thick steady light that shines across the years out of farthest childhood. All the euphoria I had felt earlier was gone now.

Haslet returned, alone this time, and sat down beside me at the desk as before. He had removed his jacket and tie and rolled up his sleeves. His hair was tousled. He looked more boyish than ever. He too had a mug of tea, the mug looking enormous in that small, white hand. I had an image of him as a child, out on some bog in the wastes of the midlands, stacking turf with his da: quake of water in the cuttings, smell of smoke and roasting spuds, and the flat distances the colour of a hare's pelt, and then the enormous, vertical sky stacked with luminous bundles of cloud.

Now, he said, let's start again.

We went on for hours. I was almost happy, sitting there with him, pouring out my life story, as the shafts of sunlight in the windows lengthened and the day waned. He was infinitely patient.

There seemed to be nothing, no detail, however minute or enigmatic, that did not interest him. No, that's not quite it. It was as if he were not really interested at all. He greeted everything, every strand and knot of my story, with the same passive air of toleration and that same faint bemused little smile. I told him about knowing Anna Behrens, and about her father, about his diamond mines and his companies and his priceless art collection. I watched him carefully, trying to judge how much of this was new to him, but it was no good, he gave nothing away. Yet he must have spoken to them, must have taken statements and all the rest of it. Surely they would have told him about me, surely they were not protecting me still. He rubbed his cheek, and gazed again into the corner of the ceiling. Self-made man, is he, he said, this Behrens? Oh Inspector, I said, aren't we all? At that he gave me a peculiar look, and stood up. I noticed again that brief grimace of pain. Bad knee. Footballer. Sunday afternoons, the shouts muffled in grey air, the flat thud of leather on leather. Now what, I said, what happens now? I did not want him to leave me yet. What would I do when the darkness came? He said I should give the Guard my solicitor's name, so he could be told I was here. I nodded. I had no solicitor, of course, but I felt I could not say so—everything was so relaxed and chummy, and I did not want to create any awkwardnesses. Anyway, I was fully intending to conduct my own defence, and already saw myself making brilliant and impassioned speeches from the dock. Is there anything else I should do, I said, frowning up at him seriously, is there anyone else I should tell? (Oh, I was so good, so compliant, what a warm thrill of agreeableness I felt, deferring like this to this good chap!) He gave me that peculiar look again, there was irritation and impatience in it, but a certain ironic amusement too, and even a hint of complicity. What you can do, he said, is get your story straight, without the frills and fancy bits. What do you mean, I said, what do you mean? I was dismayed. Bob Cherry had upward, as if out of the earth itself, and everything seems to grow thoughtful and turn away. It was almost dark when Sergeant Hogg came back, and handed me a grubby sheet of foolscap. He had been eating chips, I could smell them on his breath. I peered in bafflement at the ill-typed page. That's your confession, Hogg said. Feel like signing it? The lag next door cackled grimly. What are you talking about? I said. These are not my words. He shrugged, and belched into his fist. Suit yourself, he said, you'll be going down for life anyway. Then he went off again. I sat down and examined this strange document. Oh, well-named Cunningham! Behind the mask of the bald old codger a fiendish artist had been at work, the kind of artist I could never be, direct yet subtle, a master of the spare style, of the art that conceals art. I marvelled at how he had turned everything to his purpose, misspellings, clumsy syntax, even the atrocious typing. Such humility, such deference, such ruthless suppression of the ego for the sake of the text. He had taken my story, with all its—what was it Haslet said?—with all its frills and fancy bits, and pared it down to stark essentials. It was an account of my crime I hardly recognised, and yet I believed it. He had made a murderer of me. I would have signed it there and then, but I had nothing to write with. I even searched my clothing for something sharp, a pin or something, with which to stick myself, and scrawl my signature in blood. But what matter, it did not require my endorsement. Reverently I folded the page in four and placed it under the mattress at the end where my head would be. Then I undressed and lay down naked in the shadows and folded my hands on my breast, like a marble knight on a tomb, and closed my eyes. I was no longer myself. I can't explain it, but it's true. I was no longer myself.

That first night in captivity was turbulent. I slept fitfully, it was not really sleep, but a helpless tossing and sliding on the surface of a

Monday morning. Ah, Monday morning. The ashen light, the noise, the sense of pointless but compulsory haste. I think it will be Monday morning when I am received in Hell. I was wakened early by a policeman bearing another mug of tea and lump of bread. I had been dozing, it was like being held fast in the embrace of a large, hot, rank-smelling animal. I knew at once exactly where I was, there was no mistaking the place. The policeman was young, an enormous boy with a tiny head, when I opened my eyes first and looked up at him he seemed to tower above me almost to the ceiling. He said something incomprehensible and went away. I sat on the edge of the cot and held my head in my hands. My mouth was foul, and there was an ache behind my eyes and a wobbly sensation in the region of my diaphragm. I wondered if this nausea would be with me for the rest of my life. Wan sunlight fell at a slant through the bars of my cage. I was cold. I draped a blanket around my shoulders and squatted over the bucket, my knees trembling. I would not have been surprised if a crowd had gathered in the corridor to laugh at me. I kept thinking, yes, this is it, this is how it will be from now on. It was almost gratifying, in a horrible sort of way.

Sergeant Cunningham came to fetch me for the first of that day's inquisitions. I had washed as best I could at the filthy sink in the corner. I asked him if I might borrow a razor. He laughed, shaking his head at the idea, the richness of it. He thought I really was a card. I admired his good humour: he had been here all night, his shift was only ending now. I shuffled after him along the corridor, clutching my trousers to keep them from falling down. The dayroom was filled with a kind of surly pandemonium. Typewriters clacked, and short-wave radios snivelled in adenoidal bursts, and people strode in and out of doorways, talking over their shoulders, or crouched at desks and shouted into telephones. A hush fell when I came through—no, not a hush, exactly, but a downward modulation in the noise. Word, obviously, had spread. They did not stare at me, I suppose that would have been unprofessional, but they took me in, all the same. I saw myself in their eyes, a big, confused creature, like a dancing bear, shambling along at the steel-tipped heels of Cunningham's friendly boots. He opened a door and motioned me into a square, grey room. There was a plastic-topped table and two chairs. Well, he said, I'll be seeing you, and he winked and withdrew his head and shut the door. I sat down carefully, placing my hands flat before me on the table. Time passed. I was surprised how calmly I could sit, just waiting. It was as if I were not fully there, as if I had become detached somehow from my physical self. The room was like the inside of a skull. The hubbub in the dayroom might have been coming to me from another planet.

Barker and Kickham were the first to arrive. Barker today wore a blue suit which had been cut in great broad swathes, as if it were intended not for wearing but to house a collection of things, boxes, perhaps. He was red-faced and in a sweat already. Kickham had on the same leather jacket and dark shirt that he had worn yesterday—he did not strike me as a man much given to changing his clothes. They wanted to know why I had not signed the confession. I had forgotten about it, had left it under the mattress, but I told them, I don't know why, that I had torn it up. There was another of those brief, stentorian silences, while they stood over me, clenching their fists and breathing heavily down their nostrils.

The air rippled with suppressed violence. Then they trooped out and I was left alone again. Next to appear was an elderly chap in cavalry twill and a natty little hat, and a narrow-eyed, brawny young man who looked like the older one's disgruntled son. They stood just inside the door and studied me carefully for a long moment, as if measuring me for something. Then Detective Twill advanced and sat down opposite me, and crossed his legs, and took off his hat, revealing a flattish bald head, waxen and peculiarly pitted, like that of an ailing baby. He produced a pipe and lighted it with grave deliberation, then recrossed his legs and settled himself more comfortably, and began to ask me a series of cryptic questions, which after some time I realised were aimed at discovering what I might know about Charlie French and his acquaintances. I answered as circumspectly as I could, not knowing what it was they wanted to know—I suspect they didn't, either. I kept smiling at them both, to show how willing I was, how compliant. The younger one, still standing by the door, took notes. Or at least he went through the motions of writing in a notebook, for I had an odd feeling that the whole thing was a sham, intended to distract or intimidate me. All that happened, however, was that I grew bored—I could not take them seriously—and got muddled, and began to contradict myself. After a while they too seemed to grow discouraged, and eventually left. Then my chum Inspector Haslet came sidling in with his shy smile and averted glance. My God, I said, who were they? Branch, he said. He sat down, looked at the floor, drummed his fingers on the table. Listen, I said, I'm worried, my wife, I—He wasn't listening, wasn't interested. He brought up the matter of my confession. Why hadn't I signed it? He spoke quietly, he might have been talking about the weather. Save a lot of trouble, you know, he said. Suddenly I flew into a rage, I don't know what came over me, I banged my fist on the table and jumped up and shouted at him that I would do nothing, sign and seriousness, and I was disappointed when it turned out to be little more than a shabby office, the kind of place where obscure permits are issued by incompetent clerks. When I was led in, there was a sort of irritable flurry of activity which I took to be a general making-ready, but which was, as I discovered to my surprise, the hearing itself. It cannot have lasted more than a minute or two. The judge, who wore an ordinary business suit, was a jolly old boy with whiskers and a red nose. He must have had a reputation as a wit, for when he fixed me with a merry eye and said, Ah, Mr Montgomery, the whole place fairly rocked with amusement. I smiled politely, to show him I could take a joke, even if I did not get it. A Guard prodded me in the back, I stood up, sat down, stood up again, then it was over. I looked about me in surprise. I felt I must have missed something. Maolseachlainn was asking for bail. Judge Fielding gently shook his head, as if he were reproving a forward child. Ah no, he said, I think not, sir. That provoked another tremor of merriment in the court. Well, I was glad they were all having such a good time. The Guard behind me was saying something, but I could not concentrate, for there was a horrible, hollow sensation in my chest, and I realised that I was about to weep. I felt like a child, or a very old man. Maolseachlainn touched my arm. I turned away helplessly. Come on now, the Guard said, not unkindly, and I blundered after him. Everything swam. Haslet was behind me, I knew his step by now. In the street a little crowd had gathered. How did they know who I was, which court I would be in, the time at which I would appear? When they caught sight of me they gave a cry, a sort of ululant wail of awe and execration that made my skin prickle. I was so confused and frightened I forgot myself and waved—I waved to them! God knows what I thought I was doing. I suppose it was meant as a placatory gesture, an animal sign of submission and retreat. It only made them more furious, of course. They shook their fists, they howled. One or two strange to me, familiar and yet alien, as if it had been on an immense, transfiguring voyage, to another planet, another galaxy, since I had seen it last. I enquired after my mother. I was tactful enough not to ask why she had not come. Tell her I'm sorry, I said. It sounded ridiculous, as if I were apologising for a broken appointment, and we looked away from each other furtively and were silent for a long, awkward moment. I have a nickname in here already, I said, they call me Monty, of course. She smiled, and I was pleased. When she smiles, biting her lip like that, she is more than ever like a child. I cannot believe she is a schemer. I suspect she was as surprised as I when the will was read. I find it hard to see her as the mistress of Coolgrange. Perhaps that is what my mother intended—after *her*, the drip. Ah, that is unworthy of me, my new seriousness. I do not hate her for disinheriting me. I think that in her way she was trying to teach me something, to make me look more closely at things, perhaps, to pay more attention to people, such as this poor clumsy girl, with her freckles and her timid smile and her almost invisible eyebrows. I am remembering what Daphne said to me only yesterday, through her tears, it has lodged in my mind like a thorn: *You knew nothing about us, nothing!* She's right, of course. She was talking about America, about her and Anna Behrens and all that, but it's true in general—I know nothing. Yet I am trying. I watch, and listen, and brood. Now and then I am afforded a glimpse into what seems a new world, but which I realise has been there all along, without my noticing. In these explorations my friend Eddie is a valuable guide. I have not mentioned Eddie before, have I? He attached himself to me early on, I think he is a little in love with me. He's nineteen—muscles, oiled black hair, a killer's shapely hands, like mine. Our trials are due to open on the same day, he takes this as a lucky omen. He is charged with murder and multiple rape. He insists on his innocence, but cannot suppress a guilty little smile. I believe he is secretly proud of his crimes. Yet a kind of innocence shines out of him, as if there is something inside, some tiny, precious part, that nothing can besmirch. When I consider Eddie I can almost believe in the existence of the soul. He has been in and out of custody since he was a child, and is a repository of prison lore. He tells me of the various ingenious methods of smuggling in dope. For instance, before the glass screens were put up, wives and girlfriends used to hide in their mouths little plastic bags of heroin, which were passed across during lingering kisses, swallowed, and sicked-up later, in the latrines. I was greatly taken with the idea, it affected me deeply. Such need, such passion, such charity and daring—when have I ever known the like?

What was I saying. I am becoming so vague. It happens to all of us in here. It is a kind of defence, this creeping absentmindedness, this torpor, which allows us to drop off instantly, anywhere, at any time, into brief, numb stretches of sleep.

Joanne. She came to see me, brought me my bag. I was glad to have it. They had confiscated most of what was in it, the prison authorities, but there were some shirts, a bar of soap—the scented smell of it struck me like a blow—a pair of shoes, my books. I clutched these things, these icons, to my heart, and grieved for the dead past.

But grief, that kind of grief is the great danger, in here. It saps the will. Those who give way to it grow helpless, a wasting lethargy comes over them. They are like mourners for whom the period of mourning will not end. I saw this danger, and determined to avoid it. I would work, I would study. The theme was there, ready-made. I had Daphne bring me big thick books on Dutch painting, not only the history but the techniques, the secrets of the masters. I studied accounts of the methods of grinding colours, of the trade in oils and dyes, of the flax industry in Flanders. I read the lives of the painters and their patrons. I became a minor expert on the Dutch republic in the seventeenth century. But in the end it was no good: all this learning, this information, merely built up and petrified, like coral encrusting a sunken wreck. How could mere facts compare with the amazing knowledge that had flared out at me as I stood and stared at the painting lying on its edge in the ditch where I dropped it that last time? That knowledge, that knowingness, I could not have lived with. I look at the reproduction, pinned to the wall above me here, but something is dead in it. Something is dead.

It was in the same spirit of busy exploration that I pored for long hours over the newspaper files in the prison library. I read every word devoted to my case, read and reread them, chewed them over until they turned to flavourless mush in my mind. I learned of Josie Bell's childhood, of her schooldays—pitifully brief—of her family and friends. Neighbours spoke well of her. She was a quiet girl. She had almost married once, but something had gone wrong, her fiancé went to England and did not return. First she worked in her own village, as a shopgirl. Then, before going to Whitewater, she was in Dublin for a while, where she was a chambermaid in the Southern Star Hotel. The Southern Star!— my God, I could have gone there when I was at Charlie's, could have taken a room, could have slept in a bed that she had once made! I laughed at myself. What would I have learned? There would have been no more of her there, for me, than there was in the newspaper stories, than there had been that day when I turned and saw her for the first time, standing in the open french window with the blue and gold of summer at her back, than there was when she crouched in the car and I hit her again and again and her blood spattered the window. This is the worst, the essential sin, I think, the one for which there will be no forgiveness: that I never imagined her vividly enough, that I never made her be there sufficiently, that I did not make her live. Yes, that failure of imagination is my real crime, the one that made the others possible. What I told that policeman is true—I killed her because I could kill her, and I could kill her because for me she was not alive. And so my task now is to bring her back to life. I am not sure what that means, but it strikes me with the force of an unavoidable imperative. How am I to make it come about, this act of parturition? Must I imagine her from the start, from infancy? I am puzzled, and not a little fearful, and yet there is something stirring in me, and I am strangely excited. I seem to have taken on a new weight and density. I feel gay and at the same time wonderfully serious. I am big with possibilities. I am living for two.

I have decided: I will not be swayed: I will plead guilty to murder in the first degree. I think it is the right thing to do. Daphne, when I told her, burst into tears at once. I was astonished, astonished and appalled. What about me, she cries, what about the child? I said, as mildly as I could, that I thought I had already destroyed their lives, and that the best thing I could do was to stay away from the two of them for as long as possible—forever, even—so that she might have the chance to start afresh. This, it seems, was not tactful. She just cried and cried, sitting there beyond the glass, clutching a sodden tissue in her fist, her shoulders shaking. Then it all came out, the rage and the shame, I could not make out the half of it through her sobs. She went back over the years. What I had done, and not done. How little I knew, how little I understood. I sat and gazed at her, aghast, my mouth open. I could not speak. How was it possible, that I could have been so wrong about her, all this time? How could I not have seen that behind her reticence there was all this passion, this pain? I was thinking about a pub I had passed by late on one of my night rambles through the city in that week before I was captured. It was in, I don't know, Stoneybatter, somewhere like that, a working-class pub with protective steel mesh covering the windows and old vomit-stains around the doorway. As I went past, a drunk stumbled out, and for a second, before the door swung shut again, I had a glimpse inside. I walked on without pausing, carrying the scene in my head. It was like something by Jan Steen: the smoky light, the crush of red-faced drinkers, the old boys propping up the bar, the fat woman singing, displaying a mouthful of broken teeth. A kind of slow amazement came over me, a kind of bafflement and grief, at how firmly I felt myself excluded from that simple, ugly, roistering world. That is how I seem to have spent my life, walking by open, noisy doorways, and passing on, into the darkness.—And yet there are moments too that allow me to think I am not wholly lost. The other day, for instance, on the way to yet one more remand hearing, I shared the police van with an ancient wino who had been arrested the night before, so he told me, for killing his friend. I could not imagine him having a friend, much less killing one. He talked to me at length as we bowled along, though most of what he said was gibberish. He had a bloodied eye, and an enormous, weeping sore on his mouth. I looked out through the barred window at the city streets going past, doing my best to ignore him. Then, when we were rounding a sharp bend, he fell off his seat on top of me, and I found myself holding the old brute in my arms. The smell was appalling, of course, and the rags he wore had a slippery feel to them that made me clench my teeth, but still I held him, and would not let him fall to the floor, and I even—surely I am embroidering—I think I may even have clasped him to me for a moment, in a gesture of, I don't know, of sympathy, of comradeship, of solidarity, something like that. Yes, an explorer, that's what I am, glimpsing a new continent from the prow of a sinking ship. And don't mistake me, I don't imagine for a second that such incidents as this, such forays into the new world, will abate my guilt one whit. But maybe they signify something for the future.

Should I destroy that last paragraph? No, what does it matter, let it stand.

Daphne brought me one of Van's drawings. I have pinned it up on the wall here. It is a portrait of me, she says. One huge, club foot, sausage fingers, a strangely calm, cyclopean eye. Quite a good likeness, really, when I think about it. She also brought me a startling piece of news. Joanne has invited her and the child to come and live at Coolgrange. They are going to set up house together, my wife and the stable-girl. (How quaintly things contrive to make what seems an ending!) I am not displeased, which surprises me. Apparently I am to live there also, when I get out. Oh, I can just see myself, in wellingtons and a hat, mucking out the stables. But I said nothing. Poor Daphne, if only—ah yes, if only.

Maolseachlainn too was horrified when I told him of my decision. Don't worry, I said, I'll plead guilty, but I don't want any concessions. He could not understand it, and I had not the energy to explain. It's what I want, that's all. It's what I must do. Apollo's ship has sailed for Delos, the stern crowned with laurel, and I must serve my term. By the way, Mac, I said, I owe a plate to Charlie French. He did not get the joke, but he smiled anyway. She wasn't dead, you know, when I left her, I said. I wasn't man enough to finish her off. I'd have done as much for a dog. (It's true—is there no end to the things I must confess?) He nodded, trying not to show his disgust, or perhaps it was just shock he was hiding. Hardy people, he said, they don't die easily. Then he gathered up his papers and turned to go. We shook hands. The occasion seemed to require that small formality.

Oh, by the way, the plot: it almost slipped my mind. Charlie French bought my mother's pictures cheap and sold them dear to Binkie

Behrens, then bought them cheap from Binkie and sold them on to Max Molyneaux. Something like that. Does it matter? Dark deeds, dark deeds. Enough.

Time passes. I eat time. I imagine myself a kind of grub, calmly and methodically consuming the future, what the world outside calls the future. I must be careful not to give in to despair, to that aboulia which has been a threat always to everything I tried to do. I have looked for so long into the abyss, I feel sometimes it is the abyss that is looking into me. I have my good days, and my bad. I think of the monsters on whose side my crime has put me, the killers, the torturers, the dirty little beasts who stand by and watch it happen, and I wonder if it would not be better simply to stop. But I have my task, my term. Today, in the workshop, I caught her smell, faint, sharp, metallic, unmistakable. It is the smell of metal-polish—she must have been doing the silver that day. I was so happy when I identified it! Anything seemed possible. It even seemed that some day I might wake up and see, coming forward from the darkened room into the frame of that doorway which is always in my mind now, a child, a girl, one whom I will recognise at once, without the shadow of a doubt.

It is spring. Even in here we feel it, the quickening in the air. I have some plants in my window, I like to watch them, feeding on the light. The trial takes place next month. It will be a quick affair. The newspapers will be disappointed. I thought of trying to publish this, my testimony. But no. I have asked Inspector Haslet to put it into my file, with the other, official fictions. He came to see me today, here in my cell. He picked up the pages, hefted them in his hand. It was to be my defence, I said. He gave me a wry look. Did you put in about being a scientist, he said, and knowing the Behrens woman, and owing money, all that stuff? I smiled. It's my story, I said, and I'm sticking to it. He laughed at that. Come on,

Freddie, he said, how much of it is true? It was the first time he had called me by my name. True, Inspector? I said. All of it. None of it. Only the shame.

Supplementary Material

Thou Shalt Not Kill

JOHN BANVILLE

The following essay on The Book of Evidence*'s genesis was first delivered as a lecture at the Tavistock Clinic in November 1995, as part of a series of weekly reflections on the Ten Commandments organised by the clinic to mark its seventy-fifth anniversary. It was first published in* Arguing at the Crossroads: Essays on a Changing Ireland, *edited by Paul Brennan and Catherine de Saint Phalle (New Island, 1997), pp. 133–42, and more recently reprinted in my own* Possessed of a Past: A John Banville Reader *(Picador, 2012), pp. 349–58.*

Works of art have humble beginnings. They grow, like everything else, from a seed. Sitting at my desk recently, unable to work, I found myself thumbing through an old notebook, the one that I kept during the writing of my novel *The Book of Evidence*. The first page is dated 7 April, 1986. Here are the first few notes:

Notice in a cemetery (true): 'Planting and cultivation restricted to dwarfs.'

Browning's 'tender murderer'?

'There are no moral phenomena at all, only a moral interpretation of phenomena'

—Nietzsche, *Beyond Good and Evil*

(A small ad, clipped from a newspaper and pasted to the page:) 'Premature Baby Incubator, Vickers 59 for sale, as new. Offers, Box 402, Baby.

The living being is only a species of the dead, and a very rare species'

—Nietzsche, *Fröliche Wissenschaft*

Is it wrong to kill people? (underlined twice)

I do not think those cemetery dwarfs featured in the book, nor did the baby in its 'as new' incubator make an appearance, though they probably did lend the tale their own particular, subliminal touches of the macabre. Nietzsche is there in the pages, certainly, sometimes quoted directly, without acknowledgement—but not the two aphorisms that I have quoted from my notebook. Of course, the real origin of the book, the real gleam in the progenitor's eye, was that simple-seeming question: *Is it wrong to kill people?*

I am not a philosopher, not a psychologist, not a theologian, not a jurist. I address the subject of murder—or at least, the Mosaic injunction against murder—because I have written a series of three novels which together form an artistic meditation on the subject of a killing and its aftermath. The three volumes are *The Book of Evidence*, *Ghosts* and *Athena*. I did not set out to write a trilogy. Nor did I set out to write 'about' a murder (the work of art is never about something, though it may be about everything). I did, I suppose, have identifiable themes and ideas, which however loose and vague as artistic themes and ideas always are, could perhaps be grouped under the general heading, *The Search for Authenticity*.

The question of the authentic, of how to work authentically in a medium—art, that is—which at a certain level is necessarily fake, is one that obsesses the artist, consciously or otherwise. You take a square of stretched canvas and with infinite pains and manic concentration apply to it a series of multi-coloured daubs to make a pattern according to rigid but unknown laws: you arrange a series of sounds for voices or instruments or both combined, sounds which you may never hear outside your head (Schubert did not hear the bulk of his work performed), but which yet make a medleyed web in which an ineffable something is caught: you assemble a group of characters you have never known and will never encounter and make them dance their slow, intricate way through a story which is nothing like life—no novel is ever anything like life, though it may, as Henry James has it, *make* life—but which yet engages the reader as do those troubling dreams that come to us once in a while like succubi, drawing us into and out of ourselves, troubling our days—years, even—with the sensation of a reality more real than that which we experience in lived life itself. Where, is authentic; the territorial song of the oriole is authentic. But what of the sky painted from pigments? What of the imagined stone over which an imagined character trips as he hurries down the road to meet the love of his life? What of the stylised representation of the bird's song in a piano piece by Messiaen?

You may think these matters only of significance, or interest, to the painter, the composer, the novelist, but you only have to ponder for a moment to realise that the problem of authenticity is at the very centre of the human predicament, and perhaps never more centrally located than in our, now closing, century.

So I set out, in *The Book of Evidence*, to invent an emblematic figure who in his actions and meditations would swing between the poles of the authentic and the inauthentic. I did not attempt to create what book reviewers would call an 'original' character—there are, as we all know, no original characters. This one had a particularly luxuriant family tree, with many an odd bird squawking among its branches. Dostoevsky's Underground Man is perched there, of course, sometimes in his own words (he figures darkly in that notebook of mine; 'Can a thinking man have any self-respect whatever?' he asks, and what thinking man can give an unequivocal answer?). The narrator of Sartre's *La Nausée* flexes a blue-black wing, and Camus's Meursault is heard every so often to sound a weary note. Nabokov's Humbert Humbert flashes like a firebird. Oh, there is a whole aviary here: Goethe's Werther, Büchner's Woyzeck, Kleist's Judge Adam, Wilde's Dorian Gray, Musil's brutish killer Moosbrugger ('if society could dream collectively,' says Musil, 'it would dream Moosbrugger'), and many, many more. Out of such bits and borrowings are characters made.

I gave him a name, at once ponderous and preposterous; Frederick Charles St John Vanderveld Montgomery. Usually a novelist—my kind of novelist, that is—will infuse a character's name with as much resonance as it will bear: Godkin, Lawless, Grainger, Gabriel Swan, are some that I have employed. In this case I needed a name that would fall on the page with false resonance, or no resonance at all: Frederick Montgomery, *l'homme armée*, scion of a 'good' family, waywardly brilliant, self-regarding, dandyish, deceitful, feckless, vicious, murderous.

Freddie claims to have been in the far past, some kind of scientist, a mathematician, apparently. I am not sure that I believe him about this (I am not sure that I believe him about anything). In California, ten years before the time of the main events of the book, something occurs—or perhaps nothing occurs—and his life goes into crisis. Under this nameless affliction he is like Philip, Lord Chandos, in Hugo von Hofmannsthal's *The Chandos Letter*, who writes to his friend Francis Bacon: 'My case, in short, is this: that I have utterly lost the ability to think or speak coherently about anything at all.' My Freddie Montgomery can think, yes, and he can speak—by golly, how he can speak—but what is gone is coherence.

Meaning has fallen out of his life like the bottom falling out of a bucket. Here he is, addressing the trial judge in particular and the rest of us in general, describing a pause on his way home from the Spanish island where he has been aimlessly footling away his life for years: the paragraph occurs early on in the book, but constitutes, nevertheless, a central moment:

A washed-blue dawn was breaking in Madrid. I stopped outside the station and watched a flock of birds wheeling and tumbling at an immense height, and, the strangest thing, a gust of euphoria, or something like euphoria, swept through me, making me tremble, and bringing tears to my eyes. It was from lack of sleep, I suppose, and the effect of the high, thin air. Why, I wonder, do I remember so clearly standing there, the colour of the sky, those birds, that shiver of fevered optimism? I was at a turning point, you will tell me, just there the future forked for me, and I took the wrong path without noticing— that's what you'll tell me, isn't it, you, who must have meaning in everything, who lust after meaning, your palms sticky and your faces on fire! But calm, Frederick, calm. Forgive me this outburst, your Honour. It is just that I do not believe such moments mean anything—or any other moments, for that matter. They have significance, apparently. They may even have value of some sort. But they do not mean anything.

There now, I have declared my faith.

Freddie is obsessed with how thick is the texture of things that yet seem lacking in all substance. The world is solid as stone yet constantly quaking and shifting and sinking under him. He regards this world with the anguished fearfulness of a lover constantly in danger of losing the beloved. In this passage he is returning by ship to Ireland:

It was evening. The sea was calm, an oiled, taut meniscus, mauve-tinted and curiously high and curved. From the forward lounge where I sat the prow seemed to rise and rise, as if the whole ship were straining to take to the air. The sky before us was a smear of crimson on the palest of pale blue and silvery green. I held my face up to the calm sea-light, entranced, expectant, grinning like a loon. I confess I was not entirely sober, I had already broken into my allowance of duty-free booze, and the skin at my temples and around my eyes was tightening alarmingly. It was not just the drink, though, that was making me happy, but the tenderness of things, the simple goodness of the world. This sunset, for instance, how lavishly it was laid on, the clouds, the light on the sea, that heartbreaking, blue-green distance, laid on, all of it, as if to console some lost, suffering wayfarer. I have never really got used to being on this earth. Sometimes I think our presence here is due to a cosmic blunder, that we were meant for another planet altogether, with other arrangements, and other laws, and other, grimmer skies. I try to imagine it, our true place, off on the far side of the galaxy, whirling and whirling. And the ones who were meant for here, are they out there, baffled and homesick, like us? No, they would have become extinct long ago. How could they survive, these gentle earthlings, in a world that was made to contain *us*?

If Freddie Montgomery is obsessed by the world, half in love with its tenderness and beauty, and half in terror of its inexplicable insubstantiality, he hardly notices the people surrounding him. He compares them to mirrors into which he peers anxiously, searching for his own, hardly existent reflection (Count Dracula is another of his forebears). He comes upon a painting, and, in a passage to which he brings all his linguistic and imaginative skills, conjures a life for the long-dead woman who is its subject. Yet when, in the process of stealing the painting, he is confronted by a real, living woman, he bashes her head in, swats her out of his way as if she were no more substantial than a cobweb. *The Book of Evidence* is just what the title says it is; a presentation of the facts, not in any effort by Freddie Montgomery to prove his innocence or to excuse his murderous deeds, but as a kind of appalled act of witness. Look, he says to us, look, here is what happened! I can no more make sense of it than you can. When at the end of the book, after his capture, the police ask him why he killed the woman, he can only reply: 'I killed her because I could, what more can I say?'

As Freddie comes to realise, his *crime* was murder, but his *sin* was a radical failure of the imagination. We make others real only by imagining them: both the lover and the murderer know this. Yet where the lover and the murderer are different is that what the lover conjures into existence out of the white-hot furnace of his imaginings is a stylised image, a kind of magically detailed hologram of the beloved, while on the contrary, the murderer *makes the other real*. Here is Freddie dealing the first blow:

> I turned to her. I had the hammer in my hand. I looked at it, startled. The silence rose around us like water. Don't, she said. She was crouched as before, with her arms bent and her back pressed into the corner. I could not speak, I was filled with a kind of wonder. I had never felt another's presence so immediately and with such raw force. I saw her now, really saw her, for the first time, her mousy hair and bad skin, that bruised look around her eyes. She was quite ordinary, and yet, somehow, I don't know—somehow radiant.

This immediacy, this radiance, are what the subject of the murder and the subject of the painting have in common. Although none of the critics has remarked it, this seems to me the real scandal at the heart of *The Book of Evidence*. The living, though soon to be dead, woman is no more real to Freddie—and to us—than the painted woman: less so, in fact. The border between art and life has become blurred and not just for Freddie. We too are somehow implicated in this crime.

Freddie Montgomery, under other guises, and other names, meditates on this failure of imagination, through *Ghosts*, which is an account of his time in Purgatory; and *Athena*, his attempt to set a new life in place of the one that he took. For all the passionate *looking* that takes place in *Athena* ('looking' being for Freddie a far more important act than that other act with which it indecently rhymes), the failure remains as it must. The dead cannot be made to live again, and art cannot be put in the place of life. Even so, he is determined that something will be salvaged from the disaster he has wrought—and wrought is the most suitable word here. At the end of *Athena*, when he has been abandoned by his love, and after he has discovered that although he looked and looked and *looked* at her, he did not succeed in seeing her, he is granted a final, fleeting vision.

I saw her yesterday, I don't know how, but I did. It was the strangest thing. I have not got over it yet. I was in that pub on Gabriel Street that she liked so much. The place is fake, of course, with false wood panelling and plated brass and a wooden fan the size of an aeroplane propeller in the ceiling that does nothing except swirl the drifting cigarette smoke in lazy arabesques. I go there for the obvious reason. I was in the back bar, nursing a drink and my sore heart, sitting at that big window—I always think of windows like that as startled, somehow, like wide-open eyes—that looks down at the city along the broad sweep of Ormond Street. The street was crowded, as it always is. The sun was shining, in its half-hearted way—yes, spring has come, despite my best efforts. Suddenly I saw her—or no, not suddenly, there was no suddenness or surprise in it. She was just there, in her black coat and her black stilettos, hurrying along the crowded pavement in that watery light at that unmistakable, stiff-kneed half-run, a hand to her breast and her head down. Where was she going, with such haste, so eagerly? The city lay all before her, awash with April and evening. I say *her*, but of course I know it was not her, not really. And yet it was. How can I express it? There is the she who is gone, who is in some southern somewhere, lost to me forever, and then there is this other, who steps out of my head and goes hurrying off along the sunlit pavements to do I don't know what. To live. If I can call it living; and I shall.

The most terrifying discovery in life is that we are free. Constrained, yes, but free. I sometimes feel, in my darker moments, that the only truly interesting achievement of the human species—the most dangerous, the most terrible, species the world has ever known—is not the development of philosophy or religion, the application of science, the invention of romantic love, but the success with which we have ameliorated the horror we experience in face of our state of freedom. What stratagems we have devised to blind ourselves to the abyss that gapes always at our feet. What somersaults of logic we have performed, even on the lip of the precipice.

How are we to cope with that profoundly horrifying dictum of Nietzsche's I quoted at the outset, to the effect that 'there are no moral phenomena at all, only a moral interpretation of phenomena'? In the absence of a moral imperative, is it wrong to kill people? Religion is not much help, being itself steeped in the blood of saviours and martyrs and Philistines. Nor will art come to the rescue, as Freddie Montgomery can attest. Where, in Emerson's famous and characteristically ambiguous formulation, where do we find ourselves? As I have said, I am not a philosopher, theologian, jurist. I have no pronouncements on the problem of evil, of the just war, abortion, euthanasia, capital punishment. All that an artist can do is present the evidence. *Here is what happened, this is how it felt, this is how the light fell, how the characters spoke: it is all made up, yet strangely real.* When I think of Freddie Montgomery and his dogged search for authenticity through the three novels that are, we may say, his creation, I return again and again to a brief little passage that occurs at the end of *Ghosts*:

> I think of a picture at the end of a long gallery, a sudden presence come upon unexpectedly, at first sight a soft confusion of greens and gilts in the calm, speechless air. Look at this foliage, these clouds, the texture of this gown. A stricken figure stares out at something that is being lost. There is an impression of music, tiny, exact and gay. This is the end of a world. Birds unseen are fluting in the trees, the sun shines somewhere, the distances of the sea are vague and palely blue, the galliot awaits. The figures move, if they move, as in a moving scene, one that they define, by being there, its arbiters. Without them only the wilderness, green riot, tumult of wind and the crazy sun. They formulate the tale and people it and give it substance. They are the human moment.

It is one of the chief ironies of the trilogy that it is in those passages when Freddie contemplates the literally inhuman—the figures in paintings, or the figments of his own imagination—that he most closely approaches that state of full feeling humanness which is his one, consistent aim. Being a murderer, he must now, as he says at the end of *The Book of Evidence*, live for two. I am, he declares, 'big with possibilities'. He is pregnant with his own incipient humanity. He has learned to use his imagination, and, as Wallace Stevens has it, 'God and the imagination are one'. It is not the God of Moses, that merciless slaughterer, but the god in our own heads that injuncts us: it is the imagination that commands. Thou shalt not kill.

('Thou Shalt Not Kill', 1997)

Witness for the Defence

SEAMUS DEANE

Though a prolific reviewer himself, Banville refrains from reading cri-
tiques of his own work, professing to be all too resignedly aware of 'the
flaws, the faults, the failures' without having them enumerated for him.
And yet the acclaim afforded The Book of Evidence *on its release in*
1989, on both sides of the Atlantic, could not but have pleased his pub-
lishers at least.

Writing for The Observer, *Michael Dibdin commended Banville for*
the 'malerisch quality [of his] flowing prose whose lyricism, patrician
irony and aching sense of loss are reminiscent of Lolita'; *Patrick*
McGrath likewise remarked Banville's painterly strokes, seeing the novel
as a 'grim picture of the banality of evil, but . . . suffused . . . so richly
with wit and humanity that, despite the horror, one is inexorably drawn
into his narrator's frame'. Walter Nash, struck by the author's 'enviably
luminous, ironic elegance', adjudged the book 'to be at least seven-eighths
*of a minor masterpiece' (*London Review of Books*); Ruth Rendell was*
wistfully effusive: 'Remarkable . . . If all crime novels were like this one,
there would no longer be the need for a genre'.

In the US, John Bayley found the book 'to be more disconcerting than
either [Dostoevsky's Crime and Punishment *or Camus's* L'Étranger], *if*
only because it possesses something of the aesthetic force of both but the
*moral dimension of neither' (*The New York Review of Books*); Don*
DeLillo marvelled at its menace: 'Banville writes a dangerous and clear-
running prose and has a grim gift of seeing people's souls. The Book of
Evidence *is a major new work of fiction in which every suave moment*
calmly detonates to show the murderous gleam within'.

The New York Times *held Banville's fiction to be some deep chthonic crackle: 'Here is an astonishing, disturbing little novel that might have been coughed up from hell';* the Literary Review *opined in more celestial terms: 'I have read no other novel that illustrates so perfectly a single epiphany. It is, in its cold, terrifying way, a masterpiece'.* The Economist's *encomium read thus: 'Hauntingly beautiful and original';* the Financial Times *was no less pithy: 'reverberating and unforgettable'.*

Seamus Deane, that most astute of critics, wrote with singular deftness of the novel's 'twin worlds [. . .] and dazzling paradoxes' for The Irish Times *in March 1989. Grateful acknowledgement is made to both reviewer and newspaper for permission to reproduce in full this appraisal.*

All of John Banville's novels propose a world that exists under two aspects: the random and the orderly. The relation between these is heartbreakingly painful because the confusion of the actual is always in excess of the symmetry of the ordered world, and it is in that experience of excess that his protagonists come to grief.

Rational lucidity, of the kind we associate with mathematicians, geometers, astronomers, and a certain kind of Banvillean character, is not fine as far as it goes, because it can never go the whole way. If there is no comprehensive order, little satisfaction is to be gained from provisional, lower-grade systems.

In the zone of excess, there are frequent ambushes—sudden assaults from concealed feelings, random sensuous thrills from the physical universe. The intelligence that feels itself insulted by such dishevelment can try to survive the humiliation and place its trust in the eventual triumph of order. It can even, like Kepler, disdain the world, which is so deceptive in its appearance, and claim that the structures of appearance are quite different. Truth is truer; it's also cleaner, more crystalline, it is free of the unpredictable.

To carry on such a crusade for truth in the face of the derision and hostility of others is a heroic enterprise. But there is an alternative to that kind of courage. The insulted intelligence can, in its turn, insult the world. It can, in other words, forgo its Faustian aspirations and turn, with a sort of rancid glee, towards the Nietzschean position of the renouncer, the figure we meet in *The Gay Science*.

To renounce convention, to show contempt for what others hold to be sacred, is itself a manifestation of the proudly intelligent. Yet the violation of convention, if it is to be effective, must also be shocking. It must involve crime.

Frederick Charles St John Vanderveld Montgomery (Freddie) is a murderer and a traitor to every decent feeling. He is also, one need hardly add, a kind of genius (statistics). He has many of the characteristics of a Banville 'hero'—morally delinquent, neurasthenically sensitive, astray in the hall of mirrors he calls his consciousness, a connoisseur of his own emotions and a despoiler of those of others.

Banville's writing is fastidiously precise; it is also, because of the sheer aesthetic appeal which it sustains, an action which is grimly admonitory. All trespassers from the ordinary world into this privileged linguistic demesne will be persecuted. For the aristocratic demeanour of this writing is itself a signal that tells us the aesthetic mode is itself a form of morality which considers itself superior to all that convention offers.

The people who inhabit this world are dangerous, of course. For the sake of perfection they are willing to create havoc in the world of the ordinary. They are also insane, but their insanity, we learn to see, is provoked by a grief that the world is so cruelly divided between the orderly and the random. In effect, this division is an illusion.

What happened to Freddie was that he was born defective and then transposed his defect to the world. 'Ever since I had reached the age of reason', he says, 'I had been doing one thing and think-ing another, because the weight of things seemed so much greater than that of thoughts.' From the outset, he felt he was living a lie. In order to reconcile the difference between 'things' and 'thoughts' he committed murder, gave release to the monster inside him and gained 'freedom'. 'To do the worst thing, the very worst thing, that's the way to be free.'

This is an extraordinary novel-soliloquy, a criminal's enactment of his own trial, an account of how he finally manages to 'get life'. Imprisoned forever, he thinks himself free at last. That is the point. He can only be free in himself. Once other people are involved, he is imprisoned. He murders a girl, ruins a friend, leaves a trail of damage which is as long as his life; everything is renounced except the form which his public renunciation takes. He must be incrimi-nated in order to believe himself ultimately innocent of the one crime which he regards as lethal—the crime of not becoming himself. The manic integrity of his performance is a sign of his madness and of his reason.

The twin worlds of Banville duplicate themselves in ever more involved, frightening and dazzling paradoxes. This novel extends the range of an already astonishing achievement in fiction.

The Irish Times, 25 March 1989

Stepping into the Limelight—and the Chaos

FINTAN O'TOOLE

The following interview first appeared in the pages of The Irish Times *on 21 October 1989, less than a week before the announcement was to be made of the winner of that year's Booker Prize, a prize for which* The Book of Evidence *was shortlisted. (Kazuo Ishiguro's* The Remains of the Day *prevailed in the end.)*

The other prize for which Banville was then a contender—the more lucrative but less appealingly named Guinness Peat Aviation Book Award—he successfully carried off, though not without some demurral from the prize's final arbiter, an intractable Graham Greene. (For a fuller account of this imbroglio, see Fintan O'Toole's 'The cat among the pigeons: Greene and the GPA', The Irish Times, *2 December 1989.)*

Commenting on that year's Booker shortlist and the prize in general, many readers will remark Banville's wry surmise: 'I would [be] taken aback if [. . .] any of the books [I] write after The Book of Evidence *[ever wins the Booker Prize]. If not now, never.' Well, not then, yes; not ever? no: Banville's* The Sea *won the Man Booker Prize in 2005, a year when, as chance would have it, Ishiguro's* Never Let Me Go *was also shortlisted.*

Grateful acknowledgement is made to The Irish Times *and Fintan O'Toole to reprint what follows.*

Just when you're resigned to relative obscurity, begin, even, to enjoy it, they come and take it away from you. Nineteen years and seven books after *Long Lankin*, years of being regarded as one of the finest prose writers around and of generally not seeing his books in the bookshops outside Ireland, John Banville is in the running for both the Booker Prize and the GPA Award.

'As well as growing up as an artist,' he says, 'you also have to grow up as the man who carries the artist around inside him, and one of the things that has meant for me is coming to terms with what I can expect from my own time. And, of course, if your work has the density and oddness that mine has, then it's just foolish to expect that it will have a large immediate audience. I'd become fairly comfortable with that idea.' Now, the likelihood of a much larger audience beckons.

It's an idea that he views with the ironic humour that is so much a part of his work. 'It was only when I heard that I was on the Booker shortlist that I realised just how much I wanted to be on it, and it came as a bit of a shock. But I still have the feeling that's summed up in the story that the Welsh playwright Alun Owen told about Beckett. Owen was somehow involved in the first production of *Endgame* and after the opening they went off somewhere to wait for the reviews, which were lukewarm. Beckett was worried for the cast, for the sake of all those who might lose their jobs if the play didn't get good houses. Alun said, "Well, look, probably the critics didn't understand it." And Beckett's wife reared up indignantly and said, "I should certainly hope not." Part of me is like that. I would have been very taken aback if, say, *Mefisto* had won the Booker Prize or, indeed, if any of the books I'll write after *The Book of Evidence* does. If not now, never.'

He has got so used to expecting not to be understood that part of him still wonders if the popularity of *The Book of Evidence* isn't all a mistake, if people haven't somehow missed its darkness, its deeply troubling immersion in violence, and taken it for something else.

'I keep thinking that maybe the success is based on a misreading, except that people do see the celebration of the beauty of our brief lives that there is in the central character Freddie. But then, it strikes me that the book is about something that almost everyone feels. I heard old Lord Hailsham being interviewed by Anthony Clare and asked if he could kill someone and all he said was "I've never had the opportunity, thank goodness". And this from a bastion of High Toryism.

'The human drama of *The Book of Evidence* is that of a man coming face to face with the fact that there is no morality. The most important bit in the book is the question why did Freddie give up being a scientist, what happened? What happened is that the bottom fell out of his world. He saw that all the things that he lived by were just things that he'd invented himself. I think the appeal of the book is the fact that the reader can say "Yeah, this is right." We get up in the morning and put on our suits and drive to work and we need all this in order to live, but inside we know that all this is nonsense, that we've just invented it.'

Much of his work is concerned with this paradoxical relationship between the systems we create in order to live in the world, and the chaos that is everywhere outside of these systems. From this comes the imagery of science and mathematics in many of his novels: *Doctor Copernicus, Kepler, The Newton Letter, Mefisto*. 'One of the things that fascinated Einstein was the fact that mathematics was invented by man and yet the world obeys its rules. This means either that we only see that segment of the universe that agrees with our rules or, more interestingly, that we impose something on the universe in order to see it.'

All his books are about this tension between the rules and the chaos that surrounds them, a chaos that is all the more crushing for the elaborate, complex, mathematical correspondences, yet it begins with the sentence 'Chance was in the beginning' and ends on the word 'chance'—'In future, I will leave things, I will try to leave things, to chance.'

Banville's Copernicus and Kepler try to construct perfect working models of the universe, yet their stories merely describe an arc from the contingency and chaos of the real world back to that contingency.

This is why the novels are always as much about what is not there as what is, about the absences that surround his characters. 'All my books are about people who can't live fully. All the weight is on what is not there. *The Newton Letter* and *The Book of Evidence* are ironic successes, ironic because in both you've got this very poised voice, a perfectly controlled tone relating something that's completely chaotic. For all their assurance, the narrators completely misunderstand the story they're telling. In *The Newton Letter* it's an utter misconception about what's going on sexually, and in *The Book of Evidence* it's the violence that Freddie really doesn't understand.'

It is this sense of what is absent as the ultimately central force in the work that Banville takes from Beckett, who is not so much an influence as an example. He admires Beckett's 'courage and fortitude', but more than that he sees himself as being in a strain of Irish writing that comes from Beckett.

'There are two distinct strains of Irish literature, indeed of world literature, a sort of ego and id. One comes from Joyce. Joyce looked at the world and accepted it in all its chaos and folly. Beckett, on the other hand, can't accept the world. He stands aghast at it. Even the moments of lightness only make it all the worse. I would belong to that strain that can't accept the world. It's not really a question of influence—influence only really applies to apprentice work when you're trying out different formulas—it's to do with the way you look at the world.'

It's not just that his books deal with this tension between order, pattern, design, on the one hand, and chaos and contingency on the other, but that the writing of the books and to an extent his own life have been involved in this tension as well. There is a slight irony in the fact that *The Newton Letter* and *The Book of Evidence* have brought him most attention, because they are in a sense different from his richer, more ambitious novels.

'It seems to be a kind of pattern. *Doctor Copernicus* and *Kepler* are followed by *The Newton Letter* which is a brief, five-finger exercise. It's one of my favourites from my novels—it achieves on a technical level exactly what it sets out to achieve—it may even be a better book, but it's different, not as dense.'

It's the same with the relationship between *The Book of Evidence* and *Mefisto*. '*Mefisto* is full of strange pain and grief. Someone asked me why it was so black and I said, without thinking, that it's about grief. It was only then that it struck me that that is true, that the book has a lot to do with the deaths of my parents in the late Seventies and early Eighties. A lot of things got into it that I didn't understand, but I let them stay. The book caused me terrible problems because I finished it with the technical problems unsolved. I didn't get the tone, but I was very proud of having finished it in spite of not solving the problems.

'The tone of *The Newton Letter* and *The Book of Evidence*, on the other hand, is perfect. You can't strike them at any point and get back a dull note. But that sacrifices the density and contingency that's in *Mefisto*. *The Book of Evidence* may be better achieved but I still want that density.' He wants, like the narrator of *Mefisto* in other words, to let in more of the chaos, more of the spontaneity of life, and this is to do with the man as well as with the novelist.

'My ideas about how one should live were for a long time too solemn. I forgot about the element of play in art, as in life. It's foolish to expect readers to take you as seriously as you do yourself. Just because you've spent years of your life on something, doesn't mean that you should expect them to treat it with due solemnity. They're more frivolous than that—thank God. I've always been too safe: I've said "I don't want recognition, I don't want money" and saying that protects you. It's not that I'm now craving money and success—all of that has nothing to do with the quality of your work—but I do feel I should be open to a more chaotic world.'

One of the reasons he doesn't believe that the increased reader-ship of the Booker recognition may bring will seduce him into changing his work is that he's in the process of changing it anyway. 'I've come to an end of that idea in my work that what's central is what's not there. I'm in transition—I want to allow in more spon-taneity.'

As part of that process, he accepted a commission from Hamish Hamilton to write a historical novel based on Robin Hood (con-trary to reports, he has not left his long-time publishers Secker & Warburg: the Hamish Hamilton contract is a one-off). 'I'm doing it to see if I can write it more or less spontaneously, in six months, and then use that method for my next book. It's a risk, but I feel that I have to take that risk.'

One of the apparent contradictions of his life is that he has worked so much in journalism—as chief sub-editor of *The Irish Press* and now as literary editor of *The Irish Times*—a business that might be expected to supply all the contingency and spontaneity that he feels he needs to be exposed to.

'But I've always worked in a particular area of newspapers, as a sub-editor or an editor, where you actually have a very strange relationship to reality. Tim Pat Coogan said that a sub-editor is a man who changes other people's words and goes home in the dark.

'I remember one night when I was in *The Irish Press* having a fierce argument with one of my colleagues about the derivation of some word, looking up dictionaries and passionately hunting down the origin of this word. And there had been some terrible disaster in the North, some awful bombing I think, which everyone else was trying to cope with. Here we were obsessed with this word. That's how strange it is.'

Not that he feels that in his novels there is any kind of moral responsibility to the outside world. When writing about the murderer Freddie and his victim in *The Book of Evidence*, he was concerned primarily with the technical problems. 'Art is amoral, that is, neither moral nor immoral. I don't take a moral stance in the book, and I'm not concerned with morality. Except in the obvious sense that a work of art is a moral gesture in itself, is on the side of the good, against the chaos and nihilism of the world.

'But it's only the novel that has to answer that question. It's not asked of painting or music or even poetry. It's because the novel ostensibly deals with the world in which we live. It's still, in England, anyway, a novel idea that the novel can be a work of art.

'Maybe that's why I've never been particularly well understood in England: they assume that I'm trying to write a traditional English novel and failing, whereas I'm not trying to write that at all. Now, maybe they're right, maybe the novel shouldn't be turned into something that could have the same density and concentration that poetry strives for. But I'm not interested in writing anything else.

'I've always likened writing a novel to having a very powerful dream that you know is going to haunt you for days. If you sit down at the breakfast table and start to try to explain the dream to someone, they yawn and look at you and they can't understand what you're on about. You could just forget all about it. But if you said "I'm going to sit down for three years and I'm going to write something and at the end of it, when you read it, you will have that dream", then you're close to the impulse of my novels.'

The Irish Times, 21 October 1989

Scenes from
'The Book of Evidence: A Screenplay'

JOHN BANVILLE

Here, Freddie has returned to a crumbling Coolgrange, his ancestral home, to finesse from his mother the money he owes a drugs syndicate he has become entangled with on the same Mediterannean island where he has left his wife, Dee (named Daphne in the novel), and their infant son, Van, as collateral. The dope peddler, Randolph, to whom Freddie owed the money originally, has since passed the debt on to one Dos Santos (the 'silver-haired hidalgo' in the novel named Señor Aguirre), forfeiting an ear in the transaction. Cisco is Freddie's erstwhile chauffeur, a character who appears in the screenplay only.

These seven scenes correspond, in abbreviated form, to those of pp. 39–58 of the novel, and have been set similarly to Banville's only published screenplay to date, that of The Sea *(Enitharmon Press, 2013). In the author's Introduction to the limited edition, a few remarks bear repeating: 'In a screenplay, one writes flat, eschewing all literary flourishes and tonal colouring. A line of film dialogue is inert, practically lifeless, awaiting the animating energy that will be brought to it by actor, director, cameraman, lighting director, make-up artist . . . This is how it should be, although many novelists down the years have made themselves unhappy by expecting otherwise.' Elsewhere, Banville has spoken of his great relish for writing film scripts, describing them as 'a kind of transcendent play'.*

For permission to print these previously unpublished scenes, grateful acknowledgement is made both to John Banville and to Bernard Meehan, Keeper of Manuscripts at Trinity College, Dublin, where the typescript is catalogued TCD MS 11356/10/18, folios 35–54. Although unsigned and

undated (a rare omission on the author's part), Banville has assigned the
screenplay to the very early Nineties.

Ext. Country road—day.

FREDDIE, carrying his bag, approaches a gateway; the name
'Coolgrange' written on gatepost. He walks up drive. A dog
jumps out of the hedge at him, snarling.

FREDDIE   Get away! Jesus, get away!

A whistle from the direction of the house, and a voice calling
loudly: 'Patch! Come here, damn you!' The dog slinks away.
FREDDIE, unnerved, walks on. A big old shabby farmhouse. On
the steps outside the front door, the dog at her feet, DOLLY:
sixtyish, wearing corduroy trousers and drooping cardigan.

FREDDIE   Hello, ma.
DOLLY   Christ, it *is* you; I thought I was seeing things.

Int. Coolgrange—day.

FREDDIE enters the hallway, with DOLLY and the dog behind him.
He stops, puts down his bag, looks about.

DOLLY   Home sweet home.

They pass along the hall into the kitchen: crowded with large,
inappropriate items of furniture: armchairs, rolltop desk, etc.

FREDDIE   Are you *living* in here?
DOLLY   Pretty much, yes. The rest is falling down.
                 pause
            You might have told us you were coming.
FREDDIE   I wrote, didn't I?
DOLLY   No, you didn't.

FREDDIE   Well, I meant to.

DOLLY   Dee phoned. She says you're to call her. Why didn't you bring her?

FREDDIE, pretending not to hear, looks through the window. In a paddock outside, a girl in jodhpurs is leading a string of Connemara ponies in a circle.

FREDDIE   What are *they*?

DOLLY   (laughs)

Ugly-looking brutes, aren't they. But they pay for them, the Japs and the Germans, even the Dutch.

FREDDIE   The *Dutch*?

DOLLY   Ach, they're all over the bloody place; they own half the country now.

Pause. FREDDIE broods.

FREDDIE   And what do they want *those* things for?

DOLLY shrugs.

DOLLY   God knows; the kiddies, I suppose. Or maybe they eat them. Don't they eat horsemeat? You're the traveller, you should know.

pause

Your father would turn in his grave. Ponies, at Coolgrange!

FREDDIE   He's well turned, by now.

They laugh; he notices she is holding her left arm in a peculiar fashion.

FREDDIE   What's wrong with your arm?

DOLLY   (shrugs)

Nothing. Bit of a sprain.

She avoids his eye. They look out of the window again.

> Are you staying?

FREDDIE pretends he has not heard her.

FREDDIE   Beautiful day.

> Int. Coolgrange—day.

DOLLY, FREDDIE, JOANNE seated at kitchen table. JOANNE is a cheerful, shy, awkward girl of about seventeen. Lunch-things on the table: salad, sliced bread, cold meat, etc. FREDDIE has gin bottle at his elbow, is drinking gin from a teacup.

FREDDIE   I suppose there isn't any tonic concealed about the
           place?
DOLLY   If I wasn't on the wagon you wouldn't have the gin,
           either.
FREDDIE   On the wagon?
DOLLY   Doctor's orders.
JOANNE   Was it Spain you were in? I was there last year. In
           Torremolinos.
FREDDIE   Torremolinos!
JOANNE   It wasn't very nice, actually.
FREDDIE   No, Spain definitely is not very nice. Not very nice at
           all. Spain, in fact, is a filthy, brutal, smelly shithole.
           That's what Spain is.
DOLLY   Freddie, for heaven's sake.
FREDDIE   Same goes for Italy, Greece too. The entire bloody
           Mediterranean. And as for North Africa . . . ! One
           great shithole. The *anus mundi*, as we Latin scholars
           have it.
DOLLY   What kept you there so long, then?
FREDDIE   Just the place for me. Islands particularly. Something

about islands. The sea is a great border: you come to it, you have to stop, or . . .

Int. Bedroom—evening.

Cavernous room with peeling wallpaper, ragged curtains.
FREDDIE sitting on the side of the bed, barefoot, speaking on the phone.

FREDDIE . . . She's all right; she's got some sort of business going with ponies—

DEE Ponies?

FREDDIE Yes, Connemara ponies. The Japs and the Germans eat them, apparently.

DEE What—?

FREDDIE (laughs)
No no: they buy them for their kids or something; I don't know.

DEE Listen, I saw your friend Randolph . . .
pause

FREDDIE Yes?

DEE Freddie, someone cut off his ear.

FREDDIE What?

DEE His ear—someone cut it off.
pause
Are you there?

FREDDIE Who did it?

DEE I don't know—Cisco says it was some people he owed money to.
pause
Freddie, you weren't involved with him, were you?

FREDDIE What do you mean, involved with him?

DEE That money—you didn't get it from him, did you?

FREDDIE   What makes you think that?
                pause
DEE   Cisco says . . .
                pause
FREDDIE   Cisco says what?
                pause; silence
            Listen, you tell Cisco to watch himself, or I'll put a
            bunion on his Spanish onion.
                (laughs)
DEE   Are you drunk?
FREDDIE   (laughs)
            Drunk? What do you mean, drunk? Of course I'm
            drunk.
                pause
            Listen, don't worry, everything is going to be fine.
                pause
DEE   (coldly)
            I'll call you tomorrow.

FREDDIE is about to speak when she hangs up. FREDDIE puts the
phone down, sighs, covers his face with his hands.

Later. FREDDIE asleep, sprawled on bed. He starts awake in terror,
stares into the shadows.

FREDDIE   What do you want?! . . .

                    Int. Kitchen—twilight.

FREDDIE enters, barefoot, dishevelled. JOANNE at the range,
cooking dinner. Gin bottle and cup still on table. FREDDIE pours a
drink, knocks it back, groans.

FREDDIE   What time is it?
JOANNE   Nearly nine.

FREDDIE   At night? Christ, and I have a hangover.

Sits down at table, pours another drink.

            Living here, are you?
JOANNE   I'm a sort of dogsbody.
                pause
FREDDIE   Those horses . . .
JOANNE   The ponies?
FREDDIE   Whatever. Do they make money? I mean, is there
            money in them, selling them and so on?
JOANNE   Well, I don't know. I . . .
                pause
FREDDIE   Where's Dolly?
JOANNE   I think she's in the stables.
                pause
            You know she had a stroke?
FREDDIE   Eh?
JOANNE   It wasn't very serious, they said, but . . .

FREDDIE is not really listening.

                Int. Coolgrange—twilight.

FREDDIE, cup in hand, walks through the decrepit rooms. Notices
gaps on the walls where pictures once hung. Frowning, he moves
more quickly from room to room; the same gaps everywhere.

                Int. Stables—twilight.

DOLLY examining a pony's hoof by the light of a bare bulb.
FREDDIE enters, still barefoot.

FREDDIE   Where are the pictures?
DOLLY   What?

Scenes from 'The Book of Evidence: A Screenplay' 241

FREDDIE   The pictures, they're gone off the walls.

            pause

            Tell me they're being cleaned.

DOLLY   They're being cleaned.

FREDDIE   Is that true?

DOLLY   No.

She drops the pony's hoof, moves on to another pony.

FREDDIE   Tell me.

DOLLY   I sold them.

FREDDIE   You sold my pictures—?

            stubs his toe

            Ow! Christ!

DOLLY   *Your* pictures?

FREDDIE   My father meant me to have them. They're my . . .
            my birthright, and my son's—and Van's.

DOLLY   'Your father'—'meant you to have them'—dear God,
            that's a good one. 'Your father'—there's a pair of you
            in it.

            pause

            Your father drank this place dry and then upped and
            died and left me to settle the bill. Do you know how
            much—?

FREDDIE   Don't start all that; I've heard all that before. Just tell
            me what—

DOLLY   I'll tell you—I'll tell you what *you* did. When I was
            here fighting off the bailiffs, *you* were off stravaging
            the world. Did you ever send me a penny? Did you aye!

            pause

            How do you think I managed to hold on to this place?
            How do you think I managed to support you all these
            years?

FREDDIE   What? That was from the estate. Father left me that
           trust thing. Speaking of which—

DOLLY laughs.

DOLLY   'The estate'—that's a good one.
               pause
           He left you *nothing*.
FREDDIE   (astonished)
           The trust . . .
DOLLY   Trust, my eye!
               pause
           You poor eejit, don't you realise *I* was the one that
           supported you, *I* was the one that set up the so-called
           trust. He didn't care a damn about you, or me.
               (laughs)
           Trust! Christ.
               pause as FREDDIE absorbs this
FREDDIE   What did you get for them?
DOLLY   Not much. I went to Charlie French—
FREDDIE   Charlie . . . ? How much, ma?
DOLLY   Fifty thousand.
FREDDIE   There was a Bonnard.
DOLLY   A Bonington, you mean.
FREDDIE   And a Yeats.
DOLLY   A little small drawing.
               pause
           Beggars can't be choosers.
FREDDIE   That bastard.
DOLLY   Who—Charlie? You've a nerve, calling anyone names.
               pause
           Anyway, it's all past and gone.
               (laughs)

And so is the fifty thousand.

They walk out of the stables.

FREDDIE   Listen . . .

DOLLY   It's no good; I told you on the phone, we're broke. No more handouts. You may even have to get a job.

FREDDIE   Where did it go, the fifty thousand?

DOLLY   Into the business—where do you think?

FREDDIE   *What* business?

DOLLY   The ponies! I can't live on air, you know; I had to have something that would bring in a few bob.

    pause

FREDDIE   That girl, what's her name: that stable-girl . . .

DOLLY   Joanne?

FREDDIE   Are you paying her?

DOLLY   Don't you say a word against her, I'm warning you.

FREDDIE   I just—

DOLLY   Not a word. She's like a daughter to me—she's like the son I might as well never have had.

    pause

FREDDIE   Thanks, ma.

(from *The Book of Evidence: A Screenplay*, circa 1991)

Manuscript pages from
'The Book of Evidence'

JOHN BANVILLE

These hitherto unpublished workings lead on from those events played out in the preceding screenplay extracts, and correspond to pp. 106–13 of the novel.

Freddie's hopes of wheedling an advance on his patrimony from his widowed mother are dashed when it turns out that she has been compelled to dispose of (and for a paltry sum) the family's art collection, much of which now hangs on the walls of Whitewater House, Helmut Behrens' Palladian manor. It is there where Freddie first glimpses the work of the anonymous master that so beguiles him, Portrait of a Woman with Gloves, *and resolves to steal it. In the course of a farcically bungled theft, the Behrenses' ill-fated maid, Josie Bell, makes her second, and last, appearance. Freddie absconds with her and the painting in his hired Humber Hawk, in wide-eyed view of Whitewater's day-trippers (the 'watchers at the window') and their bus driver.*

Banville's penmanship and the fastidiousness of his writing methods (there are no erasures to be conjectured, nor any strikethroughs; rejected words or phrases are neatly square-bracketed) obviate the need for any gloss or notation of the transcribed pages en face.

Again, grateful acknowledgement is made both to the author and to Bernard Meehan, Keeper of Manuscripts at Trinity College, Dublin, for permission to reproduce in facsimile these manuscript pages (TCD MS 10252/9/2/15, folios 87–93).

I started the engine with difficulty, [and made] making the gears shriek. In my
agitation I kept getting ahead of myself and having to go back and
[begin the] repeat the simplest actions.] fumbling and snorting. The gears
shrieked. In my agitation I kept getting ahead of myself, and had to go
back and repeat [things] the simplest actions, fumbling and snorting.
The steering wheel was burning hot from the sun, and there was a glare
on the windscreen. [I let out the clutch too quickly and the car leaped
forward like a lumbering predator.] When I got off the grass on to the
drive I let out the clutch too quickly [and] so that we travelled the first few
yards in a series of bone-shaking [leaps and] lurches, the bonnet going up
and down like the prows of a [boat] ship in a storm, and the springs grunting.
The watchers at the window must have been in fits. [The maid was
wrenching at the door handle, I roared at her and she stopped.] The
maid was scrabbling at the door handle, I roared at her to stop. We [came
reached the gate, and when I slowed down I saw the maid scrabbling at
the door handle, I roared at her to stop. At last I recognised/identified
that civet smell: it was the smell of fear, hers, and mine. I turned around
to threaten her. She was crouched [in the seat] as before, [with her back] pressed into
the [seat] corner, tense and glaring, [vibrating [in fury and terror] [like a
[cornered] trapped cat.] I could almost feel her nerve-ends vibrating in the air
between us. [The bus driver was still sitting in the sun, when she saw
him she began to wind the window down. I shouted at her again, and
spun the wheel and whizzed off up the road. [It seemed to me] I had

I started the engine with difficulty, [and ^{making} made the gears shriek. In my
agitation I kept getting ahead of myself and having to go back and
[begin the] repeat the simplest actions.] fumbling and snarling. The gears
shrieked. In my agitation I kept getting ahead of myself, and had to go
back and repeat [things] the simplest actions, fumbling and snarling.
The steering wheel was burning hot from the sun, and there was a glare
on the windscreen. [I let out the clutch too quickly and the car leaped
forward like a lumbering predator] When I got off the grass on to the
drive I let out the clutch too quickly [and] ^{so that} we travelled the first few
yards in a series of bone-shaking [leaps and] lurches, the bonnet going up
and down like the prow of a ^{ship} boat in a storm and the springs grunting.
The watchers at the window must have been in fits. [The maid was
wrenching at the door handle, I roared at her and she stopped] The
maid was scrabbling at the door handle, I roared at her to stop. We [came]
reached the gate, and when I slowed down I saw the maid scrabbling at
the door handle, I roared at her to stop. At last I recognised/identified
that civit-smell; it was the smell of fear, hers, and mine. I turned around
to threaten her. She was crouched [in the seat] ^{as before,} [with her back] pressed into
the [seat] ^{corner,} tense and glaring, [vibrating [in fury and terror] [like a
[cornered] trapped cat] I could almost feel her nerve-ends vibrating in the air
between us. [The bus driver was still sitting in the sun, when she saw
him she began to wind the window down. I shouted at her again, and
spun the wheel and whizzed off up the road. [It seemed to me] I had

                              before
never/ felt another's presence with such [immediacy]/raw force. I could not
speak. At last I recognised/ identified that thin, metallic stench: it was
the sweet stink of fear, hate, and mine. [Yet still]It was not she I
was confronting, an ordinary (young)woman with mousey hair and [work-
hardened hands, [I might have been confronting a wild animal.] but something
that had leaped out of her at me. I might have been face to face
with a wild animal.] but something that [had come] leaping out [from
deep inside her.[from her very core] And the same something in me
[leaped out too] sprang forth too] but something that [had] leaped
out of her, some [nameless[essential] essence]essential, nameless thing.
Its thin part was in me, it sprang forth too,[I could feel it, yearning
towards her, with fangs bared] red and terrible, with fangs bared.] enraged and
anguished, I could feel it, yearning towards her, spitting, with fangs bared.
I [drove on] turned back hurriedly and started up the engine again. [The
wheel was slimed with my sweat. I did not dare look in the mirror.
I drove off out shakily into the road.][It was no good. That other
version of [myself] was still] Outside the window there was a pine wood, I
could feel the darkness [there under the boughs, the silence] out there, to silence.
She pummeled my shoulder with her fists, got a hand around and tried
to claw my eyes. The car was going all over the road. I pulled into the
verge and stopped, she almost tossed over the seat into my lap. I
turned to her. I had the hammer in my hand. I looked at it. [
[had] She coughed, and removed a strand of hair from her lips.

never ^{*before*} *felt another's presence with such [immediacy.]* ^{*and*} *raw force. I could not*
speak. At last I recognised/identified that thin, metallic ^{*smell*} *stink: it was*
the civet-stink of fear, hers, and mine. [Yet still] It was not she I
was confronting, an ordinary [young] woman with mousey hair and ^{*bad skin*} *[work-*
hardened hands, [[I might have been confronting a wild animal.] but something
that had leaped out of her at me. I might have been face to face
with a wild animal.] but something that [had ^{*leaped*} *come leaping] out* ^{*at*} *from*
deep inside her. [from her very core.] And the same something in me
[leaped out too] sprang forth too] but something that [had] leaped
out of her, some [nameless [[essential] essence] essential, nameless thing.
Its twin part was in me, it sprang forth too, [I could feel it, yearning
towards her, with fangs bared/red and terrible, with fangs bared.] enraged and
anguished, I could feel it, yearning [towards] ^{*out at*} *her, spitting, with fangs bared.*
I [drove on] turned back hurriedly and started up the engine again. [The
wheel was slimed with my sweat. I did not dare look in the mirror.
I drove ~~on~~. *out shakily into the road.] [It was no good. That other*
version of [myself] ^{*me*} *was still] Outside the window there was a pine wood, I*
could feel the darkness [there, under the boughs, the silence.] out there, the silence.
She pummeled my shoulder with her fists, got a hand around and tried
to claw my eyes. The car was going all over the road. I pulled into the
verge and stopped, and she about tumbled over the seat into my lap. I
turned to her. I had the hammer in my hand. I looked at it, startled. [I
[had] She coughed, and removed a strand of hair from her lips.

You must let me go, she said, or you will be in trouble.

[The first time I struck her I expected ^to feel the^ a sharp, clean
crack of ^steel^ metal on bone, but it was more like batting clay, or
putty.] [The word fontanel came into my mind.]

It is difficult to wield a hammer in a motor car, but I swept.
I had thought — if it can be called anything like thinking — that one
good blow would do it, but they are a hardy race, and do not die
easily. The autopsy would find that she had a remarkably [heavy]
strong skull — even in that, you see, she was unlucky. [Perhaps I would
have stopped after that first blow if she had not flung herself at
me across the back of the seat, clawing and (?) I was amazed.
I pushed her back, and swung the hammer sideways, and hit her
on the temple.] The first blow fell just above the hairline over
her right eye.] There was not much blood, just a dark-red glistening
^depression^ patch with matted hair. She was sitting upright, swaying a little, and
staring at me with eyes that would not focus properly those eerie
pale blue eyes which [I still] stare at me ^still^ out of the darkness [of]^of my dreams^ at
my nights, every night, every night. or Perhaps I would have stopped
then, if she had not suddenly [with a sort of low, guttural moan,]
flung herself at me ^[over?]^ across the back of the seat with a sort of large
[guttural] moan, punching and scratching, and making a sort of moaning,
rattling noise deep in her throat. I was [[amazed] astonished, and deeply
dismayed] amazed] dismayed. [A ^heavy^ sense of the unfairness of things]

You must let me go, she said, or you will be in trouble,
The first time I struck her I expected ^{to feel the} *sharp, clean*
crack of metal ^{steel} *on bone, but it was more like hitting clay, or*
putty.   *[The word fontanel came into my mind.]*

    It is difficult to wield a hammer in a motor car, but I managed.
I had thought—if it can be called anything like thinking—that one
good blow would do it, but they are a hardy race, and do not die
easily. The autopsy would find that she had a remarkably [heavy]
strong skull—even in that, you see, she was unlucky. [Perhaps I would
have stopped after that first blow if she had not flung herself at
me across the back of the seat, clawing and [?] I was amazed.
I pushed her back, and swung the hammer sideways, and hit her
on the temple.] [The first blow fell just above the hairline over
her right eye.] There was not much blood, just a dark-red glistening
patch ^{depression} *with matted hair. She was sitting upright, swaying a little, and*
staring at me with eyes that would not focus properly—those eerie
pale-blue eyes which [I still] stare at me ^{still} *out of the darkness* ^{of my dreams} *[of] at*
my nights, every night, every night. Perhaps I would have stopped
then, if she had not suddenly [with a sort of low, guttural moan,]
flung herself at me across ^[over] *the back of the* ^{my} *seat with a sort of low[,]*
[guttural] moan, punching and scratching, and making a sort of moaning,
rattling noise deep in her throat. I was [[amazed] astonished, and deeply
dismayed] amazed] dismayed. [A ^{heavy} *sense of the unfairness of things]*

[The seat where she had sat was drenched]

[It was all so unfair, all this.] [I felt a surge pity for myself.] I felt [A thick hot [surge] sweep of self-pity.] I felt sorry for myself. It was all so unfair, all this. I pushed her back, and swung the hammer [sideways] [backhand] and caught her on the right temple. [All at once I had a sense of the unfairness of [things] everything, and bitter tears rose to my eyes. [The force of the blow flung her against the door] She [slumped] was thrown against the door, and her head struck the window. A fine thread of blood [came] from her left nostril [and] ran across her cheek. There was blood on the window too, a spray of tiny drops. She closed her eyes, and gave a sort of low, guttural moan. [I struck her again, just as she [put up a hand] [was putting] up a hand to her head] Just as she was putting a hand to her head I struck her again, and hit her on the fingers, I heard one of them crack. Oh! she said, and [abruptly], as if [something] all her bones had suddenly] suddenly, as if everything inside her had suddenly collapsed, she slithered to the floor. A period of silence followed. [I could hear [my own harsh breathing] myself breathe, a harsh, [heavy sound] laboured sound]

There was silence. I opened the door and got out, and stood a moment, breathing. [For a moment I was dizzy] I expected to see [the tour bus, and] the gates of Whitewater, and the tour bus, and the driver running towards me, [I thought I had driven only a little way up the road] but [instead] [I was in the midst of a pine wood] the road [ran away] in both directions [ran between] was empty, and

[The seat where she had sat was drenched]
[It was all so unfair, all this.] *[I felt a surge pity for myself.]* I felt A thick
hot *[surge]* sweep *of self-pity.]* I felt sorry for myself. It was all so unfair, all
this. I pushed her back, and swung the hammer *[sideways]* [backhand] *and caught
her on the right temple. [All at once I had a sense of the unfairness
of [things] everything, and bitter tears rose to my eyes. [The force of the
blow flung her against the door]* She was thrown *[slumped against the door, and
her head struck the window. A fine thread of blood [came] from her
left nostril [and] ran across her cheek. There was blood on the window
too, a spray of tiny drops. She closed her eyes, and gave a sort of
low, guttural moan. [I struck her again, just as she [put up a hand]
[was putting] up] a hand to* her *head] Just as she was putting a hand to
her head I struck her again, and hit her on the fingers, I heard one
of them crack. Oh! she said, and [abruptly, as if [something,] all her
bones had suddenly] suddenly, as if everything inside her had suddenly
collapsed, she slithered* on *to the floor. A period of silence followed. [I
could hear [my own harsh breathing] myself breathe, a harsh, [heavy sound,]
laboured sound,]*

    *There was silence. I opened the door and got out, and stood
a moment, breathing. [For a moment I was dizzy] I expected to see
[the tour bus, and] the gates of Whitewater, and the tour bus, and
the driver running towards me, [I thought I had driven only a little
way up the road] but [instead] [I was in the midst of a pine wood]
the road [ran away] in both directions [ran between] was empty, and*

I had no idea where I was. On one side a [wooded] hill rose steeply, and on the other there was a [dense wall of] pine [trees] wood It all looked distinctly improbable, like [scenery] a hastily painted backdrop, especially that grand, blue distance, and the road winding away. I [and I was] still [holding] had the hammer in my hand. [I [walked to the other side and] flung it, [away] with a grand sweep [of my arm] far, far out over the [pine tops] blue pine tops. It was an [oddly] thrilling act] With a grand sweep of my arm I flung it from me, and watched [in a kind of rapture, as it flew in a thrilling arc far, far out over the blue pine tops] as it flew in a thrilling arc, far slowly tumbling end over end, far out [of] over the blue pine tops. [Then I knelt abruptly in the ditch and vomited up [the Recks] the [multicoloured] remains of [the Recks [fried] breakfast] the breakfast that Ma Reck had fed me, an age ago, in another world.] Then I bent over abruptly and vomited up the remains of the breakfast that Ma Reck had served to me, an age ago, in another world.

[When I got back behind the wheel]

I crawled back [into the car, [again, without looking into the back] keeping my eyes averted from that bundle flying behind the seat] wedged down between the seats. Blood has a thick, warm smell. I wanted to open the windows, but somehow I felt this world expose me to thy world. [When I looked through the windscreen the light was a splintered blur.] The windscreen was a blur of splintered light, I thought for a second it was

I had no idea where I was. On one side a [wooded] hill rose

steeply, and on the other there was a [dense wall of] pine [trees] wood

It all looked distinctly improbable, like [scenery] a hastily painted

backdrop, especially that grand, blue distance, and the road winding

away. I found I [was] still [holding] had the hammer in my hand. [I

[walked to the other side and] flung it, [away] with a grand sweep, [of my

arm] far, far out over the [pine-tops] blue pine-tops. It was a[n oddly]

thrilling act] With a grand sweep of my arm I flung it from me, and

watched[, in a kind of rapture, as it flew in a thrilling arc far,

far out over the blue pine tops.] as it flew in a thrilling arc, [far

slowly tumbling end over end, far out of *over the blue pine tops.*

[Then I knelt abruptly in the ditch and vomited up [Ma Reck's] the

multicoloured] remains of [Ma Reck's [fried] hearty breakfast.] the breakfast that Ma

Reck had fed me, an age ago, in another world.] Then I bent over

abruptly and vomited up the remains of the breakfast that Ma

Reck had served to me, an age ago, in another world.

[When I got back behind the wheel]

I crawled back into the car, [again, without looking into the back] keeping

my eyes averted from that bundle [lying behind the seat] wedged down

between the seats. Blood has a thick, warm smell. I wanted to open the

windows, but somehow I felt this would expose me to the world. [When I

looked through the windscreen the light was a splintered blur.] The

windscreen was a blur of splintered light, I thought for a second it was gurgled. Until I put a hand to my face and discovered I was weeping. [This I found encouraging.] It was not just that my tears seemed were a pretoken of remorse. My tears seemed not just a pretoken of remorse. but of some more common, simple urge thing, an affect for I had no name, but which was might be my last and most important link with [the community of men.] a world from which i had excluded myself. For everything was changed, where I was now I had never been before. I trembled, and [my hands shook,] all around me trembled, and there was a [sticky sluggish [sense] feeling [in]] sluggish, sticky feel to things, as if I and all [the rest had just this moment struggled [out of] [blindly into existence] out of the slime.] out of an enveloping membrane. I had not known it was possible to be alive and still feel so alone and lost.] these objects, that this car, the road, those distant meadows, as if we had all a moment past struggled blind and amazed [out of] through an enveloping membrane] out of a hole in the air. and all [the rest of] this, car, road, those distant mountains, as if we had all [just] this moment struggled [mute] [blind] and amazed out of a hole in the air. [I drove [slowly] along the middle of the road in second gear.] [I turned the key [carefully] in the ignition, [carful] [cautiously I turned the key in the ignition, convinced that, instead of the engine starting, something [would] [spill out of the [bonnet] dashboard over my legs] come gushing out over my legs from under the dashboard.] else would happen, that there would be a sudden, terrible [clamour, or] noise, or a flash of light, or that stuff, [would

smashed, until I put a hand to my face and discovered I was weeping.
[This I found encouraging.] [It was not just that my tears seemed/were a
foretoken of remorse] My tears seemed not just a foretoken of remorse,
but of some ^more common, simple thing, ^urge, an affect for I had no name, but which
was/might be my last and most important link with [the community of
men.] a world from which I had excluded myself. For everything was changed,
where I was now I had not ^never been before. I trembled, and [my hands shook,]
all around me trembled, and there was a [sticky sluggish [sense] feeling [in]]
sluggish, sticky feel to things, as if I and all ~~every~~ the rest had ^around me just this
moment struggled [[out of] [blindly into existence.] out of the slime.]
out of an enveloping membrane. I had not known it was possible to
be alive and ^still feel so alone| and lost.] these objects, ~~that~~ this car,
that road, those distant meadows, as if we had all a moment past
struggled blind and amazed [[out of] through an enveloping membrane.]
out of a hole in the air.] and all [the rest of] this, car, road,
those distant mountains, as if we had all ^of that [just this moment struggled
mute [blind] and amazed out of a hole in the air. [I drove [down] ^along the middle
of the road in second gear.] [I turned the key fearfully in the ignition,
fearful] Cautiously I turned the key in the ignition, convinced that,
instead of the engine starting, something, [would [spill out of the [bonnet]
dashboard over my legs] come gushing out over my legs from under
the dashboard.] else would happen, that there would be a sudden,
terrible [clamour, or] noise, or a flash of light, or that stuff, [would

some sort of [?] liquid, would come gushing out over my legs from under the dashboard. I wanted to open the window, but did not dare, I was afraid of what would come in, [not hard] [all outside looked like glair.] the light outside looked like glair, I imagined it in my mouth, my nostrils. | mean

I did not know where I was going, I was not going anywhere. Whitewater is, what, twenty miles from the city, but it took me hours to get there. I must have driven in circles, round and round those back roads. [I do not remember much] Of the journey I remember little. That is to say, I do not remember covering distances. [but] I do see myself [, perfectly clearly, sitting there (?clutching the wheel] sitting in a kind of crystal bubble, drifting soundlessly through a strange, sunlit landscape. [for all I know I may have kept [at] a steady seventy miles an hour] I think I went very fast, for I [have an impression of speed,] recall a sensation of pressure, [in my ears] [of a] and a dull, rushing blare. I must have driven in circles, round and round those narrow country roads. Then there were houses, and housing estates, and straggling factories, and supermarkets big as aircraft hangers. I stared through the windscreen in dreamy amazement. I might have been a traveller from the far side of the universe, unable to believe how much like home everything [looked] was] looked, and yet how different it was. I did not know where I was going, I mean I was not going anywhere. It was almost peaceful / restful, sailing along like that, with one hand on the wheel, far

some sort of [?] liquid, would come gushing out over my legs
from under the dashboard. I wanted to open the window, but did
not dare, I was afraid of what would come in, [not wind] [all
outside looked like glair.] the light outside looked like glair, I
imagined it in my mouth, my nostrils.

     I did not know where I was going, I was ^{I mean} *not going anywhere.*
Whitewater is, what, twenty miles from the city, but it took me hours
to get there. I must have driven in circles, round and round those
back roads. [I do not remember much] Of the journey I remember
little. That is to say, I do not remember covering distances. [but] I do
see myself[, perfectly clearly, sitting there(,) clutching the wheel] sitting in
a kind of crystal bubble, drifting soundlessly through a strange, sunlit
landscape. [For all I know I may have kept [at] ^{up} *a steady seventy miles*
an hour] I think I went very fast, for I [have an impression of speed,]
recall a sensation of pressure, [in my ears] [of a] and a dull, rushing
blare. I must have driven in circles, round and round those narrow
country roads. Then there were houses and housing estates, and straggling
factories, and supermarkets big as aircraft hangers. I stared through the
windscreen in dreamy amazement. I might have been a ^{lost voyager} *traveller from the*
                                                            ^
far side of the universe, unable to believe how much like home everything
[looked] was] looked, and yet how different it was. I did not know
where I was going, I mean I was not going anywhere. It was almost
peaceful/restful, sailing along like that, with one hand on the wheel, far

from everything. At the first [red light] set of lights that were against
me, drifted [to a [stop [as if it were settling] with a sigh [of brakes]
as if it [were settling on a bed of air) gently to a stop as if were
subsiding on air. It was [a suburban crossing, [one of those) at the
junction of two quiet suburban roads. To the left there was a little green
rise with a chestnut tree and a neat row of new houses. [A child
was riding a tricycle on the [side pavement.] Children were playing on the
grass, and [there was]a toddler [on a tricycle] was riding a tricycle
along the pavement. Dogs gambolled. The sun shone.] I have always had a
secret [love] for [scenes] such [as this, the [unregarded spots as this.] quiet spots
like this, the [unregarded] backwaters of human endeavour. [repositories of
hope and love] [and] yet cherished [backgrounds] where people build
and tend] [scenes of commonplace life.] (the) unremarked yet cherished
scenes of [building and] doing and tending. I sat [with my hands folded
in my lap, musing, watching the children at play. The lights changed
to green without my noticing. I was not really there, but lost [somewhere]
in some [unspecified] sunlit corner of my own childhood. There was a
knock on the window beside me, I jumped. A woman with a broad
face — she reminded of my mother — was looking in at me and saying
something. I rolled down the window. I could not understand her, she
was talking about an accident, and asking if I was all right. Then
she looked past me, and opened her mouth. Oh, the poor child, she said.
I turned my head, it seemed to turn with extraordinary slowness, like a

from everything. At the first [red light] set of lights that were against

me the car drifted [to a [stop as if it were settling] with a sigh [of brakes]

as if it [were settling on a bed of air] gently to a stop as if were

subsiding on air. It was [a suburban crossing, [one of those] at the

junction of two quiet suburban roads. To the left there was a little green

rise with a chestnut tree and a neat row of new houses. [A child

was riding a tricycle on the [side] pavement.] Children were playing on the

grass, and [there was] a toddler [on a tricycle] was riding a tricycle

along the pavement. Dogs gambolled. The sun shone. I have always harboured had a

secret [love] fondness for [scenes] places such [as this, the] unregarded spots as this,] quiet spots

like such as this, the [unregarded] unremarked [backwaters of human endeavour.] [repositories of

hope and love] [and] yet cherished [[backgrounds] places— where people build

and tend] scenes of commonplace life.] [the] unremarked yet cherished

scenes sites of building and doing and tending. I sat now with my hands folded

in my lap, smiling, watching the children at play. The lights changed

to green without my noticing. I was not really there, but lost [somewhere]

in some [unspecified] vague sunlit corner of my own childhood. There was a

knock on the window beside me, I jumped. A woman with a large broad

face—she reminded of my mother—was looking in at me and saying

something. I rolled down the window. I could not understand her, she

was talking about an accident, and asking if I was all right. Then

she looked past me, and opened her mouth. Oh, the poor child, she said.

I turned my head, it seemed to turn with extraordinary slowness, like a great stone ball on a swivel. [There was blood everywhere, I had never seen so much blood. She had dragged herself [up from [between] behind the seat] upright, and was kneeling on the floor [with an elbow] In the back now there was blood everywhere, it seemed more than just one person could have] far too much for just one person to have shed, and for a mad moment, in which [even] [a] hope] a /spark of crafty hope flared and faded, I wondered if [there had been] indeed [an accident] some sort of crash, which I had not noticed [or had forgotten], [some terrible pile-up, with bodies and blood flung] [if something had run into the back of the car] [if [there had been] some terrible pile-up [behind me which] had occurred behind me in which only the back of the car had been involved [with bodies and blood flung everywhere]. I heard myself muttering something about her being dead. But she was not dead. She had struggled up, and was kneeling with her back to the window. Her hair hung down [over] her face [in] bloodied ropes. The woman [beside me [was talking to me still] beside me was gabbling about telephones and ambulances. I turned to her angrily, smarting my eyes. Newton, I said— the words like a[...] below my voice as cultured and authoritative, bless her— will you please get on about your business!

I had not gone more than a mile when an ambulance suddenly appeared behind me, [its siren going and blue lights flashing] going like mad, with [its] siren blaring and blue lights flashing. I kept going, [the thing overtook me] and the thing drew alongside [me] and

great stone ball on a swivel. [There was blood everywhere, I had never
seen so much blood. She had dragged herself [up from [between]
behind the seat] upright, and was kneeling on the floor [with a
elbow] In the back now there was blood everywhere, it seemed [more
than just one person could have] far too much for just one person to
have shed, and for a mad moment, in which [[even] hope] a ^crafty^ *spark of*
crafty hope flared and faded, I wondered if (there had been) indeed) [an
accident] some sort of crash, which I had not noticed, ^or had forgotten^ *[some terrible*
pile-up, with bodies and blood flung] [if something had run into the
back of the car] if [there had been] some terrible pile-up [behind me
which] had occurred behind me in which only the back of the car
had been involved [with bodies and blood flung everywhere]. I heard myself
muttering something about her being dead. But she was not dead. She had
struggled up, and was kneeling with her hands to the window. Her
hair hung down [over her face] in bloodied ropes. The woman [outside [was
talking to me still] beside me was gabbling about telephones and
ambulances. I turned to her angrily, shutting my eyes. Madam, I said—
she would later describe my voice as cultured and authoritative, bless her—
will you please get on about your business!

I had not gone more than a mile when an ambulance
suddenly appeared behind me, [its siren going and blue lights flashing.]
going like mad, with [its] siren blaring and blue lights flashing. I kept
going, [The thing overtook me] and the thing drew alongside, [me] and

the fellow in it, a young man with a coarse red face, signalled to me to follow. I was dreadfully confused [surely that horror could not have had time to summon] How had it arrived so quickly? [later I would learn that it was entirely fortuitous] In fact, as I would later learn, [its appearance] it had [stumbled] come upon on me by [accident] chance) a grotesque coincidence] one of those grotesque coincidences in which this tale abounds, and which have [coloured the] touched the whole [thing] affair with a lurid, comic glow. I kept going, I think, I could not have stopped, [even if I had tried] petrified as I was with [by now] [going] fright. [and] It was returning from— yes! — from the scene of a car crash, with a dying woman in the back. The ambulance drew alongside, trumpeting like a [thing] elite angry animal, and the fellow in the passenger seat, [an elderly [person] [fellow] in a cap, gaped at the [bloodied] blood-smeared windows) a burly young man [with] in shirt-sleeves, with mottled red arms and [a] [long] narrow sideburns, gaped at the blood-streaked window beside me, He spoke to the driver, (pointing) and then made a complicated set of signals, nodding at me encouragingly. They thought I was a doctor, you see, on my way from the same accident. They shot ahead [of me. Why do ambulances always look, from the rear, as if they are sweeping the ground?] I followed in their wake, [my eyes fixed] clutching this big square thing trundling along, shooting up dust and rolling [fatly] on its springs. Then abruptly it braked, and swung into a wide gateway, and an hand appeared out of the side window and

the fellow in it, a young man with a coarse red face, signalled to me
to follow. I was dreadfully confused [surely that woman could not have
had time to summon] How had it arrived so quickly? [Later I would
learn that it was entirely fortuitous] In fact, as I would later learn,
[its appearance] it had [stumbled] come upon on me by [[accident] chance] a
grotesque coincidence] one of those grotesque coincidences in which this
case abounds, and which have [coloured the] touched the whole [thing]
affair with a lurid, comic glow. I kept going, I think I could not
have stopped, [even if I had tried] petrified as I was by now with panic fright. [and]
It was returning from—yes!—from the scene of a car crash, with a
dying woman in the back. The ambulance drew alongside, trumpeting like
a [huge] large white angry animal, and the fellow in the passenger seat, [an
elderly[, ferrety] pointy [fellow] in a cap, gaped at the [bloodshed] blood
smeared windows] a burly young man [with] in shirt-sleeves, with
mottled red arms and [a] [long] narrow sideburns, gaped at the blood-
streaked window beside me, He spoke to the driver, [pointing,] and then
made a complicated set of signals, nodding at me encouragingly.
They thought I was a doctor, you see, on my way from the same accident.
They shot ahead [of me. Why do ambulances always look, from the
rear, as if they are sweeping the ground?] I followed in their wake,
[watching] [my eyes fixed] this big square thing scudding along, whooshing up dust and
rolling fatly on its springs. Then abruptly it braked, and swung into
a wide gateway, and an hand arm appeared out of the side window and

[waved] beckoned me to follow. [Perhaps it was the sight of that fat arm] [But already I was past the gate, [hurtling down] I drove on, past the gate, plunging the pedal to the floor, and the sound of the siren dwindled behind me, to a mournful plaint, and I was free again. A kind of manic laughter bubbled up inside me.

She was slumped on the back seat, [moaning, trying to speak] her head hanging, her hands resting at her sides,

Suddenly the sea was on my left, far below. I went down a [enormous] steep hill, then along a straight level road beside railway tracks. A white hotel, [turreted] castellated, with pennants flying, rose up on my right, enormous, mad, and empty. The road [ended] came to an end in a marshy patch of scrub and thistles, and here I stopped, [finally, as if it were the destination I had been] in the midst of a vast and final silence. I could hear her behind, breathing. [I wanted to turn and abase myself before her and cry out sorry, sorry, oh, I am so sorry!] When I turned to her she lifted her [sibyl's] head, droopily and looked at me. [with a kind of weary] Help me, she [said] whispered, help me, and a babble of blood burst in her mouth. What did I feel? [I cannot remember feeling anything, [except]] Remorse, fear, a terrible — [no, no that's a lie] but no, I must not lie. I cannot remember feeling anything, except still that sense of strangeness, of being in a place I recognised but did not know. I got out of the car, and felt giddy for a moment, and had to lean against the door with my eyes shut.

[waved] beckoned me to follow. [Perhaps it was the sight of the fat arm]
[But already I was past the gate, [hurtling down] I drove on, past the
gate, plunging the pedal to the floor, and the sound of the siren
dwindled behind me, ^{to} a mournful plaint, and I was free again. A
kind of manic laughter bubbled up inside me.

She was slumped on the back seat, [moaning, trying to speak.]
her head hanging, her hands resting at her sides.

Suddenly the sea was on my left, far below. I went down
a [narrow] *steep* hill, then along a straight cement road beside railway
tracks. A white hotel, [turreted] castellated, with pennants flying, rose up
on my right, enormous, mad, and empty. The road [ended] came to an
end in a *marshy* patch of scrub and thistles, and here I stopped, [finally, as
if it were the destination I had been] in the midst of a vast and final
silence. I could hear her behind, breathing. [I wanted to turn and
abase myself before her and cry out sorry, sorry, oh, I am so sorry!]
When I turned to her she lifted her sibyl's head *slowly* and looked at me.
[with a kind of weary] Help me, she [said] whispered, help me, and
a bubble of blood burst in her mouth. What did I feel? [I cannot
remember feeling anything. [except]] Remorse, fear, a terrible—[no,
no that's a lie] but no, I must not lie. I cannot remember feeling
anything, except still that sense of strangeness, of being in a place I
recognised but did not know. I got out of the car, and felt giddy for
a moment, and had to lean against the door with my eyes shut.

[The sleeve of my jacket was stained with blood] My jacket was bloodstained , I wriggled out of it and flung it [on the ground] away, into the bushes. They never found it, I wonder why. I remembered the pullover in the boot, and put it on. It smelled of axle-grease and sweat. Something was falling on me : [I stared about me and suddenly realized that "it was rain] a delicate, silent fall of rain, [looked up in the glistening sunlight] sparkling] I looked up in the glistening sunlight. [and saw a smear of cloud] There was a smear of cloud directly above me. [Then I turned and walked swiftly away, and was a long way off when I remembered the picture, lying face-down in the boot] Who had sent this gentle benison ? The thought came to me: I am not human. Then I turned and walked away.

29. X. 87

[The sleeve of my jacket was stained with blood] My jacket was
bloodstained, I wriggled out of it and flung it [[on the ground] away,]
into the bushes. They never found it, I wonder why. I remembered the
pullover in the boot, and put it on. It smelled of axle-grease and
sweat. Something was falling on me: [I stared about me and suddenly
realised that it was rain] a delicate, silent fall of rain, [looked up
in the glistening sunlight] sparkling] I looked up in the glistening
sunlight. [and saw a smear of cloud] There was a smear of cloud
directly above me. [Then I turned and walked swiftly away, and was
a long way off when I remembered the picture, lying face-down in
the boot] Who had sent this gentle benison? The thought came to me:
I am not human. Then I turned and walked away.

29.x.87

Appendix

List of Emendations

There follows a record of the more substantive emendations made by the author to the first edition of *The Book of Evidence*, and which have been adopted for this revised, anniversary edition. The rejected reading of the copy-text (that is, the first edition) appears to the left of the square bracket. The page and line numbers which precede these rejected readings and their emendations are those for this revised volume. (Example: 5:1 denotes page 5, line 1 of the present edition.) As mentioned in 'A Note on the Text', em dashes have been favoured over the en dashes used throughout in the original edition as published by Martin Secker & Warburg Limited in 1989.

5:1   lord] Lord
5:14   guard] Guard
7:16   *battenberg*] *Battenberg*
7:27   honour] Honour
8:2   worship] Worship
8:19   sidle up to] approach
14:13 punch] Punch
15:11 *guardia*] *Guardia*
17:14 masterbuilder] master builder
19:5   concision] conciseness
19:21 in his teeth] between his teeth
19:29 broad soles] broad-rimmed soles

20:16 with this one's hands, and that one's eyes, and yet
       another's sobs] with this one's hands and that one's eyes
       and yet another's sobs
21:31 sucking a wooden spoon] sucking on a wooden spoon
22:10 a sleek bored old cat] a sleek, bored old cat
22:25 The child, who] The infant, which
25:9   That peasant] The *campesino*
28:7   handmade] expensive
31:7   a large, a gargantuan gin and tonic] a large, a gargantuan,
       gin and tonic
32:11 pleasantly, almost voluptuously vulnerable] pleasantly,
       almost voluptuously, vulnerable
33:7   he was my friend, and –] he was my friend, and—
33:29 still queasily smiling] still smiling uneasily
37:31 lordship] Lordship
40:2   toward] towards
44:8   around] round
45:32 after a moment] and after a moment
47:23 regard] weight
49:4   with that grin. You can think] with that grin—you can
       think
51:9   grey] pale
52:7   parboiled] boiled
57:28 out the window] out of the window
59:5   distrait] distraite
60:28 an impressive volume of mathematical theory] an
       impressive volume on mathematical theory
63:9   calvados] Calvados
65:24 attending at a ritual disrobing] attending a ritual disrobing
68:28 white] blue
72:23 frowning importantly] frowning
73:28 large deserted places] and large deserted places

83:4   thinking of, I fumbled] thinking of, but I fumbled
84:11 the dreamy housewives] dreamy housewives
84:14 walking] trotting
87:1   in a corner] into a corner
88:30 dripped] spread
88:31 passed over] passed across
91:5   —what is the word—] —what is the word?—
95:14 out the windows] out of the windows
95:22 like this] just like that
95:31 to see him] to see him there
96:11 for her to see] for her to see, not once
104:24 flayed alive in here] flayed in here
104:32 do it] do it!
108:6 sweep] curve
110:2 aircraft hangers] aircraft hangars
113:11 smear] smudge
117:2 disturbed] feeling disturbed
117:24 sergeant] Sergeant
119:13 discoloured wads] and discoloured wads
120:11 why it was so deserted there?] why the place was so
       deserted?
120:28 a for-sale sign] a For Sale sign
121:14 queasy] uneasy
122:1 in a dreamy detachment] in dreamy detachment
122:5 a caution] an official caution
122:9 that would take] that had taken
122:14 loon] waxwork model of myself
122:16 something] wrongdoing
122:22 nursing] tending
124:1 went to the pub] went back to the pub
124:8 I needed to make] and that I needed to make
124:10 he'd heard] he had heard

125:13 leer] laugh

126:25 trouser pocket] trousers pocket

131:5 and I shut my eyes tight] and shut my eyes tight

132:18 since I got up] since I had got up

133:12 out the front-door] out at the front door

133:25 all out there] out there

134:18 dangerous] untrustworthy

134:19 a great, gaunt, shadowy place] a great gaunt shadowy place

135:3 unlock] break into

135:8 reverently] carefully

135:17 my face] half of my face

135:24 if the gas] and if the gas

135:26 tombal] steamy

136:7 garbage bag] rubbish bag

137:17 a large, square, lofty room] a large square lofty room

138:29 what did they say exactly] and what did they say exactly

138:31 talked] had talked

139:14 into the shop, my stomach wobbled] into the shop. My stomach wobbled

140:11 she was wearing] for she was wearing

141:16 for so long, sometimes, that I forgot] for so long that sometimes I forgot

142:32 and she] and Josie Bell

145:1 Pommerol] Pomerol

148:14 with a cigarette] with yet another cigarette

149:9 glistening] gleaming

149:10 the sun shining in my face] the sun in my face

149:15 I could hear the blood] I could feel the blood

154:15 metal] precious metal

155:5 clutching his coat around him] clutching his coat about him

155:26 a quick look around him] a quick look up and down the street

157:15 avid] eager

157:29 smeared on the sky] trembling in the sky

162:1 the oak wood] an oak wood

163:6 on my forehead] on to my forehead

164:16 come back] return

165:5 the big, gaunt drawing-room] the big gaunt drawing room

166:31 a scrubbed, eager, slightly anxious air] an eager, slightly anxious air

168:16 extravagant waiterly flourishes] extravagant, waiterly flourishes

171:10 of course, they were trying] of course—they were trying

172:10 my moment of drama] my moment in the spotlight

174:15 her voice] Madge's voice

178:23 I said. I'm sorry] I said, I'm sorry

181:16 between the shoulder-blades, and I almost stumbled] between the shoulder blades and I almost stumbled

182:18 babe] baby

185:29 that you think] you think

186:11 inspector] Inspector

189:5 that same, faint, bemused little smile] that same faint bemused little smile

190:9 qualm] stab

190:12 lumpy] bare

190:26 not my jailers, but my keepers, rather] not my jailers but my keepers, rather

194:24 not for wearing, but to house] not for wearing but to house

194:26 he was wearing] he had worn

194:29 and left it] and had left it

196:2   the anger evaporated, and I sat down] the anger
evaporated and I sat down

197:16 He pretended not to hear] This also he pretended not to
hear

199:5   I had killed. It had rained] I had killed. ¶ It had rained

200:26 Billy] Eddie

203:18 them] the two of them

204:1   Stoney Batter] Stoneybatter

204:21 I looked out the barred window] I looked out through
the barred window

206:17 someday] some day

About the Author

William John Banville was born in Wexford, Ireland, on 8 December 1945, the youngest of three siblings. He was educated at Christian Brothers schools and St Peter's College, Wexford. After college Banville worked as a clerk for Ireland's national airline, Aer Lingus, before joining *The Irish Press* as a sub-editor in 1969. Continuing with journalism for over thirty years, Banville was Literary Editor at *The Irish Times* from 1988 to 1999.

Banville's first book, *Long Lankin*, a collection of short stories and a novella, was published in 1970. His first novel, *Nightspawn*, came out in 1971, followed by *Birchwood* (1973), *Doctor Copernicus* (1976), *Kepler* (1981), *The Newton Letter* (1982), *Mefisto* (1986), *The Book of Evidence* (1989), *Ghosts* (1993), *Athena* (1995), *The Untouchable* (1997), *Eclipse* (2000), *Shroud* (2002), *The Sea* (2005), *The Infinities* (2009) and *Ancient Light* (2012). His non-fiction book, *Prague Pictures: Portraits of a City*, was published in 2003 as part of Bloomsbury's 'The Writer and the City' series. In 2012, an anthology comprising extracts from Banville's fifteen novels to date, together with selections drawn from his dramatic works and various reviews, was published under the title, *Possessed of a Past: A John Banville Reader*.

Among the awards Banville's novels have won are the Allied Irish Banks Fiction Prize, the American-Irish Foundation Award, the James Tait Black Memorial Prize, the *Guardian* Fiction Prize, the Lannan Literary Award for Fiction and the Kerry Group Irish Fiction Award. In 1989 *The Book of Evidence* was shortlisted for the

Booker Prize, and was awarded the first Guinness Peat Aviation Award; in Italian, as *La Spiegazione dei Fatti*, the book was awarded the 1991 Premio Ennio Flaiano. *Ghosts* was shortlisted for the Whitbread Fiction Prize in 1993; *The Untouchable* for the same prize in 1997. In 2003 Banville was awarded the Premio Nonino. In 2005, he won the Man Booker Prize for *The Sea*. In 2011 Banville was awarded the Franz Kafka Prize. Two years later, in 2013, he was awarded the Irish Pen Award for Outstanding Achievement in Irish Literature. In 2014, Banville was awarded Spain's most coveted literary prize, the Asturias Award for Literature. He was also made a Chevalier de l'Ordre des Arts et des Lettres by the French ministry of culture.

Under the pseudonym Benjamin Black, Banville has published the following crime novels: *Christine Falls* (2006), *The Silver Swan* (2007), *The Lemur* (2008), *Elegy for April* (2010), *A Death in Summer* (2011), *Vengeance* (2012) and *Holy Orders* (2013). The first three of these books were adapted by Andrew Davies and Conor McPherson for the BBC/RTÉ co-production *Quirke*, and broadcast in 2014, with Gabriel Byrne in the title role. Earlier in 2014, *The Black-Eyed Blonde* (a Philip Marlowe novel) was published, again under the pseudonym Benjamin Black.

Chronology

1945 Born in Wexford, Ireland on 8 December.

1962 First story, 'The Party', written.

1966 'The Party' published in *The Kilkenny Magazine*.

1969 Joins *The Irish Press* as sub-editor.

1970 First book, *Long Lankin* (a collection of short stories and a novella), published. Reissued in revised form in 1984.

1971 First novel, *Nightspawn*, published. Reissued in 1993.

1973 *Birchwood* published. Wins the Allied Irish Banks Fiction Prize and the Irish Arts Council Macaulay Fellowship.

1976 *Doctor Copernicus* published. Wins the Whitbread Prize, the James Tait Black Memorial Prize, and the American Ireland Fund Literary Award.

1980 *The Spoils of Poynton*, a radio dramatisation of Henry James's novel of the same name, broadcast by BBC Radio 4 on 15 March.

1981 *Kepler* published. Wins the *Guardian* Prize for Fiction.

1982 *The Newton Letter* published.

1984 A film version of *The Newton Letter*, entitled *Reflections*, broadcast by Channel 4 and RTÉ.

1986 *Mefisto* published.

1988 Appointed Literary Editor of *The Irish Times*.

1989 *The Book of Evidence* published. Shortlisted for the Booker Prize. Wins the Guinness Peat Aviation Book Award and the Marten Toonder Award.

1990 Begins a long-standing tenure as reviewer-essayist with *The New York Review of Books*.

1991 *La Spiegazione dei Fatti* (the Italian translation of *The Book of Evidence*) awarded the Premio Ennio Flaiano.

1993 *Ghosts* published. Shortlisted for the Whitbread Fiction Prize.

1994 *The Broken Jug*, an adaptation of Kleist's *Der zerbrochne Krug*, premiered at the Peacock Theatre, Dublin on 1 June. *Seachange*, a film adaptation of the author's uncollected story 'Rondo', broadcast by RTÉ.

1995 *Athena* published.

1996 *The Ark*, a story for children, published.

1997 *The Untouchable* published. Wins the Lannan Literary Award for Fiction. Shortlisted for the Whitbread Fiction Prize.

1999 Adapts Elizabeth Bowen's *The Last September* for the screen.

2000 *Eclipse* published. *God's Gift*, an adaptation of Kleist's *Amphitryon*, premiered at the O'Reilly Theatre, Dublin on 12 October. *Doctor Copernicus*, *Kepler* and *The Newton Letter* published together in a single volume under the title *The Revolutions Trilogy*.

2001 *The Book of Evidence*, *Ghosts* and *Athena* published together in a single volume under the title *Frames*.

2002 *Shroud* published. Longlisted for the Man Booker Prize. *Stardust: Three Monologues of the Dead* broadcast by BBC Radio 3's *The Verb* on 11 May. *Dublin 1742*, a play for children, performed at The Ark in Dublin on 5 June. The stage production of *The Book of Evidence* premiered at the Watergate Theatre, Kilkenny on 10 August.

2003 Awarded the Premio Nonino. *Prague Pictures: Portraits of a City* published as part of Bloomsbury's 'The Writer and the City' series.

2004 *Kepler*, a radio play, broadcast by BBC Radio 4 on 11 August.

2005   *A World Too Wide*, a radio play about Shakespeare's 'sixth age of man', broadcast by RTÉ on 8 February. *The Sea* published. Wins the Man Booker Prize. *Love in the Wars*, an adaptation of Kleist's *Penthesilia*, published.

2006   Awarded the Premio Grinzane-Francesco Biamonti Prize. *Todtnauberg*, a radio play about the 1967 meeting between Paul Celan and Martin Heidegger, broadcast by BBC Radio 4 on 20 January. *Christine Falls* published under the pseudonym Benjamin Black. 'Beckett's Last Words', a lecture to mark the centenary of Samuel Beckett's birth, broadcast by RTÉ on 22 June; the text was later published as a limited edition. *The Sea* shortlisted for British Book Awards Author of the Year. 'First Light', an early version of the opening section of what became *The Infinities*, published as a limited edition. *The Sea* awarded Irish Novel of the Year (Bord Gáis Energy Irish Book Awards).

2007   Awarded the Madeleine Zepter Prix Littéraire Européen. Made a fellow of the Royal Society of Literature. *Loving*, a two-part radio dramatisation of Henry Green's novel of the same name, broadcast by BBC Radio 4 on 18–25 March. *The Sea* nominated for the Man Booker International Prize. *The Silver Swan* published under the pseudonym Benjamin Black.

2008   *Conversation in the Mountains*, the script of *Todtnauberg*, published. *The Lemur* published under the pseudonym Benjamin Black.

2009   *The Infinities* published.

2010   *The Infinities* wins the Kerry Group Irish Fiction Award. *Elegy for April* published under the pseudonym Benjamin Black. *The Sea* shortlisted for the Irish Book of the Decade (Bord Gáis Energy Irish Book Awards).

2011   Awarded the Franz Kafka Prize. Co-scripts (with Glenn

Close and Gabriela Prekop) the film *Albert Nobbs*. *A Death in Summer* published under the pseudonym Benjamin Black. Contributes two short character sketches to the National Portrait Gallery's *Imagined Lives: Portraits of Unknown People*.

2012 Shortlisted for the Asturias Award for Literature. *Ancient Light* published. *Vengeance* published under the pseudonym Benjamin Black. The anthology *Possessed of a Past: A John Banville Reader* published. *Ancient Light* awarded Irish Novel of the Year (Bord Gáis Energy Irish Book Awards).

2013 Awarded the Irish PEN Award for Outstanding Achievement in Irish Literature; the Austrian State Prize for European Literature; the XIII Premio Leteo; and the Premio Liber. *Holy Orders* published under the pseudonym Benjamin Black. *The Sea: A Screenplay* published as a limited edition. Presented with the Bob Hughes Lifetime Achievement Award (Bord Gáis Energy Irish Book Awards).

2014 *Bowen and Betjeman*, a radio play, broadcast by BBC Radio 4 on 14 February. *The Black-Eyed Blonde* (a Philip Marlowe novel) published under the pseudonym Benjamin Black. Awarded the Asturias Award for Literature. Awarded the insignia of Chevalier de l'Ordre des Arts et des Lettres. *Love in the Wars*, an adaptation of Kleist's *Penthesilea*, premiered at the Fisher Center for the Performing Arts at Bard College, New York on 10 July.

Picador Classic

On 6 October 1972, Picador published its first list of eight paperbacks. It was a list that demonstrated ambition as well as cultural breadth, and included great writing from Latin America (Jorge Luis Borges's *A Personal Anthology*), Europe (Hermann Hesse's *Rosshalde*), America (Richard Brautigan's *Trout Fishing in America*) and Britain (Angela Carter's *Heroes and Villains*). Within a few years, Picador had established itself as one of the pre-eminent publishers of contemporary fiction, non-fiction and poetry.

What defines Picador is the unique nature of each of its authors' voices. The Picador Classic series highlights some of those great voices and brings neglected classics back into print. New introductions – personal recommendations if you will – from writers and public figures illuminate these works, as well as putting them into a wider context. Many of the Picador Classic editions also include afterwords from their authors which provide insight into the background to their original publication, and how that author identifies with their work years on.

Printed on high quality paper stock and with thick cover boards, the Picador Classic series is also a celebration of the physical book.

Whether fiction, journalism, memoir or poetry, Picador Classic represents timeless quality and extraordinary writing from some of the world's greatest voices.

Discover the history of the Picador Classic series and the stories behind the books themselves at www.picador.com/classic.